Written by Doris Durbin

The Captain Chronicles:
The Captain Takes a Wife (Book 1:1875)
The Captain Seeks the Lost (Book 2: 1876)

Edited by Ed and Doris Durbin:

**How Firm a Foundation:
A History of the First Baptist Church of Blairsville, Georgia**
Written by Eva Decker, Mary Sue Moon, and the History Committee

The CAPTAIN Seeks the Lost

The Captain Chronicles, 1876

Doris Durbin

WESTBOW PRESS
A DIVISION OF THOMAS NELSON
& ZONDERVAN

Copyright © 2015 Doris Durbin.

All rights reserved. No part of this book may be used or reproduced by any means, graphic, electronic, or mechanical, including photocopying, recording, taping or by any information storage retrieval system without the written permission of the author except in the case of brief quotations embodied in critical articles and reviews.

This is a work of fiction. All of the characters, names, incidents, organizations, and dialogue in this novel are either the products of the author's imagination or are used fictitiously.

WestBow Press books may be ordered through booksellers or by contacting:

WestBow Press
A Division of Thomas Nelson & Zondervan
1663 Liberty Drive
Bloomington, IN 47403
www.westbowpress.com
1 (866) 928-1240

Because of the dynamic nature of the Internet, any web addresses or links contained in this book may have changed since publication and may no longer be valid. The views expressed in this work are solely those of the author and do not necessarily reflect the views of the publisher, and the publisher hereby disclaims any responsibility for them.

Any people depicted in stock imagery provided by Thinkstock are models, and such images are being used for illustrative purposes only. Certain stock imagery © Thinkstock.

ISBN: 978-1-4908-8581-0 (sc)
ISBN: 978-1-4908-8582-7 (hc)
ISBN: 978-1-4908-8580-3 (e)

Library of Congress Control Number: 2015910109

Print information available on the last page.

WestBow Press rev. date: 08/24/2015

In honor and memory of my parents,
Floid and Wilmoth Schneider

And to Ed, always

"Choestoe" is a Cherokee name that means "The Place of the Dancing Rabbit." In Cherokee folklore, the rabbit is a trickster. I should have known that in a place called Choestoe things would not always be what they seemed.

*—Harry Richardson's journal,
July 30, 1876.*

CONTENTS

Acknowledgments ix
Prologue xi

Day One: Monday
    Chapter 1   News of a Stranger 1

Day Two: Tuesday
    Chapter 2   Fishing: Truth and Lies 13
    Chapter 3   Kidnapped 22
    Chapter 4   Harry Goes to War 29
    Chapter 5   Into the Mountains 39
    Chapter 6   Michael Makes a Change 47
    Chapter 7   Prospector's Hut 58

Day Three: Wednesday
    Chapter 8   Sarah Speaks Her Mind 70
    Chapter 9   Finding What Was Lost 81
    Chapter 10   Annie? 91
    Chapter 11   Saving Harrison 100
    Chapter 12   A Ghost from the Past 115
    Chapter 13   "You're Not Alone" 120

Day Four: Thursday
    Chapter 14   What They Found in the Smokehouse 126
    Chapter 15   Making Arrangements 141
    Chapter 16   A Homecoming 148

Chapter 17	Laying Out the Bodies	155
Chapter 18	A Visitor Comes Forward	163
Chapter 19	The Wake	169
Chapter 20	The Deacon's Undoing	178

Day Five: Friday
| Chapter 21 | Two Funerals and a Reunion | 195 |

Day Six: Saturday
| Chapter 22 | A Conference on the Porch | 203 |

Day Seven: Sunday
| Chapter 23 | New Beginnings | 209 |

End Notes ... 213
Reader's Guide ... 217

ACKNOWLEDGMENTS

I am indebted to friends who read the manuscript and offered suggestions, including my sisters, Carol Turnage and Joan Schneider-Cooper, as well as Brenda Adams, Cathy Brackett, Howard Wells, Faith Bell, James Hooper, Eva Decker, JoAnn Hamby, Jim Eddins, Laureen Batchelor, Carol Knight, Marybeth Harris, and Donna Howell.

The story of the two snakes swallowing each other came to me from Mr. Charles Roscoe Collins. The Collinses in the story are entirely fictional, but people named Collins lived in Choestoe in 1876, and there really was a Collins Store.

I am grateful to Eddie Alexander, owner of Alexander's Store, who took the time to tell us about the history of his store and of the way things were done in the old days in the Choestoe area; to Sylvia Dyer Turnage for information about Choestoe history; and to Melinda Tipton Stites for information about the name's origin.

My deep appreciation goes to photographer Chris Hefferen for his cover photos.

I am grateful to all the people who read the first book in the series and kept eagerly asking, "When's the next book coming out?" You've been a great source of encouragement.

Most especially, as always, I thank my husband for his inspiration, support, ideas, and expertise in history. We've learned not to discuss the books when we're driving, because we get so caught up in fictional possibilities that we miss real exits and end up miles off course. Thank you, Ed, for making this journey with me!

PROLOGUE

The noise was deafening. Cannons thundered and rifles popped and exploded while men screamed in agony. Smoke filled the air, making it hard to tell which soldiers wore blue and which wore gray. The Southerners were in retreat up the steep mountainside, and Harry was trying to hold the line, or, failing that, at least rescue the fallen. Suddenly at his feet he saw Ned Spiva with a bullet wound in his leg. Ned was bleeding badly, and the leg appeared to be broken. Harry knelt and used his sash to wrap Ned's leg and staunch the bleeding. Through the smoke he saw Liam Banks walking dazedly, looking lost, with blood running into his eyes from a cut on his head. He was a walking target.

"Liam, come here!"

"C-C-Cap'n?" stuttered Liam.

"Come with me, Liam," he said. "Here. Help me get the Sergeant over my shoulder."

Liam helped as Harry stooped and pulled the semiconscious Ned up and over his shoulder. "Now help me carry him up the hill."

Liam walked beside Harry, supporting him, and together they struggled up the long hill to get behind what remained of their company's lines, carrying Ned. On the ridge, when they reached the tents where the doctors were working, the sight was even more horrifying than the scene on the battlefield. Doctors were amputating limbs so fast that a pile of arms, legs, hands, and feet lay on the ground beside the operating table. Amid the screams, smoke, and thunder of cannons, there was the smell of sulfur.

"Please, Harry. Don't let them do that to me," said Ned, when Harry eased him to the ground near the tents.

Harry nodded at his good friend, then looked quickly around and saw an orderly hurrying past pushing a wheelbarrow.

"Private, I need that cart!" he commanded.

"But sir, the doctor…"

"Get him another one," Harry ordered. "And bring me paper and a pen. Do it now!"

"Yes, sir!" The boy dropped the cart and ran back, looking frantically for what the Captain needed.

Harry loaded Ned into the cart then pulled the bandana from around Ned's neck and used it to tie up the wound on Liam's head.

"All right, you two. You're out of this war. Liam, Take Ned and get in that line of men heading south down the back of the ridge." Harry pointed at a line of wounded soldiers that was being evacuated. "You take Ned all the way home to Dalton, then go back to your mother in the mountains. If anyone questions you, tell him you're following Captain Richardson's orders. After you get down off the mountain, go where Ned tells you to go; he'll know the way."

The orderly was back with paper, pen, and ink. Harry wrote two quick notes and signed them with a flourish, releasing the two men from duty.

"I didn't know you had that authority," Ned said with a weak smile when Harry gave the notes to him.

"I don't," Harry confided. "Don't tell anybody."

"God be with you, Harry," said Ned.

"And you." He turned to Liam. "You can do this, Liam. When you get to a town, both of you see a doctor. Hurry, now. Get out of here."

Liam obeyed without hesitation. Harry turned and ran back through the tents and retreating soldiers, but now every face had a strange, eerie glow. As he passed the last tent, he saw a ghostly nurse stirring an iron caldron that seemed to be filled with blood. When she looked up at him he saw that it was Molly.

"What are you doing here, Molly?" he gasped.

"I've just delivered your baby," she said, smiling strangely. Harry felt himself choking with fear and looked wildly around for his wife.

"Sarah!" he cried.

"Sarah! Sarah!" Harry called aloud and sat up, at first confused and then relieved to find himself in his own bed with Sarah by his side.

Sarah sat up, startled, then she held him and patted him. "Shhh, shhh. It's all right, Harry. Everything is all right."

"I'm sorry, honey. I'm sorry I woke you," said Harry, holding her tightly, still catching his breath.

"Was it the same dream?" she asked.

"Mostly, only worse."

"Poor Harry. Everything is all right. Go back to sleep now."

Harry lay down on his side and gathered Sarah close to him, his chest against her back and his arms around her. He sighed with relief, happy that his wife was safe in his arms, feeling his heart rate gradually returning to normal. To Harry, one of the greatest comforts of marriage was having his wife to hold onto when the nightmares came. In some mysterious way her presence made him whole again, took away the fear. He wondered how he had ever lived without her. "How's Annie?" he asked softly.

Sarah placed Harry's hand on her gown so he could feel the baby kicking. "She's kicking up her heels. I think she's already learning to dance," said Sarah.

"Good," sighed Harry, relaxing toward sleep.

"Harry?" asked Sarah after a minute.

"Hmm?"

"What if it's a boy?"

Harry thought for a moment. "He'll be pretty annoyed when he finds out we named him Annie." When Sarah giggled, Harry said, "Don't worry, it's a girl."

"How do you know?"

"She kicks like a girl," said Harry.

"So you say," Sarah replied. "I'd say she kicks like a mule."

"Same thing. Girl—mule."

Sarah swung her heel back and kicked Harry on the shin.

"Ow! See?" laughed Harry. "Just like a mule! Well, if that's the way you feel about it…" He rolled over, pulled the quilt up over his shoulder, and keeping his back close to Sarah's, settled back to sleep.

Sarah lay quietly, listening to her husband's soft breathing. When he had the nightmares he always awoke in a panic, then he usually went back to sleep fairly quickly afterward while she lay awake. It was a recurring dream about the terrible day when everything went wrong in the battle of Missionary Ridge, when the Confederate forces were defeated and Harry was captured. The dream always stayed true to events until Harry managed to get Ned and Liam off the battlefield. Then things went strange, and the severed limbs of soldiers came crawling after him, or he fell into a pit of fire, or he found his own body lying dead in the field, covered with maggots. She wondered how tonight's dream could possibly have been worse. Finally, she slept, too.

Choestoe,[1] Georgia, July 1876
Day One: Monday

CHAPTER 1

News of a Stranger

Captain Harry Richardson slung the sack of feed onto his horse's back just behind the saddle and strapped it into place. When the horse sidestepped, he said, "Hold on there, Smokey. This is for you." Then he laid a homemade, double-sided sack across in front of the saddle. It held the rest of his purchases: flour, sugar, coffee beans, and other staples. "That ought to do it," he said to Seth Collins, who had helped with the carrying and now stood by the hitching rail in front of the Collins General Store.

On the porch, three men sat in weathered wooden chairs around a checkerboard that rested on a keg. Blacksmith Eb Ward and a visitor named Jimmy were hunched over the game of checkers. An older man named Oliver, who was Seth's father and owner of the store, sat back, whittling a figure out of wood and telling a story. Harry and Seth stopped to listen.

"I was walkin' out to the cornfield last week, and as I passed by the corner of the rail fence around the yard, I heard a rustlin' in the leaves, and when I looked over in there, what do you think I saw?"

No one else answered, so Jimmy spoke up. "What did you see?" All the locals had heard the story before so they knew where it was going. Harry smiled, watching Oliver reel in the newcomer while the others kept silent.

"There was two snakes down there in the corner, and each one had the other one by the tail. They were swallowin' each other."

"No! You don't mean it!" said the man, sitting back in rapt attention to Oliver, who was nodding seriously. "Two snakes swallowing each other. So what did you do?"

"Do? I didn't do anything. I just watched." Oliver polished the carving on his sleeve, frowned at it, and then blew away some dust.

"So what happened?" Jimmy insisted.

Oliver spun out the tale. "Well, the snakes swallowed and they swallowed and they swallowed, until each snake had the other one right up to the neck." He paused, letting the silence stretch out.

"Then what happened?" asked Jimmy. "Go on!"

Oliver looked solemnly around at the others. He had Jimmy in the palm of his hand. "Well, they swallowed one last time, and"—he snapped his fingers—"just like that, both snakes were gone!"

All the men laughed appreciatively, and Oliver chuckled, clearly enjoying his own story.

Jimmy looked sheepish. "You got me that time." He turned to Eb, who was waiting for him to make a move. "My turn?" he asked. Then he moved a checker.

Eb grinned, jumped the last three of Jimmy's checkers and won the game.

Jimmy turned to Oliver. "You did that on purpose. You distracted me! You two were working together!"

As the friendly arguing on the porch continued, Seth walked over to hold Smokey's head while Harry mounted. Seth had spent the morning loading a wagon for the weekly trip to Gainesville. He would trade locally made products like honey, tanned hides, chestnuts, and farm produce for things that the mountain people needed to buy, such as coffee beans, cloth, and canned goods.

"I sent that telegram for you when we got to Gainesville last Wednesday," Seth told Harry. The telegram was addressed to a doctor in Atlanta, and Seth was curious. "You and Sarah ready for that new baby?" he asked.

"Ready as we know how to be," Harry answered. "I'm ready for the child to be born and safe in its mother's arms, that's for sure. Then I can stop worrying." It was clear that Harry was nervous about the whole thing.

He and Sarah had been married less than a year, and this was their first baby.

"Everything will be fine. You'll see. Old Doc Carter has delivered lots of babies in his time."

"Yeah. I just wish he lived a little closer—maybe right next door. I'm gone a lot." Although he didn't say it, Harry also wished he had a little more faith in the old doctor. He wasn't sure how up-to-date the doc's medical knowledge was, and as often as not, the old man seemed to be just a little bit drunk. As long as everything was going well, he'd be fine at delivering the baby, but Harry wasn't sure how much help he would be if anything went wrong.

Harry had hoped his friend Walt could be here at the right time, but Walt was still in medical school in Atlanta, and Atlanta was far away. Compared to Doc Carter, Walt lacked experience, but at least he had the latest information. Just in case Walt was available, Harry had sent the telegram asking him if he could come.

"If you aren't home, Harrison can go for help."

"That's right. We're counting on him. I don't know what we'd do without that boy." Harrison was Harry's thirteen-year-old son. Harry had not known the boy existed until he had shown up, abused and in need of a home, just three days after he and Sarah were married. It had been something of a shock, but Harry had accepted responsibility for the boy, only regretting the years he had missed knowing him. Harrison had been moody lately, and that was another cause for concern.

"Let me tell you a secret, Captain," said Seth, with the air of one who is older and wiser, even though he and Harry were both in their early thirties. Seth already had three children, so that made him an authority. "You won't stop worrying after the baby is born. You'll worry about that child from now on. Might as well get used to it."

"You're obviously a very wise man," said Harry. "How are you at delivering babies?"

Seth grinned. "When the time comes, do what I do. Go get a granny-woman, and then stay outside and pace."

"Who's the visitor?" Harry asked, with a nod toward Jimmy.

"Oh, he says he's a writer and he's collecting stories. He carries a little notebook all the time to write things down."

Harry laughed. "Well, he's found a gold mine in Ollie, hasn't he?"

The men on the porch had stopped teasing Jimmy, and Oliver walked over to hand the little carving to Harry. "Give this to Harrison." It was a small, rough, circular carving of two snakes swallowing each other. Oliver knew that Harrison was learning to carve.

"Thanks, Ollie," said Harry. "He'll like that." He put the carving in his shirt pocket.

Eb spoke up. "Preacher, a stranger was here looking for you this morning. Did he find you?"

"No," answered Harry. "What was his name?"

"He didn't say." Eb hesitated and exchanged a glance with Jimmy. "He was a big man and looked a little wild, like he's been on the trail awhile. He had shaggy, light brown hair and a scruffy beard. I hope I did the right thing. I told him where you lived."

"Well, it's no secret where I live. Anyone would have told him." Harry frowned. "What worried you?"

"I don't know—just something about him. He seemed kinda sneery... sorter shifty-eyed."

"What exactly did he say?"

"Just wanted to know if we knew the preacher named Harry. The one they call the Captain. Wanted to know where you lived."

"I'm going home now. I'll see if he's there. Thanks, Eb. What kind of horse did he ride?"

"Well, that was the funny thing. He was on a beautiful gray horse with a fine saddle. The horse seemed a lot nicer than the man, if you take my meanin'." He wouldn't say it, but he thought the man could be a horse thief. "The horse was unshod, and it was favoring a forefoot. You'd think if a fella was going on a long trip he'd shoe the horse first. I offered to shoe it for him, but he wasn't interested. He seemed to be in a hurry."

"Maybe he just didn't have any money," said Harry. "Well, thanks. I'll keep a lookout." He nodded to Seth, turned his horse, and headed for home. There was probably a reasonable explanation. Maybe the man looked rough because he was down on his luck and had traveled a long way, and he was looking for Harry because he hoped the preacher would help him with food and shelter. He wouldn't be the first. Or maybe it was someone Harry had known during the war.

There was no reason to feel worried, and yet Harry did. If the man had really been looking for him since this morning, he should have found him already. Except for this trip to the store, Harry had been at home all day. He had been putting the finishing touches on a cradle he had built and helping Sarah arrange their tiny cabin to make room for the baby. If their calculations were right, they had three weeks to go, but, as people kept telling him, babies didn't always follow a schedule. Their lives were about to change in a big way. Maybe that's why the news about this stranger gave him an uneasy feeling. There was too much going on right now. He didn't want to deal with anything else.

It was less than a mile from the store to home, and Harry frequently walked it, even when there were heavy sacks to carry, but not today. He had wanted to make the trip as quickly as possible. Most of the mountain folks walked to the store, and he wanted to live like everyone else. When he walked, Harry was on the same level as the people he met, and they had time to talk. Lots of the people didn't even own a horse, or if they did, it was used for work only and, in their opinion, not worth saddling to save a walk of just a few miles. The valley was cut through with paths that wound alongside creeks and through woods, and the roads that existed were poor. Many people had to cross creeks on narrow foot-logs, so walking was the easiest way for them.

Even though people were accustomed to walking, isolation was a way of life here, for tiny cabins and small farms were scattered far and wide among the hills and coves of the Choestoe area and the mountains beyond. After the Cherokee Indians had been removed from the area, land had been parceled out by way of a lottery. Some people had drawn lots for land on steep mountainsides, and that was where they lived and tried to farm.

Harry had recently conducted a wedding for a sixteen-year-old girl who had never been farther than ten miles from her home at the foot of Yellow Mountain. She had never even been to Blairsville, which was the nearest town. It was hard for Harry to imagine a life so isolated.

It was a difficult task to get to know all the people in the four small churches Harry served, but the circuit-riding preacher was becoming known and respected by people all over the area. He was frequently the bearer of news and messages from one family to another, and he was almost always welcome. A few people back in the hills preferred to be left alone.

One such was Mrs. Ivalee Banks. She lived in a cabin with her grown son Liam several miles from the nearest neighbor. Harry had first met Liam when Harry was just ten years old and was living temporarily with his Aunt Winifred in Choestoe after his mother died. Winifred taught at a one-room school, which both Harry and Liam attended. The boy stuttered so badly that he could hardly communicate, and Harry had stood up for him when other boys taunted him. For two years they were fast friends, exploring the woods, fishing, and hunting together. Liam was a crack shot, and they always brought home food for the table. Those golden days ended when Harry moved back to Marietta to live with his father. Years later, their paths had crossed again during the war, and Harry had made Liam the sniper in his company. It was Liam who had taken a wounded soldier named Ned Spiva all the way to Ned's home in Dalton when they were both medically discharged.

The church people had warned Harry not to approach the Banks cabin without an escort that the boy knew, or he might be shot. They said the boy hadn't been right in the head since the war, and he no longer talked much at all. (They still called Liam "the boy" even though he was Harry's age.) An older deacon named Eldridge Payne had volunteered to escort Harry when he went to visit him the first time. They had stood some distance from the cabin, partly behind a tree, and when Eldridge had shouted, "Hey, Liam! I've brought a friend to see you!" he had been answered with gunfire. He didn't dare go any closer. Harry was sure the shots were only warnings. If Liam had intended to shoot Eldridge, he wouldn't have missed.

"Step right out there where he can see you," urged the deacon.

Harry thought it ironic that the deacon who was hiding behind the tree was advising him to step right out there, but apparently the deacon thought it was safe. Harry didn't think Liam would shoot him, so he stepped out in front of the tree and shouted, "Corporal Banks! What's for supper?" and his old friend had rushed out the door to meet him, first saluting, and then hugging Harry happily.

Eldridge Payne had gone away amazed, and the news had spread throughout the community. Later Harry had returned, bringing Ned and Harrison with him. It was there that Harrison had first learned to carve. Liam lived in a room full of carvings. And as time went by, Sarah had also come to know Liam's mother, Ivalee. But Liam still lived the life of a hermit, and he still didn't talk much at all.

During this past winter, people had appreciated Harry's willingness to come whenever he was needed, in all kinds of weather. Each season had its special hardship as well as beauty. Harry had found the mud of the spring thaw an even bigger impediment to travel than the ice and snow of winter. But whether on horseback or on foot, he had been out and about, meeting people, getting to know them, sitting by their bedsides when they were ill, celebrating births, providing consolation at deaths, and ministering to his flock by being there.

The churches held services one Saturday and Sunday each month on a rotating basis. Each week he preached at a different church, arriving on Friday evening or Saturday morning to preach both Saturday and Sunday services, always staying at the home of one of the members, even if that home was a one-room cabin full of children. He came home on Sunday evenings, and he had made the trips so often that, before long, Smokey knew the way. One winter night when Harry fell asleep in the saddle, Smokey had carried him home. The weekly schedule was broken on occasional fifth Sundays, when there was a communion service followed by singing and dinner on the grounds at the Choestoe Church.

Harry's wife Sarah had been constantly by his side in the early days, walking with him or riding behind him on his horse, or, when the condition of roads allowed it, riding in the wagon. Sarah had grown up on a plantation near Macon, and being a circuit rider's wife in the North Georgia mountains had not been an easy transition for her. Harry was proud of how well she had met the challenge. But recently, at the advice of the old doctor, she had stopped traveling.

No one could blame Harry if he tried to stay a little closer to home during the week, now that the baby was almost due. Family had to be cared for, too. And it was clear to everyone that Harry adored his wife and his half-grown son and took his family responsibilities seriously.

As he returned home from the store, Harry rode slowly and studied the dusty clay for tracks. His days as a soldier and later as a cavalry officer in the West had given him experience that came in handy, and the smell of dust in the hot July air brought back memories. Not that North Georgia was anything like the western desert. Although the rugged western lands had their own kind of magnificent beauty, this rolling landscape with its clear, rushing creeks, lush, green forests, and distant blue hills would always feel like home to Harry.

Harry followed the prints of an unshod horse and saw where it had turned onto the path to his cabin, but it had not gone all the way to his door. He saw droppings where the horse had stood for a time among the trees some distance from the house, but now the horse was gone. There was evidence that the man had helped himself to hay and grain from Harry's little barn. Harry had not met the stranger on the road, which raised the disturbing possibility that the man had already been watching the house when Harry had left for the store. Harry reached the house, dismounted, looped the reins around the hitching post, and then looked around for a weapon. He was not in the habit of carrying a gun now and usually didn't need one. He lifted the double sack of groceries off the horse's neck and hefted it across his shoulder. It would be better than nothing.

Harrison's dog Sparky, staying cool under the steps, wagged a greeting. The front door was wide open, and Harry heard a deep male voice inside the house. He entered cautiously and was relieved to find his good friend Ned Spiva there, showing Harrison a new rod and reel he had ordered through the mail.

"Look at this, Harry. Those trout don't stand a chance," Ned said exuberantly. Then, noticing Harry's expression, he added, "What's the matter with you?"

Harry shook his head. "Nothing. Just didn't know who was here."

Sarah came to greet Harry at the door. He hung his hat on a hook, set the sack of groceries on the floor, and took his very pregnant wife into his arms. Then he looked intently at her. "How are you? You feelin' okay?"

"Yes, Harry. I'm fine," she said with some concern. "Same as I was when you left an hour ago."

Ned spoke up. "Harrison and I are going to try out the new rod and reel tomorrow. Want to come?"

"Don't know. Not sure I want to be away that long," he answered, still looking at Sarah.

"I'm staying with Sarah," said Winifred, who was standing at the wood stove at one end of the room, apparently cooking supper. "You boys need to get out from underfoot and go have some fun. Give us girls time to visit."

"Is that what you want?" he asked Sarah, frowning.

"Yes, Harry. It will be good."

"All right, then. Count me in," he said to Ned, but he still seemed distracted. "I've got to see to the horse," he said. "Harrison, would you put these groceries away, please? And Ned, you could give me a hand, if you don't mind."

Ned put down the fishing gear and followed Harry outside.

"What's the matter?" asked Ned, now fully alert. Ned was a man who didn't miss much, and he knew Harry well. They had been friends since they served together in the war, and, at different times, each one had saved the other's life. Ned had recently married Harry's Aunt Winifred, so the old friend was now family, too.

When Harry started leading the horse to the barn and didn't respond immediately, Ned offered this observation. "Is this about Sarah? You know, Harry, every person on the earth got here the same way. Women have babies, and most of the time everything is just fine."

"But this is not just any woman. It's Sarah," Harry said.

"I know. And you're Harry. Don't forget that. I've seen you charge into cannon fire without breaking a sweat, and here you are shakin' in your boots over this baby. You need to have a little courage, man!"

"When it's Winifred's turn, I'll remind you of that." Harry tied the horse, removed the sack of feed, and started unsaddling him, his firmly closed mouth the only indication of his annoyance.

"Yeah. Well, Winifred may not get a turn," Ned answered. "We may have waited too late to start a family." Harry did the math in his head. Ned was forty-three; Winifred forty-one.

"Oh," said Harry, pausing to look at Ned with concern. "I'm sorry. I didn't know—I didn't think. Anyway, this has nothing to do with courage. Risking my own neck was one thing. At least I could *do* something. Standing by while Sarah risks her life is something else entirely. And I'm not sure she's fine. She's awfully tired. What if something's wrong? There's nobody I can ask about that." Harry put the saddle in its place on a sawhorse, picked up a brush, and started grooming the horse.

"Anyway, this isn't just about the baby. Eb says a man was looking for me today. Have you seen a fellow on a gray horse?"

Ned shook his head.

"Well, Eb thought he looked suspicious. I followed his tracks and it looks like he might have been watching my house. I'd just like to know who he is and what he's up to."

"You think he might have some connection to Dawson?" Ned was referring to a counterfeiter he and Harry had helped to capture back in the fall.

"I don't know, but I wouldn't think so. Dawson's still in jail, and I don't know of anybody else who has a grudge," Harry responded, and then delivered a dig at Ned, who was the area's new revenue agent. "The local moonshiners might not like me much, me being friends with the revenuer and all, but this was not a local man. Eb would have known him if he was. I didn't want to worry Sarah, but I'm not sure I want to leave her and Winifred alone all day, just in case this man is still hanging around."

"Well, let's ask her if she saw him. It may be nothing. What does Eb know, anyway?"

"He knows about horses and men. That's enough," said Harry. He stood back to admire the sheen of the horse's coat, then put the brush away on a shelf. They started walking slowly back to the house.

"About Dawson," said Ned.

"Yeah. What about him?"

"I still don't figure him for the boss, do you?" Ned was frowning.

Harry shook his head. "I never thought he was smart enough. Do you think there's still somebody out there that we didn't catch?" he asked.

"I think so. Not only was Dawson not smart enough, he wasn't cold-blooded enough. He tied Whittaker up instead of killing him."

"I know. Everybody seemed really scared of the boss, and they weren't scared of Dawson. And Dawson hasn't said a word to clear himself, which could mean he's scared to talk, even in jail. But if there's a boss still out there, he's made a clean get-away. Why would he bother us now?"

"I don't know. You're right. It's probably nothing to do with him."

When they returned, Winifred and Sarah had moved to the front porch to escape the heat of the tiny cabin. Winifred was sitting in one of the two rockers and Sarah was in the porch swing. Ned sat beside Winifred in the other rocker, and Harry joined Sarah in the swing. Harrison was sitting on the steps with his shaggy, flop-eared dog at his feet. He was whittling on a small block of wood with his pocketknife.

"Harrison is coming home with us tonight," said Winifred. "He wants to spend some time practicing with the reel."

"That'll be good," said Ned. "If he figures it out, he can teach me."

Sarah was wearing a dark green calico dress with a bow on the front. It was a maternity dress designed to expand with her as she grew, but she had hated the bow from the beginning because it kept sticking farther and farther out in front of her, and she found it embarrassing. But she hadn't had to adjust the bow lately, so maybe she was as big as she was going to get. Fortunately, Harry didn't seem to mind the way she looked. There was nothing but adoration in his eyes and a little worry. He took her hand and kissed it.

"Eb said a man was looking for me. Did he come by here?"

"He came right after you left," said Sarah.

Harry frowned. Maybe the man had been waiting for him to leave the house. "Who was he? What did he want?"

"He didn't say his name. He asked for water. His horse was limping, and he wanted to know if you had a pick and some grain or fodder you could spare. He used your pick to dig out the stone in the horse's hoof, fed the horse, and went on his way."

"Did he say anything else?" asked Harry. "Did he ask about me?"

"Not really. We didn't talk that much." Sarah fanned herself with a piece of folded newspaper. She didn't complain, but Harry knew it had to be hard on her, being pregnant in this heat. The weather had been unusually hot and dry this summer in the mountain area. The humidity had been building lately, and old-timers were saying they were due for a storm. Lucky they weren't still down in Macon, where it would be even hotter. At least in the mountains the nights were cool.

"He asked if my husband was the preacher they called the Captain, and he asked about our family, if this was the first child, or if we had any other children. I told him about Harrison. He said he was heading for North Carolina and had to get on the road, so he couldn't stay longer. I gave him something to eat, and he took it with him. Not long after that, Ned and Winifred walked over. What's wrong, Harry?"

"Nothing. I heard some fellow was looking for me, that's all. Eb didn't like the look of him. Did you see him, Harrison?"

"No, I was down at the Joneses' house. Mr. Jones asked me and Lindy to help pull some corn." He blushed a little, which was a clue to everyone that thirteen-year-old Lindy Jones meant something special to Harrison.

Winifred spoke up to draw attention from the boy. "And that's why you have fresh corn for supper," she said.

"Ahh," said Harry, nodding. Suddenly he smiled, happy that everything seemed normal. The stranger had gone on his way, and now he knew why Harrison had been moody. He had a girlfriend.

"Oh, yes," he said, patting his shirt pocket and then pulling out the little carving. "Here's a present from old Mr. Collins, at the store." He tossed the carving to Harrison. "Something you can make."

Harrison examined the circular carving. "Two snakes swallowing each other?" he asked.

"You'll have to get Mr. Collins to tell you the story." Then when Harrison looked disappointed, he gave a summary: "They swallowed and swallowed and swallowed until both snakes were gone!"

"I guess one of them should have let go," said Harrison.

"Yes, but then he would have been eaten, and the other would have survived."

Harry turned to Ned. "So what do we need to do to get ready for this big fishing trip?"

Harry put his worries out of his mind and got down to the business of planning tomorrow's holiday. It would be good to spend some time with Harrison. Harry felt that time was short, and he had a lot of catching up to do if he wanted to be a good father to Harrison. As soon as the cold weather had given way to spring, he and Ned had made a special effort to teach Harrison what they knew about surviving in the woods: how to make a camp; how to build a fire; and how to find the way if he ever got lost.

For his thirteenth birthday, Harry had given him the pocketknife and a flint for starting fires, and they had camped out and eaten fish they caught in the stream. Harrison was growing up fast, and Harry felt he had barely had a chance to know him. A day of fishing would be a good thing.

Day Two: Tuesday

CHAPTER 2

Fishing: Truth and Lies

Harry, Ned, Harrison, and the dog Sparky were following Stink Creek away from the valley floor and upward into the hills. Harry couldn't imagine why such a clear, beautiful stream should be called Stink Creek, and he said as much to Ned, who shook his head in agreement. The water sparkled, rushing over half-submerged rocks through sunlight and shade, and the air was filled with the lush, earthy scent of woodland moss, wildflowers, and wet clay. Sparky bounded along with them, darting from one person to another for attention, then exploring the edge of the woods, occasionally racing off after a bird or rabbit or something unseen, always returning, panting and happy.

Harry felt happy and wondered why he had waited so long to explore this beautiful path along the stream. He had been working too hard, that was all. It was hard to take a day off when his time was filled with traveling, preaching, and visiting in the homes of his church members. Not to mention preparing sermons, tilling the land with a borrowed mule to make a garden, cutting stacks of firewood to be ready for next winter, caring for the horses, and making a home with Sarah. And now there would be a baby. It was good to take a day off. The fishermen walked for some time until they reached a place where the land was level and the creek was wide and fairly shallow.

"This looks like a good place for trout," said Ned. "I'll need some quiet. Why don't you'uns take the dog and go a little farther up the way with your poles?" Trout were skittish, and fly-fishing required a different strategy than just using a cane pole.

Harry and Harrison agreed and continued walking. When they rounded a curve and came to a quieter, deeper pool, they decided to stop. Sparky settled next to Harrison, enjoying the shade. After they had fished for a few minutes, Harry figured it was time to talk, but this whole business of being a father was still new to him, and his own father had not been a very good role model. He'd never told Harry anything about anything. Harry didn't know where to start. He took a breath and plunged in.

"You've been awful quiet lately. Is there something on your mind? Something you want to talk about?"

Harrison looked at his father, surprised that Harry had noticed, but it would be a relief to tell him the secret he'd been carrying around since they'd met. "I don't know," he answered. "I'm not sure I should talk about it."

Harry thought the boy probably had questions about growing up and was embarrassed to ask anything. "Well, I don't think anything you'd say would surprise me."

"You're wrong," said Harrison. "It would. You'd be pretty disappointed in me." The boy pulled up his hook to check the bait, and then swung the line back out into the water.

Harry looked at the boy curiously. "Is this about men and women?" He hesitated. "You know—life, relationships—babies?" Harry felt his own face redden, but Harrison just grinned, and there was that mischievous look that reminded Harry so much of Molly, Harrison's mother.

About fourteen years earlier, Harry and Molly had spent one night together before he left school to join his regiment in the Civil War, and Harrison had been born as a result. Not many weeks after Harry left, Molly was told he had been killed in battle, and shortly thereafter, she had married Charlie. Their paths had never crossed again. He had only found out that he had a son when the boy came to find him after he had married Sarah, less than a year ago.

"I think I've figured most of that out already, Dad."

Harry wondered how much Harrison had figured out just living in the two-room cabin with him and Sarah. Harry and Sarah had their own room, and Harrison had a bedroom in the loft over the other room. The newlyweds had been discreet. Still, it was close quarters.

"I know a cow needs a bull to make a calf. Is that what you're talkin' about?"

"Well, yeah, I guess. Sort of." Harry pulled his hook out of the water to see if he still had any bait. A limp worm still dangled from the hook, so he lowered it back into the water and looked away.

"How do fish do it?" Harrison asked innocently, enjoying his father's discomfort. Harry looked exasperatedly at him, and the boy grinned.

"I have no idea," admitted Harry. "So if that's not it, what are you worrying about?" he demanded. "You aren't involved with this little Jones girl in some way you shouldn't be, are you?"

"*No*, Dad." This time the boy was embarrassed. "Not like that. I'm only thirteen, you know."

"Yeah, and I was only nineteen. Well, what, then?" asked Harry, getting irritated.

Harrison hesitated, then said, out of the blue, "I want to be baptized."

The total change of subject took Harry by surprise, but this was a conversation he was prepared for. In some ways, the role of Baptist preacher was more comfortable than that of father. After all, he had a degree in theology from Mercer University, and he knew all the right words to say about what Baptists believed, but no one had ever taught him how to raise a son.

Harry had talked with Harrison about his faith before. The boy had accepted Christ, but before he could be baptized and officially become a member of the church, he was required to make a public profession of faith. Harry had told him that whenever he was ready to do that, he would baptize him in the river not far from the church, but Harrison kept putting it off. Now Harry pulled his line out of the water and laid the pole on the bank so he could give the boy his undivided attention.

"You've got me completely confused," said Harry. "It's wonderful if you want to be baptized. Why would you think I'd be disappointed in you?"

Harrison struggled with the words. "Because I can't. Because I'm not good enough yet," he said at last.

"But son, no one is good enough." Harry frowned and tried to explain the gospel story one more time. "We've all sinned. That's what the Bible says. We've all sinned and come short of the glory of God. But Christ, who was without sin, took our punishment. And by His grace we are saved through faith."

"And I believe all of that. But what if you believe, but you plan to go right on sinnin'?" asked Harrison. "What then?"

Harry studied his son. "I can't really tell you what to do if I don't know what you're talking about. And I can't believe you're doing anything that bad. What's worrying you?"

The dog edged closer to the boy, inviting his attention. Harrison petted him, hesitating to answer his father. Finally he blurted it out.

"I've lied to you, over and over again. But it wasn't my secret to tell, and I promised I wouldn't, so I had to lie. I've been lying from the very beginning, and it's wrong." Harrison was upset now, and he looked like the scared little boy he had been when Harry had taken him in almost a year ago. "You've been so good to me, and I feel terrible about it. I don't want you to be disappointed in me. I don't want you to ever be sorry I'm your son."

"Hey, hey. Calm down," Harry said sympathetically, squeezing the boy's shoulder. "Whatever it is, you can tell me. Look at me." Harry turned the boy's face so that they were looking at each other, eye to eye, and he spoke firmly. "There is nothing you can do that is so bad that I'll stop being your father. Do you understand me? You don't need to carry this guilt around with you anymore. Just tell me what's on your mind. I'll help you deal with it, whatever it is."

The boy looked relieved. He sniffed, wiped his eyes with his shirtsleeve, and started to speak, but still seemed hesitant. He slanted a glance at his father before asking, "First, could we talk about my mother?"

"Your mother," said Harry, surprised again. "Of course. You mean—"

"My real mother. Molly."

So the secret had something to do with Molly. Harry studied the boy solemnly. Maybe it was something about the way his mother had died. All that Harrison had ever said about Molly was that she had died two years before he ran away from Charlie. When Harry had asked him for details about how she had died, Harrison had shied away from the subject. He said she just got sick and died. He didn't want to talk about it. He didn't want to talk about Molly at all. Harry had never pressed the issue after that.

"Sure," said Harry. "Tell me about Molly."

The Captain Seeks the Lost

"Did you know she was a nurse?"

"No, I didn't," said Harry, "but I'm not surprised. Her father was a doctor. She used to help him in his office."

Harrison nodded. "That was my grandfather. We lived with him and Meme when I was a baby."

"Your grandparents were very kind to me," said Harry. "Dr. Rogers was my family's doctor. My mother was sick a long time, and Dr. Rogers took care of her until she died, and he knew about my father's problem." Harry shifted. He still wasn't comfortable talking about it. "He knew that my father had a drinking problem, and sometimes, when my father had been drinking, he hit me."

Harrison gave a nod that indicated he knew how that felt.

Harry went on. "When I finally left home, I stayed with the doctor and his wife for a short time. They had a big house, and the family lived upstairs, and his office was downstairs. He let me have a small room near the kitchen to call my own. It meant a lot to me, having his support. In some ways he was like a second father to me—a father who wasn't drunk and didn't hit me."

"And that's where you met Mama," said Harrison. "Tell me about that."

"Well, we were just kids when we met. Molly was thirteen and I was fifteen when I moved in with them. I didn't live there very long. Dr. Rogers helped me get into the Georgia Military Institute, and then I moved out.

"Molly and I stayed friends, though, and I went to the Rogers' house whenever I had a holiday and my school was closed. And as time went on, and we got older, when I needed a date for one of the dances, I would take Molly, because I felt comfortable with her. She was just a friend—like a younger cousin. And we had a lot of fun together. She was funny and outrageous, and she could always make me laugh. And, boy, could she dance! I never really understood how she felt about me. She was ahead of me in some ways, even though I was older."

Harry paused, wondering how much to say to this thirteen-year-old son.

"She loved you," said Harrison.

"Yes, she did. Before I really understood how she felt or figured out how I felt about her, I was graduating and going off to war. I didn't think the war would last long. None of us did. I was gonna go out there and fight a few battles, and then come home and get on with my life. Then I could think about getting married. I'd do things the right way. Court Molly, if she would have me. I wasn't sure if we would end up together, but if things went well, I'd ask her to marry me. Get her father's blessing. Have a wedding. I never intended to get involved with her that way before we got married—it just happened."

Harry sighed. It would be wrong to blame Molly for the way things had ended between them, although she really had instigated it, and how did you explain all of that to a thirteen-year-old? "The war changed everything. Everything. Things got out of hand, and our lives were never the same afterward."

"Did you love my mother?" Harrison asked. It was a direct question, and it deserved a direct response.

"Yes, I did. Like I said, I was young, but I cared very much for her, and I think if we'd had time—but, we didn't, because of the war—and we were scared, and we were afraid we'd never see each other again after that night. As it turned out, we didn't. After I left, I wrote her letters. I asked her to marry me—and she never wrote me back. Before long, I heard she had married someone else. Then the war went on, and one thing led to another, and I never got to see her again."

Harry was quiet again while he concentrated on checking his bait and placing the line where he thought some fish should be waiting. "You know I was in a Yankee prison, don't you?"

Harrison nodded.

"Well, I got out of prison by agreeing to serve in the cavalry, out West, and when the Civil War ended, I stayed on in the cavalry. It was a job, and jobs were scarce in the South, and I thought there was nothing for me to come home to, anyway. Molly was married and my old school had been burned to the ground, and I didn't know anyone any more. Everything had changed."

"If you had known about me—"

"If I had known about you, I would have come back as soon as I could, and I would have married your mother," Harry assured him. "You can believe it."

Harry stopped talking, feeling he had said enough. He lifted the fishing pole, checked his hook again and saw that the bait was gone, then dug around in the can of dirt, pulled out another worm, and baited the hook. Then he pointed his fishing pole closer to a shady spot near some rocks. It looked like a good place for fish to hide. He changed the subject.

"There must be some fish in there. Something got my bait. Have you felt any bites yet?" he asked Harrison.

"Haven't noticed any."

Harry decided it was Harrison's time to talk. "So, what was it like when you lived in Marietta with your grandparents?" he asked. "What do you remember about your mother?"

Harrison was now baiting his own hook. "I don't remember much about Marietta. I was too small, but I'll tell you what I know. Meme took care of me most of the time while Mama worked with Grandpa, and he taught her how to help him in the office and how to be a nurse. He paid her a salary, and that's what we lived on. Mama said Charlie wasn't there much."

"Where was Charlie?"

"At first he was in the army—not fighting, but something to do with supplies, I think. Then he was out of the army, but he was gone a lot, prospecting for gold."

"Really!" said Harry. "When I knew him at GMI, the story was that his father was a big-time prospector up in Dahlonega. He had made a fortune in gold, and that was how Charlie could afford to go to the school."

Harrison snorted. "I think that was mostly lies. What Mama said was that he had a choice between military school and jail, and he went to school."

Harry had never heard that story, but it made sense. "But Charlie's father was really a prospector, wasn't he? Is that why you moved to Dahlonega?"

"I guess so. It's where Charlie was from, anyway, and his parents lived there. We moved there after the Yankee soldiers took over Marietta. Mama's parents stayed in Marietta, but we moved to Dahlonega. They thought it would be safer for us there. I guess it was. Grandpa and Meme died when Sherman's soldiers finally burned the town and left. Mama said Grandpa wouldn't leave his hospital, and he got killed."

"How were things in Dahlonega?"

"Well, we weren't rich. It's true that Charlie's father hunted for gold, but he never seemed to find any. And he was crazy as a Bessie-bug. He was always going on about the treasure he had lost.

"Charlie's mother was a poor old washerwoman, and Mama ended up supporting the whole family by working for the doctor there. She said no matter where she went there would always be work for a nurse. It might not pay much, but it put food on the table.

"And we ended up living in a small house right in town, not far from the doctor, and Mama worked for him and minded the patients in his little hospital while he was out tending to people. She learned to be a midwife, and she's—I guess she was good at it. People started calling on her as much as the doctor, and he didn't mind. He was happy to have the help. He would let her use one of his horses so she could go out and deliver babies, and she only asked him to help if there was some kind of problem. I was thinking how nice it would be if she could be here to help Mother."

Harry grimaced. "Wouldn't that be a thing, now," he said. "Think how much gossip that would stir up: The mother of my oldest son delivering the baby of my new wife. That would be enough to keep Alotta Payne talking for years." Carlotta Payne was the church's biggest gossip, and Harry secretly called her Alotta Payne when talking to his family. He looked up, then, to see a frown on Harrison's face, and he realized he had hurt the boy's feelings.

Harrison spoke up. "But you've been so worried about Mother. It would have been a good thing, wouldn't it, Dad? If Mama could have helped her?"

"Yes, son. It would have been fine. I'm sorry. I know how much you must miss her, and I'm sure she was a good nurse. I'm really sorry." Harry watched him sympathetically, wishing he hadn't made the comment. The boy had seen so much hardship in his short life, and Harry felt guilty that he had never been there to protect him from it. He asked, "This thing you've been keeping secret. Is it about your mother?" Harry hoped the boy would finally tell him what had caused her death.

The boy nodded and seemed almost relieved to tell Harry. "You see, when I told you—" He started to speak, only to be interrupted by Ned, who came huffing around the curve in the path at that moment.

"Well, that was a complete disaster," said Ned. "On the first cast I got the line caught in the branches hanging over the creek, and I've spent all this time trying to get it untangled. I had to cut the line." He looked at the other two, finally realizing he had interrupted something.

"I'm just gonna walk a little farther up the creek. Come when you're ready," he said. Then he turned abruptly and stomped on, his exasperation clear.

Harry waited until Ned was out of sight.

"I'm sorry about that," he said at last. "Go ahead and tell me."

But the mood was broken. Harrison shook his head. "I need to talk to somebody else first."

Harry was disappointed. "You'll have to do what you think is best. I'm here if you need me."

"I know, Dad. We'll talk soon."

Then, without further conversation, they gathered their gear and followed Ned up the path. After a few minutes of walking, they met him coming back toward them. He looked very serious.

"I think I know why they call this Stink Creek. There's a little branch coming down into the stream up here, and it smells like mash." Ned looked from Harry to Harrison. "I hate to interrupt the fishing…"

"But you need to check it out. We'll all go," said Harry. They followed Ned, and, still carrying their bamboo poles, began walking up the hill, passing a shallow spot that served as a ford and continuing until they came to the place Ned had described where another branch fed into the stream. There, they followed a narrow trail that led farther uphill beside the little tributary. The dog ran on ahead through the woods.

CHAPTER 3

Kidnapped

Two bootleggers stood at the edge of a clearing in the woods. They were dressed in dark clothes and holding the reins of saddle horses and the lead ropes of pack mules that were heavily loaded with jugs of whiskey. One of the men was tying canvas over the loads to hide what they were carrying.

The man who had made the moonshine stood facing them in the clearing, counting his money. No one talked over the peaceful sound of trickling water and distant birds. Beyond a rough lean-to, under the green cover of mountain laurel and rhododendron, the twisted copper tubing of a whiskey still could be seen. The quiet was suddenly broken by the crunch of dry leaves as another man picked his way cautiously through the trees toward them, leading a gray horse.

"It's Charlie," he called out, before anyone could react.

"Well, it's about time you showed up," said the tallest of the bootleggers in a voice that was low, slow and steely. He was black-haired and had dark eyes that smoldered dangerously, like banked coals.

"Sorry I'm late," said Charlie. "The horse was going lame and I had to get that taken care of. I'll help with moving the rest."

"You should have been here yesterday, with or without the horse. You're too late. This is the last load. We don't need you."

"Look, Gibson, I said I was sorry," argued Charlie.

"I know you're sorry. Too sorry to do the job I hired you to do. You got a free guide from Dahlonega through the mountains—that's all—and then you took off. I don't need your kind of help."

The Captain Seeks the Lost

"Are you tellin' me I came all this way for nothin'? Aren't you gonna pay me somethin'?"

"I'm tellin' you I'm not sure why you came all this way, but it wasn't to help me with the whiskey." Gibson reached for one jug of whiskey, untied it from the pack mule, and held it out. "You can have one jug—on one condition. I never want to see you again. You haven't earned any money."

Charlie walked forward and took the jug. He saw that Gibson was holding a gun in his other hand.

"Okay, okay. I'm gone," said Charlie, raising his empty hand in surrender. He tied the jug onto a loop of twine that hung from the pommel of his saddle, mounted his horse, and rode up the trail. But after he crossed a low ridge and was out of sight, he left the trail and circled back around through the trees.

"That man is trouble," said the second bootlegger. "I'm glad you sent him packing. He'd bring the law down on us."

"Yep. I'm glad to see the back of him," Gibson agreed.

The moonshiner stuffed the roll of bills into his pants pocket and approached the other two men, offering his hand. "Thanks for your business," he said.

"Any time, Pete," said Michael Gibson, friendly now that the stranger had gone. "It's good white liquor, just like your grandpa used to make. Will you have more to sell later?"

"No, that's my last run. I'm moving west with Alice. Just needed the extra money to pay for the trip."

"Well, if you change your mind, let me know. I can always use another supplier." Gibson tipped his hat, mounted his horse, and leading the pack mule, headed up the trail. The other bootlegger followed him.

Pete turned back to his still and straightened things to make it look as if the still hadn't been used in awhile. It would take some time to get rid of the smell of mash that still hung in the air, but he had buried all he could of it and had washed the rest out in the creek. A few good rains and no one would be the wiser. He took a pine branch and was brushing out the tracks of the riders when he heard one of them return. He looked over his shoulder to see Charlie leading his gray horse into the clearing.

"Hey, Pete. Would you check that money again? I think Gibson gave you my share."

Pete shook his head. "No, it was the amount we agreed on." He continued sweeping.

"I was afraid you'd say that," said Charlie, bringing the butt of his pistol sharply down on the back of Pete's head. Pete dropped like a stone and found himself lying flat on his face in the dirt. At first he was too stunned to move; then he heard the scrape of Charlie's boots as he knelt to look at him. Pete kept his eyes shut and held still, hoping Charlie would think he was unconscious or dead. Charlie kicked him in the side, just to see. "You can give that one to Harry Richardson. And that—and that."

The last kick was to Pete's head, and then there was no need to pretend: everything went dark.

Down the hill, a dog barked, and a boy's voice called "Sparky! Come here!"

Swearing softly, Charlie turned Pete just enough to pull the roll of bills from his pocket, then quickly mounted his horse and left the clearing. He kicked the horse into a canter until he was beyond the ridge and out of sight. The last thing he needed was a dog chasing him. A dog and a boy. But maybe things were working out for him after all. He was pretty sure that the voice he had heard was that of young Harry—or Harrison, as they called him now. Yep, maybe things were working out okay.

A moment later, Harry and Ned came into the clearing, followed closely by Harrison. Sparky reached Pete and sniffed at the injured man's body, barked excitedly, and then sniffed again.

"Stay back a minute," Harry warned his son, then, after taking a cautious look around the clearing, he hurried to check on the man.

"It's Pete Nix," he said. "He's breathing. Let's turn him over."

Harry and Ned carefully turned the man over while Harrison joined them and held the dog back.

"Pete!" said Ned urgently, trying to wake the man. He didn't respond. "He's got a knot on his head—more than one knot. Somebody hit him hard, and not long ago." Ned scanned his surroundings quickly. "What do you think, some kind of fight between moonshiners? What was Pete doing up here, anyway? You think this is his still?"

Pete was a regular attender at the Choestoe Church and not someone Harry would have expected to find in the moonshine business. "His family used to make liquor, but I thought that was history. I wouldn't have thought he'd be involved," answered Harry. "Trying to get some extra cash, maybe? He and Alice want to move to Colorado."

Harry turned to Harrison. "Son, take the dog and the gear, and hurry on down to the house. If you see Mr. Jones or someone else who can go for the doctor, send him, but if there isn't anybody else, can you do it? Saddle up Smokey and go toward the store and turn at—"

"I know where he lives," said Harrison, already picking up the fishing poles and calling the dog to follow. "Come on, Sparky."

Harry called after him. "We'll carry Pete down to the house. Get the doc to meet us there." The boy hurried away with the dog at his heels, following the curve of the hill down toward the wider stream and back along the path toward the cabin.

Harrison hadn't gone far when there was a thrashing sound in the laurel thicket on the bank beside him, and Charlie emerged on his horse just in front of him.

"Charlie!" gasped the boy, horrified.

Charlie sneered. "Now, is that any way to greet your father?"

The boy dropped the fishing poles as he turned and ran, but Charlie spurred the horse and caught up with him, and, leaning out of the saddle, reached down and grabbed him by the belt and hauled him up onto the horse in front of him. When the boy fought to get away, Charlie twisted him around and slapped him across the face.

"Always have to do everything the hard way, don't you?" he said, putting one hand over the boy's mouth to stop the yell that was emerging and clamping the boy's head tightly to his chest. With his other hand, he shifted the boy's weight, so that he was roughly cradled in front of him, then he pulled at the reins and wheeled the horse around.

As he kicked the horse and sent it hurtling down the narrow trail, he muttered, "I've finally got you where I want you, Harry Richardson." Harrison wasn't sure whether Charlie was talking about him or the Captain. Either way, it wasn't good.

The saddle horn was digging into Harrison's leg with every motion of the horse, and Charlie was holding him so tight he could barely breathe. Charlie was a big man—as tall as the Captain, but heavier—and he smelled like sweat and whiskey. Charlie's stench and Harrison's own fear of choking almost made the boy gag. He took a slow breath through his nose and tried to calm himself. When he did that, he felt anger rise to take the place of his fear.

Harrison wasn't the scared little boy he had been last September when Charlie had beaten him and he had left Dahlonega to find Harry. He was stronger now, and he had a real father who cared about him. He had to think like a man—a brave man like Harry. If the Captain were in his place, what would he do?

Harrison felt himself grow cold inside as he started planning how he would get away, and he tried to pay attention to where they were going. He would have to find his way back. They had been following the creek down toward home, but Charlie turned the horse to ford the creek in order to follow another trail that headed upward into the mountains.

As long as they had been going toward home, Sparky had been content to run along behind, but when the horse turned to ford the creek and follow the mountain path, the dog stood at the edge of the water and started barking.

Charlie cursed, turned the horse and stopped, facing the dog. Then, coolly and deliberately, he shifted the reins to the hand that had been covering Harrison's mouth, drew his gun, and shot the dog.

Harrison screamed, "No!" and tried to push free of Charlie's hold as the dog ran yelping back down the trail toward home. Charlie fired again into the dust at the dog's feet, but missed, then clamped his hand around Harrison's mouth even harder than before and turned the horse again.

"If you don't hold still, I'll break your scrawny neck," Charlie growled into Harrison's ear.

Harrison held still. He was crying now, in pain from Charlie's rough treatment and sure that his dog was injured, maybe dying. Sparky had been able to run, but that terrible, screaming yelp meant he was hurt.

Harrison wished he had a weapon. He had dropped everything he had been carrying, but he still had his pocketknife and his flint in his pockets, and they might be handy—if Charlie didn't find them. He had the little carving tied on a string around his neck. He had brought it in case he had time to whittle. That wasn't much to work with. But he was strong and fast, and he knew a little about how to get around in the woods. Harry had seen to that. And he could fight.

First he had to make Charlie believe he was already beaten, so the man wouldn't think he needed to prove who was in charge by hitting him again. (Harrison had spent most of his life figuring out how to avoid being beaten by Charlie.) He had to hold still now, because if Charlie tightened his grip any more, he might just break Harrison's neck without meaning to. When they got where they were going, he had to watch for his chance to get away.

And somehow he would find a way to kill Charlie so that this could never happen again. Harrison groaned loudly, hoping Charlie would believe he had given up, or would at least ease up a little bit so he could breathe better. Charlie thought he was still just a little boy, so Harrison acted like it, but deep inside, the cold, angry part of him was waiting and watching for a chance to get away.

* * *

Back in the clearing, Harry kicked a wide, gray, oak plank loose from the side of the lean-to and brought it over to use for a stretcher. Then he and Ned carefully moved Pete onto it and they used Pete's suspenders to tie him down. For a brief moment, Pete regained consciousness, and, although he was very groggy, he recognized Harry and Ned.

"What happened to you, Pete?" asked Harry.

"Man beat me up." He felt his pocket and found it empty. "Robbed me."

"Do you know who it was?" asked Ned.

"Big guy. Ask Mike Gibson." Pete seemed confused. He blinked slowly.

"Was it a bearded man on a gray horse?" asked Harry.

"Yeah. That's the one. He hates you, Harry. Said to give all these kicks to you." Pete smiled feebly. "I don't know why he didn't just kick you directly. Don't see why I had to take the message."

"What was his name?" asked Harry.

Pete tried to shake his head, but the movement hurt him. "I heard it. I'll think of it," he said, and then he passed out again.

"We need to get him to the doc," said Harry.

"He might not make it," said Ned grimly. "He's been hit pretty hard."

They were just starting down the path when they heard two distant gunshots and the terrified yelping of a dog.

"What was that? Sparky?" Harry's eyes met Ned's and, holding the stretcher between them, they hurried down the trail as fast as they could go. The narrow clay path was partially covered with leaves and pine needles, and tracks were not always easy to follow, but it was clear that an unshod horse had intercepted Harrison at the place where the fishing poles had been dropped, and, farther down, the horse had turned at the ford to cross the stream and follow the mountain path. And where the horse had turned, there was blood on the ground.

"He shot the dog, and the dog ran for home," said Harry. "But there were two shots. Harrison?" he asked bleakly.

"I don't think he shot Harrison," said Ned. "Why would he? He may have taken Harrison with him, but we can't be sure of that, either. Maybe the man took off and Harrison carried the dog home. We have to follow the blood."

Ned looked gravely at Harry, who was studying the trail. "I know what you're thinking, Harry, and you can't go after him now. We need to check on the women and make sure they're safe, and see if Harrison's there, and get Pete to the doc. Even if this man has taken Harrison, you can't go after him unarmed and on foot. You might be walking into an ambush. And if he's headed up into the mountains, we'll need horses and men and supplies."

Harry knew Ned made sense, but every instinct made him want to follow the horseman into the hills anyway. He felt a sick dread, knowing his son might have been shot or kidnapped and might be getting farther away with every minute that passed. But he wouldn't know that for sure until he checked to see if the boy was at home. And Ned was right: Sarah and Winifred might also be in danger. He helped Ned lift the still-unconscious Pete, and, following the drops of blood, they walked rapidly down the path toward home.

CHAPTER 4

Harry Goes to War

Sarah and Winifred had spent the morning washing and rinsing clothes in washtubs that were set up under a shelter off the back porch. Earlier in the year, with the help of some men from the church, Harry had built a system to bring icy cold water down from a spring on the hillside behind the house using pipes made of hollowed white pine logs. Now there was no need to carry water in buckets from the spring. There was a cistern with a hand pump on the back porch.

Sarah considered herself a lucky woman, indeed. There was a big iron caldron or "wash pot" that stood on three legs so that a fire could be built under it for heating the water, and there were two wooden washtubs on a low table for washing and rinsing the clothes. Water still had to be carried by bucket from the pump to the wash pot or the washtubs, but at least she didn't have to carry it all the way from the spring. Normally, this made it possible for Sarah to do the washing without Harry there to help, and that was important, given the time he spent traveling all over the area. Now that she was "in the family way" she needed assistance, and Winifred had come to help.

The two women had used a washboard to scrub the clothes, rinsed them, and rung them out by hand, and then had hung them on clotheslines in the back yard. Now they were sitting on the front porch. Sarah was putting the final touches on a crocheted baby blanket she had assembled from granny squares, and Winifred was stringing green beans and using a sewing needle to thread them onto lines so that they could hang them from pegs around the porch to dry. Dried "leather britches" beans would taste good in the winter when fresh fruits and vegetables were not available. The green beans would join strings of June apple slices that were already hanging to dry.

Right now, Harry and Sarah had an abundance of fresh vegetables from their own garden and the gardens of church members, and it was a big job to get the food put by before it could go to waste. People couldn't pay the pastor much, but they were willing to share what they had and see to it that he and his family didn't go hungry. For supper there would be a variety of fresh vegetables from the garden, and if the men had had any luck, there would be fish. If not, they would have ham or sausage from the smokehouse.

"I don't know how I would have managed this past year without your help, Winifred," Sarah said.

Winifred shrugged off the compliment. "I haven't done anything."

"But you have. You've taught me so much! I didn't know what it meant to be a preacher's wife—how to deal with the gossips, how to lay out a body for a wake. I was completely unprepared for all of that, and I truly don't know how I would have survived without you. So, thank you."

"You're welcome. I'm glad you're here to keep Harry happy." Winifred looked mischievous. "Otherwise, he would have been left to the devices of Alotta Payne and her clingy little flirt of a daughter."

"Winifred! Shame on you!" Sarah stifled a laugh as she looked quickly around to make sure no one could possibly be standing nearby and listening. "I think Harry could have fended Abigail off—" She broke off to stare into the distance, where the dog Sparky was dragging himself into the yard, whining and shaking.

"Sparky's hurt!" she said. The two women dropped what they were doing and hurried to see what was wrong. One of the dog's front legs was bleeding. Winifred ran to get a rug, wrapped the dog in it, and carried him to the house.

"Poor thing," said Winifred. "It looks like he's been shot. He's all bloody." The women used wet rags to clean the dog up as much as they could, and Winifred wrapped a dry cloth around the injured leg. The dog growled a warning when they caused him pain, then wagged his tail pitifully, as if in apology. They tried not to hurt him.

"Poor Sparky—poor boy, it's all right," murmured Sarah, stroking his head while Winifred wrapped the leg. "I don't know how this could have happened. He never leaves Harrison's side." Then Harry and Ned came into the yard, carrying someone on a plank.

"Oh, no. Harrison's hurt," said Sarah.

"That's not Harrison," said Winifred. "It's a grown man."

The women left the dog and hurried to meet the men.

"Is Harrison here?" demanded Harry, as soon as he was close enough to be heard.

"No," said Sarah. "Isn't he with you? Harry, what happened? The dog is hurt!"

Harry and Ned lowered Pete to the ground in the shade of a tree. Ned knelt beside him to see if he was still breathing.

"He's still alive. Barely," Ned reported.

Then Harry looked gravely at his wife. "Someone robbed Pete and beat him. We think it was that man that came here yesterday." Harry hesitated to give the worst news. "And we think he's taken Harrison."

"Why would he do that?" gasped Sarah.

"I don't know, but it's personal. He hates me, whoever he is." Harry looked carefully around. "We need to get inside." He spoke to Winifred and Sarah. "Go into the house and stay there. Get some food together that I can take on the trail. And get my revolver, Sarah." Harry turned to Ned. "Let's move him into the house."

Once inside, they lowered Pete to the floor, and as Harry walked quickly around, gathering the things he would need, he continued to talk to Ned, reeling off thoughts as they came to him. "I need to saddle Smokey and go. You'll have to get your horse. Then go down to the store and tell people we need help. Ring the church bell. Get somebody to go for the doctor. Somebody needs to get Alice and tell her about Pete. And we need a handpicked posse. We don't need a crowd of church people wandering in the woods, stomping out the tracks and getting lost. Get Liam if you can. He's the best tracker I ever knew. And find Mike Gibson. Pete thinks he knows something about the man. And he knows all the trails around here."

"You trust him?"

"Yeah—with everything except moonshine. He's a good man at heart. He wouldn't do anything to hurt Harrison."

Ned nodded, agreeing. "Whoever this is, he couldn't have planned this ahead. He couldn't have known we'd be fishing up there, or that you'd send Harrison for help. He just took advantage of an opportunity. You think you know who it is?"

Harry paced the floor in the living room. "If Dawson's still in jail and there's not some other member of the gang that we didn't catch, it has to be Charlie. He's the only man who's ever hated me this much. It's personal, and it makes sense that he would take Harrison. I just don't know why he would suddenly do this when we haven't heard a word from him the whole time Harrison has been here. He took Harrison to the station himself. I telegraphed him that I had the boy. When I didn't hear anything, I thought he was glad to be rid of him."

"Maybe he's just crazy."

"Crazy as a Bessie-bug—that's what Harrison said about Charlie's father," mused Harry. "But there's something more. Harrison was starting to talk to me today. There's something he couldn't bring himself to tell. Then we ran out of time."

"That was my fault."

"No. All of this—all of it—is Charlie's fault—if it's Charlie."

While Ned knelt beside Pete to check on him, Harry walked to the fireplace to get the rifle that was hanging on pegs above the mantle. It was a new '73 model Winchester that Raymond Whittaker had sent him as a reward for his help in breaking up the counterfeiting ring. He lifted it down from the pegs and walked to the bedroom to retrieve a leather pouch and ammunition that he kept in his trunk. As he slung the leather strap over his shoulder he had the feeling he was going back to war. And, in a way, he was. He got out his gray cape and his bedroll and rolled them tightly together so he could strap them behind his saddle. Other things went into his saddlebags: a few extra clothes, a flint lighter, a canteen, and a roll of bandages. He prayed that he wouldn't need the bandages. He would get some rope from the barn.

He was still standing by the bed when Sarah came in, frowning. She brought a small cloth sack filled with food. "I don't know how much you want to carry, Harry."

Harry looked into the sack and saw cold cornbread, beef jerky, and dried apples. "That will be enough, right there." He took Sarah into his arms and held her tight. "I don't know when I'll be back."

"Don't worry about me, Harry. I'll be fine. Just get Harrison back."

"Take care of Sparky," said Harry, and suddenly there were tears in his eyes. "It would really hurt Harrison to lose that dog." He wouldn't consider the possibility that he might lose Harrison, too.

"I'll do that, Harry," Sarah said. "And Ned wants to talk to you," Then, stepping away from Harry, she looked him in the eye. "This will be all right. You'll take care of it like you always do. I know it."

Harry nodded and squeezed Sarah's hand, and she left the room to be replaced by Ned, but Sarah lingered at the door, and Winifred was right behind her.

"What is it?" asked Harry, knowing Ned.

"Just a reminder. You're emotionally involved here. That's dangerous. It can cause you to make mistakes and get hurt. You need to pretend this boy is a stranger and be the Captain. Then you'll do what's best for him and for all of us. And I'll do everything you ask me to do, Harry."

At that, Harry smiled faintly. "You've made your point. But he's getting farther away with every minute that passes."

"You assume that, but the man could be hiding out in the woods behind this house, waiting for us to take off so he can take Sarah hostage, too. We don't know enough, Harry."

"You're right—anything's possible." Harry thought for a moment. "Forget everything I said. We shouldn't leave Sarah and Winifred unprotected. One of us should stay here with them. If Harrison comes back, or you need me for some other reason, send someone after me. And if I'm not back in two days, see if Liam can come with you, and come and find me, but get somebody to stay with the women. Right now, go get Albert Jones, and send him after the doctor and let him tell people what's going on. He can tell them to be on the lookout for Charlie, but to look after their own families for now. If we need help, we'll let them know. As soon as you get back, I'll go."

Ned nodded, satisfied. "That sounds like a good plan."

Harry was loading cartridges into the Winchester. "And when I find Charlie, I'll do whatever I have to do to get my son back." He slammed the last cartridge home, looking grim.

"Nobody will blame you." Ned nodded his approval, then hurried from the room.

"Sarah?" called Harry. He picked up his saddlebags. "You heard. You keep the Colt. If anyone threatens you or Winifred, you know what to do."

"Yes, Harry."

Harry marched past them, carrying all of his gear, heading for the barn to saddle his horse.

Winifred exchanged a glance with Sarah. "This is a Harry I've never seen. Ned told me what he was like in wartime, but I never really understood."

"Whoever this man is, he'll be sorry he came to Choestoe," said Sarah.

"Yes, he will."

"We should send some clothes for Harrison," said Sarah, looking toward the ladder to the loft. She was in no condition to climb up there, so Winifred climbed up the ladder to Harrison's small room in the loft. She quickly picked out a change of clothes for the boy from things that hung from hooks on the wall. There was no telling what condition Harrison would be in when Harry found him. He might be filthy, injured, and cold.

Winifred examined the meager contents of his room, wondering what else the boy would need. On a shelf near the bed was the small, framed picture of Molly, Harrison's mother. It had been one of the few possessions he had carried with him when he left home. On impulse, Winifred took the picture and wrapped the clothes around it. Then she went back down the ladder. She carried the clothes to the barn and gave them to Harry.

"For Harrison," she said.

Harry nodded and added the clothes to one of his saddlebags. Feeling the picture frame, he asked, "What's this?" then saw that it was the picture of the boy's mother. "You keep this for him, Winnie," he said. "Keep it safe for him."

"All right."

"And, Winnie, I won't be able to help Alice and Pete. Will you see that someone does what's needed?"

"Yes. Some of the ladies will take them food and sit with them. Everyone will want to help."

"If I'm gone awhile, someone will need to get old Preacher Brown or Elder Dyer to fill in for me until I get back. If Pete doesn't make it and there needs to be a funeral…"

"We'll take care of everything, Harry."

From the house, Sarah called out, "Pete's awake!" Harry hurried back inside to talk to him. When he knelt beside him and put his hand on the man's forehead, Pete opened his eyes.

"How're you feeling, Pete?" Harry asked.

Pete blinked several times, looking around to get his bearings. His eyes focused on Harry.

"I've been better. Where am I?"

"You're at my house. Do you remember what happened?"

Pete felt for his money. "Yep. A low-down skunk named Charlie beat me up, and I guess he robbed me, too." He looked around the room. "Do you think I could get some water?"

Harry helped him sit up and offered him a dipper of water. When he moved, Pete held his side, and Harry suspected he had some cracked ribs.

Winifred came and knelt beside him. "Ned has gone to get help," she said. "You rest for a few more minutes while we wait for them." Pete nodded and drank deeply then they helped him lie back down. He was weak, but he was definitely showing signs of recovering.

Harry went back to the barn. Within just a few minutes he had saddled his horse and added the rope to his saddle and a nosebag with some grain to the saddlebags, then he led the horse over to the house, where Sarah waited on the porch. She was holding his blue cavalry coat, and she was trying not to cry.

"Maybe you should take this," she said, walking down the steps to meet him. "It's cold on the mountains at night."

"All right," said Harry, understanding that she needed to give him the coat whether he needed it or not. She felt he would be safe in that coat with the bullet hole in it, for it had protected him once before.

"Thank you." He took the coat, rolled it up, and wedged it under the straps between his saddle and the bedroll. Then he smiled and spoke gently. "You tell little Annie to wait 'til I get back, okay?"

Sarah nodded and bit her lip to stop it trembling, then held tight to Harry. "Come back to me, Harry."

"I will," he promised, and he kissed her firmly on the mouth.

Ned rode his horse into the yard. "Albert's on his way to get the doctor and Gibson, and to let people know what's going on. You can go."

With no further need for words, Harry mounted his horse and rode quickly out of the yard.

Ned stood watching him ride away, then he turned back to consider the small cabin, thinking about how best to keep everyone safe.

"Sarah," he said at last. "How would you feel about moving down to our house until things are settled? We'd have more room there, and Charlie hasn't been there. He knows this house."

Sarah nodded. "That's a good idea. Let me get some things together."

Winifred went to help her, and Ned followed them inside to check on Pete. He was lying still, resting, and his color looked better.

Ned didn't disturb him. "I'll hitch up the wagon," he told Winifred.

After a while, Albert drove up in his buckboard with Pete's wife, Alice, on the seat beside him. "The doctor wasn't home," Albert said.

Alice ran inside and knelt beside her husband, then stooped over to kiss his face. He opened his eyes, smiled, and assured her he would be all right.

After a few minutes, Ned and Alice helped Pete get up and walk, and now he wanted to go home, so they settled him on the seat of the buckboard with his wife beside him, supporting him. After talking briefly with Ned, Albert clucked to the horses and turned the wagon around.

"We're moving down to my house," Ned called to Albert. "If anyone needs us, that's where we'll be."

Ned helped Sarah get up into the wagon and loaded her suitcase and her bag of knitting. Then, with Winifred's help, he put the injured dog into a wooden crate and loaded that into the wagon, too. Finally, they were ready to leave the smaller cabin and head for Ned and Winifred's house.

"What about the clothes on the line?" asked Sarah.

"They aren't dry yet. We should just leave them," said Winifred. "We can come back later."

Sarah had a bad feeling about leaving her home. She was afraid this was the end of something important and things would never be the same again. Without her family she felt alone and afraid, and she could only imagine how Harrison felt, wherever he was.

"We should leave a lamp on," she said, "in case Harrison comes back in the dark."

"I'll do it," Ned said, and he went back inside to light a lamp. He found a large container of lamp oil and filled the receptacle in the lamp so that the flame would last awhile, then lit the lamp and turned the wick down low. He left the lamp on a porcelain-topped table where it would be safe. Then he went to all the windows and pulled the curtains closed. No point in making it easy for Charlie to see that no one was home.

When they reached the other house, Winifred announced that the spare bedroom was Sarah's for as long as she needed it and helped put her things in there.

A few minutes later, the sound of the church bell arose in the distance. Sarah was glad that things were in motion and the community would be involved, but she was also very happy that she wouldn't have to deal with people that came by. Ned would be here to organize the searchers as well as protect Sarah, and Winifred could handle everything else.

"Albert's going to send for Michael Gibson and have him come here," Ned reported to Sarah and Winifred. "He may know something about this man. Charlie may be taking the boy back to Dahlonega. Michael knows all the roads and trails that lead there, and he has men who can help. Maybe they can head Charlie off."

Winifred nodded. "Raymond Whittaker is in Dahlonega. He might be able to help, too. Wonder if Michael would talk to him."

"I think he might," came a voice from the doorway. And there was the dark-eyed bootlegger, holding his hat in his hands and looking somber. "I heard about Pete and came as fast as I could," he said.

"Pete said to ask you about the man who hit him. Big man with a beard, name of Charlie," said Ned.

"That would be Charlie Baldwin. I hired him down in Dahlonega to help me with some work, but I fired him this morning."

"Why?" asked Ned.

"Because he's no good—the kind of person that gives men like me a bad name," said Michael with a look that was both ironic and defiant. He was aware of his own reputation as a bootlegger, and he knew that Ned was aware of it, too. "On the way here, he asked me a lot of questions. I figured he had plans of his own, but I had no idea what he was up to. He must have hung around after I left. Then, when everyone else was gone, he went back to rob Pete."

Michael looked solemnly at Ned. "I want you to know that I'm sorry for bringing this man here, and for what he did to Pete. This is personal for me. The man betrayed my trust. I'll help you any way I can." Michael offered his hand.

"Thank you," Ned said, gripping his hand firmly. Ned and Michael knew each other from a distance, but they weren't close friends. Both men had been soldiers, and they respected each other for that, but they were on opposite sides of the law when it came to liquor taxes. A few months ago, when some bad liquor was circulating that was making people sick, Michael had helped Ned track down the source. That had been the beginning of friendship.

"The main thing is to find the boy," said Ned. "Harry is trying to track them, but I thought you might have ideas—"

"The boy?" interrupted Michael, looking lost.

Ned filled in the missing information. "Harry's son is missing. We think Charlie took him."

"I didn't know."

"Harry and Charlie are old enemies. Come on in," said Ned. "We'll talk."

Very quickly, the two men talked about the situation and ways to organize men to search. For now, Ned's biggest responsibility was to protect the women and maintain a headquarters so that there could be communication. Michael agreed to head south toward Dahlonega, just as he had planned to do, but with all of his men taking separate trails and keeping watch for Charlie and Harrison. Ned didn't ask what Michael's business was, and Michael didn't offer the information. For the time being, the bootlegger and the revenuer had put aside their differences. There were bigger issues at stake here. Harry needed their help.

After a few minutes, Sarah retired to her room and closed the door, feeling tired and helpless. And her back had been aching since they washed the clothes. She needed to rest.

CHAPTER 5

Into the Mountains

Charlie urged the gray horse off the path and into a clearing that was surrounded by low brush and overhanging limbs. He held still for a moment, listening, then, satisfied that no one was following, he dismounted, pulling the boy off the horse and dropping him roughly onto the ground. Harrison, dazed by the rough ride and the harsh treatment, looked quickly around to see where they were. He could see only green leaves in all directions.

When Charlie reached for a braided leather cord that was tied in a loop on the saddle, Harrison shielded his head with his arms, behaving like a little boy expecting a lashing.

"That's right. Show me a little respect," said Charlie. "But I don't have time to whip you now." He grabbed Harrison's hands and tied them together with the cord, and he kept hold of the long end of it, using it like a leash. "I'm letting you keep your hands in front so you can hang on. You're gonna ride behind me on the horse. I can't cradle you like a baby any more. You're too big and heavy."

As if Harrison had been comfortable being "cradled" by Charlie! He was covered in bruises, and he was afraid his legs wouldn't work if he tried to stand. But he needed to stand.

"I need to pee," said Harrison.

"Well, that's another good reason to have your hands tied in front. Go ahead, I won't stop you. Just don't try to run."

Harrison managed to stand and turn his back to Charlie before he awkwardly unbuttoned his pants and relieved himself. He could hear Charlie doing the same thing. He fumbled to get his pocketknife out of his pocket while Charlie wasn't looking, which wasn't easy with his wrists tied together. Then he wedged the knife under the cords that tied his hands. The small knife seemed secure against the inside of his wrist, and it didn't show. After he had buttoned his pants again, he stretched his legs and arms as well as he could. Nothing seemed to be broken, only sore.

"Hurry up. We don't have all day." Charlie yanked on the tether so that Harrison was forced to face him. Harrison glanced and saw that the knife was undisturbed.

"I'll explain things to you," Charlie said. "We're going a long way. Sometimes it will be steep. You'll need to hold onto the saddle. If you fall off, I might just drag you or let you run along behind. If you give me any trouble, I might shoot you like I did the dog, or I might decide to tie you up and sling you across the horse like a sack of grain. So you try real hard not to fall off or give me any trouble. And if you scream, I'll stuff a dirty handkerchief in your mouth, and if you choke on it, that's okay with me.

"If you behave yourself, things will go a lot easier for you. Understand?" Charlie looked threateningly at the boy. When Harrison didn't respond, he repeated the question. "I said, 'Do you understand?'"

"I understand," Harrison said quickly. Anything to keep Charlie from losing his temper. "Where are we going?"

"That's for me to know. Somewhere Harry will never find you." He seemed to be in a mood to talk, but Harrison knew he needed to be careful. Charlie always found a way to twist things, and even the most innocent remark could send him into a rage.

"Why?" asked Harrison. "Why are you doing this?"

"Because Harry's had everything his own way long enough."

"If you wanted me back, why didn't you just tell him?"

"Because I didn't know where you went at first. You're lying mother made up such a load of stories." Charlie's face kept changing: first arrogant, then angry, then smug. "You know what gave it away? That letter you wrote her." Charlie smirked, remembering. "I've always been good at finding her mail."

Harrison didn't say anything. He was pretty sure Charlie had stolen the letters that Harry and Molly had written to each other all those years ago. Everything bad that had ever happened to him had been Charlie's fault.

Charlie kept talking. "That snoopy treasury agent, Whittaker, came around one day, and the next thing I knew, she was going there and talking to him, and so I searched her things, and there was this letter from you, only the envelope was addressed to Mr. Whittaker from some little girl."

So Lindy's letters had reached Molly. That part had worked, anyway. But maybe it hadn't been such a good idea.

Charlie was getting angry now, and that was dangerous. The longer he talked, the louder and more threatening his voice became. "There you were, asking Molly to come and help your *new mother* with the baby and signing your name 'Harrison.' Your name was never Harrison, and you don't have a *new mother*! You have the same mother you've always had, and she's my wife, and YOU ARE MY SON. I'm the one who was there for the first twelve years of your life. What does Harry think I'll do, just look the other way while he takes my son?"

Harrison spoke in Harry's defense. "He didn't think you cared. He saw the way you beat me. He thought you were glad to get rid of me!" Then, alarmed that he had mentioned the beating and afraid it would give Charlie ideas, Harrison rushed on. "Besides, he's been so busy, he never even thought about you."

"He never even thought about me. Well, there's the truth. Harry has never once thought about me. Never cared. And how many times did he look in on you and your mother in all those years? Tell me that! How many times?"

"He never even knew I existed," said Harrison.

It was a true statement, but Charlie took it to be a complaint.

"You're absolutely right. He never knew any of us existed. There was only the great Captain Harry, ruler of the world. Well, I'm going to let him know that I exist. I'm going to take everything away from him, just like he took everything away from me. I'll make him pay."

"But you still have Mama," said Harrison, beginning to worry. "Harry didn't take her away." And there was the truth that Harrison hadn't told Harry. His mother, Molly, was still alive.

"But he's going to. She left me. She thinks she's going to find Harry. And I'm going to make sure she never does. But first, we'll lead Harry on a merry chase. And while he's looking for you—well, I'll see what other things I can do to make his life interesting." Charlie put a foot into the stirrup and swung himself into the saddle. Then he moved the horse closer to a big gray rock. "Step up on the rock and put your foot in the stirrup," he commanded, and he removed his foot from the stirrup so that Harrison could use it.

As Harrison attempted to mount, Charlie pulled the boy's tied arms and swung him onto the horse behind him. Harrison managed to get his leg up over the horse's rump and hold onto the back of the saddle, and before he felt settled at all, the horse was moving, and all he could do was hang on. While they were moving, Charlie looped the end of the leather cord through his belt and tied it fast. Now if Harrison fell off, he would be dragged under the legs of the horse. He held on for dear life—with one hand. With the other, he worked at the pocketknife until he got it free of the cord.

Harrison had to use both hands to open the blade, but he managed it. Now he could get to work on the straps that held his left hand. Once that one was free, he'd figure out how to get completely free without Charlie noticing. But Charlie would notice when he cut the tether that held him. He could almost hear Harry's voice in his head as he made his plans. *And then what, Harrison? What will you do next?* That thought made him stop.

What would happen if he got his hands free? He could slide off the back of the horse and run—and Charlie would catch him. And then he'd know Harrison had a knife, and he'd take it away, and he would do something terrible to him as punishment. Harrison thought of all the possible ways he could get off the horse and try to get away, and every way he imagined it, it ended up the same. Charlie caught him every time. It would be better to keep the knife a secret and wait until Charlie was asleep to sneak away. Then he could get a head start and be gone before Charlie knew it. He closed the knife silently and carefully slid it back under the leather cords between his wrists, and he waited.

And Harrison watched where they were going. They had been following a stream for most of the time. It wasn't Stink Creek; it was one they had come to after they followed the mountain path for a while, and it was leading ever higher into the mountains. Sometimes Charlie would cross the creek and ride for a while in another direction, then he would cut across rocks or through woods and end up back at the creek. Sometimes he rode right into the creek and traveled in the water.

Harrison knew he was trying to send trackers off on a wild goose chase whenever he could. But he still kept coming back to the creek. This was his road map. He would follow the creek until some other landmark caused him to change courses. Harrison planned to watch and remember so that he could find his way back down when the time was right.

After what seemed like hours of following the creek and taking detours, then riding in the water, Charlie did something different. He rode in the creek for a while, and then he pulled the horse up onto the soft clay of a low creek bank. When they stopped, he lifted Harrison down.

"Walk around a minute. Stretch your legs," said Charlie. Harrison was baffled by this sudden kindness until he realized that their shoes were making tracks. This was another ploy, another way of misdirecting Harry. Harrison stood still. If Charlie was leaving tracks to make it seem like they were continuing on this route, they must be turning. They must have gone past their turnoff this time, and now they'd be backtracking through the water to the place to turn.

"Can I get a drink?" he asked.

"I don't care. Just don't fall in," said Charlie. "And don't go anywhere. I'd hate to have to shoot you." Charlie untied the tether from his belt and tied it back to the saddle while he went into the bushes for a minute. He had his gun in his hand, and he made sure Harrison saw it.

Harrison knelt by the clear stream and bent down, holding his tied hands in front of him, trying to get some water into his mouth. He tried to think what he could do to signal Harry that something was different. While he knelt by the creek, he lifted the carving out of his shirt and yanked on the string. The string broke, leaving the circle of wood in his hand and the string hanging loose around his neck. Now he had two things he could use to mark the way: the carving and the string. He pulled the string loose and dropped it into the mud between his knees. It was too white. Charlie would see it. He quickly rubbed the string in the clay, then formed it into the shape of an arrow, pointing back the way they had come, and he dropped the carving into his pocket. He rinsed his hands in the water and stood back up, putting his shoe on top of the string. Then he waited for Charlie to help him get back on the horse. He hoped two things: that Harry (and not Charlie) would see his arrow, and that the arrow was pointing in the right direction.

* * *

Harry figured that Charlie had about an hour's head start. As he followed the trail, he was cautious at first, making certain he wasn't riding into an ambush, but it became clear as he continued the journey that Charlie was keeping a steady pace, following the stream. After following several false leads off to one side or the other, Harry knew that Charlie was trying to confuse him, and that he always returned to the creek. Then Harry started ignoring the side trails and increased the pace, making up for lost time.

Even when the trail went cold for a while, Harry continued, and eventually it would reappear. Using this strategy, there was the danger that Harry would unexpectedly catch up with the gray horse, unprepared, or that the real trail would diverge from the present course and Harry would have to backtrack, and that would cost him time. He tried to remain vigilant.

He figured there were times when Charlie rode the horse into the stream, and he watched for wet tracks emerging. At one such place he got down from his horse and examined the wet hoof prints to try to estimate the passage of time. It was true: He was gradually catching up. And at one place he saw two sizes of footprints on the soft clay where both Harrison and Charlie had dismounted. He was on the right track.

The trail disappeared again, and there was no obvious detour. As Harry continued up the stream, he began to hear a distant roar. He rode slowly, watching, and he was sure he knew the source of the sound: there was a waterfall up ahead. He continued following the path along the creek, and it was more difficult now, for the banks were thick with mountain laurel and fallen trees. As he grew closer, the roar of the falls grew louder. Then the stream widened out, and he saw the waterfall in the distance. It was magnificent, an almost vertical fall of water pouring from a great height down the face of a rocky cliff and into a wide pool. There would be no more following of this stream. Not from here. Not without backtracking and finding a detour that would lead up into the cliffs from one side or another, avoiding the falls. Still, Harry searched as close as he could to the waterfall. He dismounted and tied Smokey where there was a little grass, and he walked. Could there be a path that went behind the falls? No, there wasn't one. Was there a path that led to the top? Apparently not. Harry scouted all around the waterfall to no avail, finally coming upon what looked like a game trail that led up into the cliffs, but it was too steep for a horse.

Harry walked to where he had tied Smokey, mounted the horse and turned back. He would go back to the last evidence of tracks and start there. He had to do it now, while the sun lasted, and before the trail grew cold. Rain might come in the night and wash away every trace. Harry rode back, studying the ground as he went, wishing he had taken the time to bring Liam with him. He hoped that if he didn't return soon, Ned would bring him. If Harry couldn't do this, Liam might be their only hope, but if Liam was as addled as he sometimes seemed, that was a slim hope, indeed.

Harry didn't see a single trace of the gray horse's tracks beyond the point where the shoe prints appeared, and he didn't see where any other tracks left the stream farther up the creek. The only hoof prints on the path beyond this point were Smokey's. He looked more closely at the shoe prints, trying to figure what had happened here. Charlie had walked off into the woods, and Harry saw why. Call of nature. Charlie had not bothered to cover it up, just as he had not bothered to hide their tracks. It was odd, unless he wanted these things to be seen.

Harrison had knelt by the stream, probably getting a drink of water. Harry walked carefully around the tracks so as not to disturb them. Then he knelt beside the marks made by Harrison's knees. And there, pressed into the ground by another footprint, was a perfect arrow made of string, pointing back the way they had come. It was a message from Harrison—no doubt about it.

Harry was proud of his son for keeping his wits about him and using his resources. He hoped he could find him and tell him how proud he was before it was too late. Harry rode Smokey into the creek, as he was sure Charlie had done, and headed back downstream, looking carefully for any sign that another horse had left the stream.

He had lost time. He had to hurry. And yet Harry took his time, looking on both sides of the stream for any indication that a horse had left the creek. It was almost dark when he finally saw it. It was a place where the bank was made of a long flat, rock and there would be no tracks. But the rock was wet where a large animal had come out of the water, and there were faint brush shapes in the water on the rock, where someone had tried to cover his trail.

And there, just where the rock gave way to dirt and undergrowth, something round had been dropped on the ground. Harry stopped his horse, dismounted, and stooped to pick up the object. It was a rough carving of two snakes swallowing each other. Harry squeezed it into his palm and thanked God. The boy was still alive, and Harry was on the right track. Then he looked once more at the carving, and he wondered if he and Charlie had always been the two snakes swallowing each other, and if one would ever let go, or if they would both be destroyed. Not if he could help it.

Harry used what remained of the daylight to set up his camp. It would be a cold camp, because a fire would give away his location, but there was a rough meadow by the creek, he had food to eat, and the horse could graze. Before he quit for the night he followed the trail across the meadow and up to the edge of the mountain. He saw how the path twisted and turned, going upward. He would have preferred to keep following, but the light was fading too fast, the terrain was too rough and steep, and the trail too hard to follow. One misstep in the dark could mean a broken leg for him or the horse. It would be best to wait, get some rest and try again tomorrow. He would wait, pray and try to sleep.

CHAPTER 6

Michael Makes a Change

Michael Gibson liked Ned Spiva, Harry Richardson, and their wives. That was the trouble. They were all good, interesting people—the kind of people he would have liked to call his friends. He had met them all at his Uncle Greg's house after the capture of the counterfeiters last year, when they had celebrated with a picnic. Harry and his friends had played music, and the rest of them had danced. Some people had complained about the preacher's behavior, but Michael liked that about Harry. Even though he was a preacher, he wasn't afraid to play the fiddle and dance. There was just this one obstacle to their friendship: Michael was on the wrong side of the law.

Michael came from a long line of mountain people who made liquor by the light of the moon because what they were doing was illegal. It was not illegal to make whiskey, sell it, or drink it. It was illegal to avoid paying tax on the product, though, and that's what the moonshiners did.

All the way back to George Washington's time there had been an excise tax on whiskey, and the Whiskey Rebellion had been a result. And all the way back to that time there had been moonshiners who had taken to the hills to avoid paying the tax. Michael didn't think that would change any time soon.

Michael's illegal activities had never hurt anyone, as far as he knew, and his resistance to the law was a matter of principle as much as family tradition. Michael thought the tax wasn't fair. He didn't believe the government had the right to burden poor mountaineers with taxes when they were barely making a living. Moonshiners had found a way to make money from the corn they grew, and they felt they should be allowed to keep it.

For better or worse, "white lightning" was part of the mountain culture. Many people kept a jug of whiskey on the dinner table, usually for social drinking, but if not for that, for "medicinal purposes." Different churches took different stands on the issue. One old preacher expected to find a pint of white liquor at his place at the table whenever he came to eat, while others preached that drinking was a sin. It was complicated.

Michael respected people on both sides of the argument. He didn't drink much himself, and he felt that people had a right to their own opinions on the subject. But government interference made him mad, and so he fought it the only way he could. He got the liquor to market. As far as he was concerned, he represented the poor and oppressed, and what he was doing was not wrong. It was a crime, because the law said it was, but his conscience was clear.

He was also very good at getting away with it. He kept some tax stamps on hand, just in case he needed to put them on the jugs at the last minute. Some bootleggers had been known to keep tax stamps in their boots, in case of emergency, thus the name "bootlegger." But most of the time Michael managed to buy and sell the liquor without anyone paying the tax.

Even though his conscience was clear, being a bootlegger put a solid barrier between him and these fine, upstanding people he admired. And it put him in the company of men who didn't respect the law. Almost all of his friends were outlaws of one kind or another. Some of them were decent enough men, like himself, but others were like Charlie—not only bad, but also dangerous. And not all moonshiners made a good product. Some cut corners that made the liquor unfit to drink, and people had died or been blinded by bad liquor. Others just drank too much, fought too much, and lived too rough. Michael was beginning to think he needed to make some new friends.

He knew the reputation of Captain Richardson. He was a brave, honorable, and capable man. And Ned Spiva was an honest revenuer. He did his job fair and square. He had no favorites and took no bribes. Not only that, but he had already proven he could be compassionate. Just a few months ago, when word came to Ned that a poor moonshiner needed to finish planting his corn before going to jail, or his family would go hungry next winter, Ned postponed having him arrested, giving the man just enough time to get the work done. Most of the mountaineers liked Ned, all things considered, but even if they didn't like him, they respected him. They knew he couldn't be bought.

For Michael, nothing was simple any more. In addition to making some new friends, he was beginning to consider the possibility that he needed to find another way to make a living. Maybe he was just growing up, getting tired of fighting the system, needing to settle down. Whatever the reason, here he was, working with lawmen to try to catch this criminal named Charlie, secretly delivering messages to the regional Treasury Supervisor himself. Michael was surprised to find that this kind of law enforcement appealed to him, especially if he got to help catch that scum named Charlie and rescue the Captain's son. For once he was on the side of law and order.

Now it was the middle of the night, the time when he usually did most of his work. Michael was riding his horse ahead of another horseman along a dark, narrow road that cut its way through the forest. The second rider was leading a pack mule. Other similar riders had taken different trails to reach Dahlonega, and all were on the lookout for Charlie Baldwin and Harrison. So far, they hadn't seen anyone.

Suddenly, a rider came out of the woods to block their way, and at the same time, men on foot surrounded them. "Stop, in the name of the law!" commanded the rider.

Michael could see that the man wore a badge. He reined in his horse and sat perfectly still, waiting to see what would happen. Someone lit a lantern, and at that signal, other lanterns were lit so that his cargo could be searched.

"It's all legal," Michael said calmly.

The man who was searching under the canvas on the pack mule agreed. "It's stamped," he said.

The rider seemed doubtful. "You sure?" he asked.

The searcher continued to examine jugs of whiskey by lantern light.

This felt like a trap, and for a brief moment, Michael questioned his trust in Ned Spiva. His temper flared. Had Ned set him up? Then he knew

Ned hadn't had time to stir up this much resistance, even if he had wanted to. There had to be another explanation.

"Yep, it's all legal," said the man.

"Then you're free to go," said the horseman.

"Wait a minute," said Michael. "I need to talk to you."

The young man rode up beside him.

"I need to see Raymond Whittaker," Michael said.

"What business do you have with Agent Whittaker?"

"I have a message for him from Ned Spiva. May I?" He got permission to reach into his coat pocket, then showed him the envelope.

"All right. Follow me." The horseman turned to lead Michael down the road.

Michael called back to the bootlegger behind him, "Deliver the load and go home when you're ready." The man nodded and then continued his slow pace while Michael urged his horse forward to follow the other horseman. After a short moonlit ride, they came to a larger road, and where the two roads met there was an encampment.

"Wait here," said the rider, and Michael did.

The other man dismounted and walked into the camp, meeting a guard. After a low conversation, the guard nodded, and they waved for Michael to approach. Michael dismounted and allowed the guard to search him. Michael was wearing a holstered pistol.

"You'll have to leave your gun with me," said the guard.

"All right," agreed Michael, allowing the guard to take it.

"Now, give me the letter," the guard said.

Michael reached into his coat pocket and withdrew the letter.

"I'll be right back," said the guard.

Michael waited with the first horseman while the guard took the letter into a tent. He wondered what rank the guard had held in the army. He was quite sure the man had seen military service. A light flared inside the tent, and after a moment, the man came back out.

"Mr. Whittaker wants to talk to you," he said. "Come this way."

Raymond Whittaker was less formal than the guard. He had been asleep. After reading the letter, he had quickly pulled pants and shirt on over his long underwear, and now he emerged from the tent shoeless, still buttoning his shirt.

The Captain Seeks the Lost

"Don't you guys ever sleep?" he asked, extending his hand.

"Not lately," said Michael, shaking his hand and meeting his gaze. Whittaker's sharp eyes took the measure of a man, like Ned's did. Michael did not say anything else.

"Well, this is an interesting development," said Whittaker. "Let's sit by the fire and talk." He dismissed the guard with a wave, then reached into the tent to pick up his shoes.

"Wait just a minute," Michael called to the retreating guard, then he spoke to Whittaker.

"There will be other men with liquor coming through on different roads," said Michael. "They're legal, too. I don't want anybody to get shot."

"All right," said Whittaker. "Anything else?" Whittaker sat down by the fire and started putting his shoes on. He motioned for Michael to sit down, too.

"They should keep watch for a big man with a beard, probably on a gray horse. The man's name is Charlie, and he's wanted for kidnapping a thirteen-year-old boy. The boy's name is Harrison. He also robbed a man named Pete Nix up in Union County and beat him so bad he might not live."

Whittaker motioned to his guard "Did you get that? Spread the word. And don't shoot Charlie, either. They might need him to find the boy." Then he directed his attention back to Michael. "This Charlie. Is it Charlie Baldwin?"

"Yeah. You know him?"

"You could say so. He's the man who informed on you. Said tonight should be the time for us to catch a big fish from up in the mountains."

"A big fish." Michael repeated. Then he kept his silence when he really wanted to describe Charlie with a few choice words. "When did you see him?" he asked at last.

"A couple of days ago. He came to my office in Dahlonega."

"He probably came to you right after I hired him. What do you know about him?"

"Scum of the earth," answered Whittaker matter-of-factly.

"But you believed him. I believed him, too. He said he wanted to work for me, but I think what he really wanted was for somebody to guide him through the mountains to Choestoe. He's stirring up trouble for Harry Richardson."

"That's what Ned's letter says," nodded Whittaker. "But legally, the boy is Baldwin's son, isn't he?"

"You do know him, then."

"I know he's a prospector who grew up in this area. And I know his wife, Molly. I know she's afraid of him—with good reason—and she sent the boy to Harry."

Michael blinked and considered his response. "You say you know Molly. I thought Molly was dead. And Harry thinks she's dead. Are you saying she's not?"

Whittaker nodded. "It's a long story. I was on the same stagecoach with the boy when he went looking for Harry. I didn't know who he was or anything about him, but he was traveling alone, and he told me was looking for his father. I gave him my card and told him to contact me if he didn't find his father."

"That was good of you."

Whittaker shrugged. "You would have done the same thing, I think. He's a nice kid, but he was scared, and he looked like he could use a friend. Later, I got the story from Harry. I found out that when the boy came to him, he was all beat up. The story he told was that Molly had died, and Charlie had re-married and had another child. He said Charlie had taken him to the station and left him there. Harry took the boy's word for it. Later, we wondered if Molly had died of natural causes, or if Charlie might have killed her.

"I promised Harry that I would check on the second wife and child to make sure they were safe, and I would see if I could find out what had happened to Molly. What I found out when I went there was that Molly was still alive. There was no second wife and child, and it was Molly herself who had taken the boy to the station because she feared for his safety. I told her she needed to tell Harry the truth. She said she wanted to let him have some time with his wife before she got in the way. She knew he would come to her rescue if he thought she was in trouble."

"That's probably true," said Michael. "Still—"

"I agree. Harry had the right to know. I'm guessing that Charlie didn't know where the boy had gone, and when he found out, he must have been extremely angry."

"I don't know why he thought it would help him to stir up all the revenuers to catch me," said Michael.

"Well, if we had arrested you, you'd be out of the picture, and so would all your men," said Whittaker.

"Or maybe he wanted to keep *you* busy and out of the picture. Would he know that you're Harry's friend?"

"He might know I've been trying to help Molly. I've given her some letters from Harrison. He could have found one of those. That could be what got him stirred up." Whittaker shook his head, thinking aloud. "He's not planning to come through here then, is he? Not with the woods full of my men, all waiting and watching. Unless he thought we'd let him pass, because he gave us the tip."

"No. He might do that if he was alone, but I can't see him bringing the boy through here," said Michael. "He must have something else planned. If he's a prospector in the mountains, and he grew up in Dahlonega, he knows these roads, anyway, so why did he need me to show him anything? I just don't get it."

"Maybe he just meant to rob you, and he found out Pete was an easier target," said Whittaker. "You look pretty tough."

Michael shrugged that off. "Whatever his plans were at the beginning, right now I think he's using the kid to get to Harry," said Michael.

Whittaker nodded. "That's what I'm afraid of. He might be setting a trap, using the boy as bait."

"Anyway, I don't need to go all the way through to Dahlonega now that I've talked to you. I'll ride back tonight and try to warn Ned. I might be able to help him."

There was some commotion on the outskirts of the camp that drew Whittaker's attention. The guard came back and spoke into his ear.

"Really!" Whittaker responded, looking surprised. "Bring her to me. You don't need to search her. She'll be armed, but she's not after me. And you can return Mr. Gibson's gun, too." Then he turned to Michael. "Apparently nobody is sleeping tonight. You're about to meet Molly."

Both men stood as the guard ushered Molly Baldwin into the firelight. Michael was curious about this woman from Harry's past, and when he saw her, his first thoughts were *How did Harry let her get away?* and *How did she get involved with a bum like Charlie?* She was small and slender, wearing a dark gray riding habit. It consisted of an elbow-length cape over a tailored coat and a long split skirt. She wore short black boots and a black hat with a scarf that tied under her chin. She quickly untied the scarf and removed the hat, letting long, curly blonde hair fall down to her shoulders. She was beautiful, but there were dark circles under her eyes. Michael caught himself staring at her and had to remind himself that this was Harrison's mother, and she was in trouble.

Whittaker greeted her like a concerned uncle. "Molly! Dear girl. Are you all right? Come to the light and let me look at you."

"I'm fine," she insisted, but Michael could tell she was anything but fine. She was tired and anxious. "It's my son. I'm worried about him. Charlie came home while I was out on a case. He tore the house up, and he's in a rage. I don't know what he'll do!"

The guard hurried over with a camp chair, and Whittaker offered that to Molly. "Here, sit down and take a breath. Start from the beginning." He made sure the chair was steady, then he helped her to get settled, taking her hat and offering her water. "How long has it been since you slept?" he asked sympathetically.

"It doesn't matter! Listen to me! Harry is in trouble. Young Harry, I mean. They're calling him Harrison. Charlie found the letters he wrote to me. Until then, Charlie never knew where I'd sent him." Molly pulled a handkerchief out of her sleeve and used it to wipe dust from her face. "I told Charlie if he tried to find the boy, I'd tell the sheriff how he beat him. He beat him so bad the last time, it's a wonder he didn't kill him. I knew he would eventually.

"The older my son gets, the more he looks like Harry. Charlie has always hated Harry, and he must have been in a terrible temper when he found out that's where I sent him. The house is torn up, and dishes are broken. He didn't know where I was. He must think I've left him and gone to Harry."

Michael spoke up. "It's lucky you missed him. He might have killed you."

Molly looked at him for the first time, seeming surprised, as if a tree had spoken. "Or I might have killed him. Who are you?"

"Michael Gibson, ma'am."

Agent Whittaker introduced him. "Michael is a friend of Harry's. He's brought news."

"Then tell it," she demanded.

The two men looked at each other. When no one responded immediately, she knew the news was bad.

She frowned and steeled herself. "What? Is my son dead?"

"No, no! It's not like that," said Michael.

"Then, what?"

"Charlie's taken the boy. Harry's tracking them."

Molly seemed relieved. "Then there's hope. If anything can be done, Harry will do it." She looked at Michael with concern. "What about Harry's wife? Is she still all right?"

"So far as I know. She seemed tired, but she was doing all right when I saw her."

"I'll go to her. Harrison was worried about her. He said Harry was worried, too. I'll go to her, and we'll wait together." She stood.

"You've still got a long ride ahead. Don't you want to get some sleep first?" asked Raymond Whittaker. "You can have my tent and sleep a few hours before you set out."

"No, I'll go now. Sarah may need me. Harrison may need me."

"Then I'll ride with you," said Michael.

"Good," she said, taking her hat back and tying it firmly under her chin. "Do you know any shortcuts?"

"I might know a few," he said, smiling.

"Then let's get going," she said. She offered her hand to Agent Whittaker. "Thanks, Raymond. And apologize to your wife for me. I'm afraid I woke her up."

"She's always happy to see you," he responded.

"Mr. Whittaker, if you wouldn't mind writing me a pass, I'd appreciate it—just in case we meet any more of your men," said Michael.

Whittaker grinned, took a pencil from his pocket, scribbled a note on the back of Ned's letter, and handed it over. Then he fished in his pocket and brought out a small, star-shaped badge. "If they don't believe it, show them this," he said.

"All right," said Michael, wondering.

"You can give it back to Ned when this is all over. Good luck to you both. Tell Ned I'll keep an eye out at this end, and if he needs me he has only to send word and I'll come."

"I'll do it," said Michael.

"And Michael," Whittaker said thoughtfully. "A piece of advice: One of these days the law will catch up with you. Before that happens, maybe you should make a change. I've heard you're a good man. If you're interested, I might have a job for you here."

Michael nodded, looking surprised. "I'll give that some thought."

Michael retrieved his gun and mounted his horse, then he set off with Molly Baldwin to ride back through the mountains. Molly rode her horse astride, but she certainly didn't look like a man. She rode well, and she seemed very capable of taking care of herself. Her job as a midwife must mean a lot of traveling at all times of day and night. She was interesting and intelligent, as well as beautiful. *And married*, he reminded himself.

After they were some distance from the camp and had passed the place where he had originally been waylaid, Michael stopped. "Hold on just a minute. I need to see what Mr. Whittaker wrote."

Michael pulled out the note, struck a match, and read the following: "Michael Gibson is my temporary deputy, charged with the safe conduct of Mrs. Baldwin to Choestoe and back. Please give him any help he requires." Raymond Whittaker's signature followed it. And on the other side of the paper, Ned had spent as much time giving Michael a character reference as he had in explaining Harry's problems.

When the match burned down to his fingers, Michael hurriedly blew it out.

"Well, I'll be," he said.

What a strange and complicated world.

"Have you been blinded by the light?" Molly asked.

"You mean, like Paul, on the road to Damascus?" he asked ruefully.

"No," she answered, looking curiously at him. "I mean have you lost your night vision? Lighting a match was a bad idea. Maybe we should wait a few minutes."

"No, you just lead the way for the time being. I'll follow you. We stay on this road for another hour, anyway."

And Michael Gibson, who had never let anyone take control in his life, let his horse follow Molly's while his eyes adjusted to the moonlight—and the sight of the woman who rode ahead of him.

He thought about the badge in his pocket. What a strange and complicated world.

CHAPTER 7

Prospector's Hut

Harrison carefully dropped the round carving as they left the stream and started across the meadow. He kept re-thinking and second-guessing everything he had done. He hoped he had not wasted the string and the carving. He hoped Harry would see them and come for him. And he hoped Charlie would stop somewhere soon. The poor horse was favoring that foreleg again, and that made the ride even rougher. Harrison was so tired of trying to balance himself on the back end of this horse that all of his muscles ached. His wrists were raw, and his hands kept going to sleep from the tightness of the cords; he was hungry, and he wanted to go home.

Harrison hoped Charlie wouldn't find the knife before he had a chance to use it. It would be better to drop it as a clue for Harry than to lose it to Charlie. Maybe it would have been better if he had left it in his pocket. He still had his flint in the other pocket, and so far, it hadn't occurred to Charlie to search him. So maybe he would untie him when they stopped, and find the knife and take it away. Harrison had no way of knowing how to do the right thing.

It seemed that they might really be leaving the creek this time. They were taking a long detour away from it, through a rocky meadow and up a narrow trail that kept switching back and forth, going up the side of a mountain. Eventually, the path leveled off, and then they were making their way back to the stream again—at least Harrison thought it was the same stream. When they got close to the stream he heard the roar of rushing water, and then he understood the detour. They had made their way around a waterfall. Now they were on the mountainside above the falls, where the air was moist from rising mist.

They passed through more thick woods and rhododendron, crossed the creek above the falls, and then followed a smaller branch of the creek until it emerged into another rocky clearing. Here, the flow of water had narrowed until it was just a little stream, but it rushed down the slope as if hurrying to get to the falls.

Finally, at sunset, after what seemed like endless hours of riding, they reached their destination. There was a little gray shack on the far edge of a clearing, backed up at an angle against the rocky side of the mountain. Charlie stopped the horse in front of the shack, then turned so they could look back the way they had come. From the clearing there was a view of forested mountains going from green to blue in the distance, range after range. This mountain they had been climbing was not the tallest one, but it was hard to tell which one was tallest, and none of the mountain shapes seemed familiar, so Harrison couldn't get his bearings from them. But he did know where "west" was from the sunset, and he knew the cabin faced northeast. The little stream ran toward the north, and if he could follow that, and if it was the same stream as before, and if he could get around the waterfall, he could find the way home. There were so many "ifs."

There was an immense silence here. The sky was changing to red and pink and purple as the sun settled into the west, and in all that grand, sweeping view, there was only forest and mountains, with no sign of human habitation. They could have come to the end of the world.

Now Harrison was really worried, because he didn't see anything he recognized, and even if he managed to follow the right stream, how could he ever find his way back home through all that forest, all those mountains that looked alike, all that distant, unending blueness? And how could Harry ever find him? He tried to think what Harry would do, but the voice he heard in his head was that of his mother, who had told him time and again that when things were out of control, when there was so much to do that you couldn't think where to start, you should just *do the thing that's nearest*. And the thing that was nearest was to get off this horse.

"Can I get down now?" he asked Charlie, who was sitting there, looking at the view and watching to see if anyone was following. "I have to go again," he said.

"Yep. Get down. Make yourself at home. We're gonna be here awhile, waiting for dear old Harry." Charlie untied the leather cord from his belt and let it drop. Then, ignoring the boy, he got down, untied the jug of whiskey that still hung from the horse's saddle, and carried that with him. "There's food in the house," he added. He let the reins drag so that the horse wouldn't wander too far, walked up the one rickety step onto the sloping porch, and went into the cabin.

Harrison slid down off the horse's rump, hoping the poor thing was too tired to kick him. When his feet touched the ground he had to grab the horse's tail to keep from falling. "Easy boy, easy," he murmured, patting the horse as Harry had taught him to do. He managed to keep his balance and walk away, turning his back on Charlie and the house. He relieved himself, and while he pretended to fumble with the buttons, he dropped the knife back into his pocket. He was rubbing his wrist, trying to hide the shape of the knife that was impressed into his skin, when Charlie's voice behind him made him jump.

"What's the matter?" Charlie said.

"This rope is rubbing my arms raw," said Harrison, continuing to rub his wrist.

"Well, I'd untie you, but I don't think you're exactly trustworthy. I think you might try to find your way home, and that wouldn't do. If you got lost up here and a bear ate you, you wouldn't be any use to me at all."

The boy muttered, "Being useful to you has always been my highest goal."

Charlie looked curiously at him. "You've changed since you've been gone."

Harrison shrugged. "I'm older." Then he asked, "What's for supper?"

"Nothing, if you're not careful," warned Charlie.

"Whatever you say, Charlie," said Harrison. He nodded toward the horse. "You need to take care of your horse."

"Why don't you do that for me."

"Untie me and I will," said Harrison. "Do you have a brush and some feed?"

"Well, no. What do you think this is, a livery stable?" said Charlie. "Use the horse blanket if you want to wipe him down, then come on in if you want any supper."

Harrison stuck his hands out in front, waiting for Charlie to untie the ropes.

"All right," said Charlie. "Just wait 'til I get my food, so I can watch you. Come with me."

It turned out that Charlie had stashed some canned food in the hut in a box under a loose floorboard. The hut was so dilapidated that it would be hard to find a floorboard that wasn't loose. Harrison wondered if he regularly used this place when he was out prospecting, or if he had actually made plans for this kidnapping, but he didn't ask. He had already antagonized Charlie enough.

He watched while Charlie used a straight metal can-opener to punch a hole in the lid and then cut it open around the edge. Then he pulled the jagged top back so that he could eat out of the can with a rusty spoon. He opened two cans—one of beans and one of peaches—and carried them out onto the porch. He sat with his feet on the step and then finally untied Harrison's hands. Harrison rubbed his wrists and moved his arms and hands around to relieve the stiffness. Charlie pulled out his pistol and set it on the porch beside him.

"Okay, take care of the horse. See that you do it right, like the great Captain Harry taught you. And if you behave yourself, I won't shoot you, and I'll let you eat."

"Yes, sir, Mr. Baldwin," said Harrison, with a bow. He just couldn't seem to help himself. He would never have talked back to Harry, but this was not Harry. He felt that Charlie didn't deserve his respect.

And Harrison did take care of the horse exactly as Harry had taught him, removing the saddle and placing it on the porch where it wouldn't get rained on, and rubbing the horse down with the saddle blanket. Then he checked all the horse's hooves, paying special attention to the sore one. He thought it was just bruised, not seriously injured. The light was fading, and it was hard to see it clearly, and he wasn't exactly an expert.

"I think the horse needs to stand in the cold creek for a little while. That would help the sore hoof," he said.

"All right, just stay in sight," said Charlie, enjoying his food, and curious to see what the boy would do next. "But you can't leave it too long. As soon as the sun gets below that ridge, it will be dark here."

Harrison walked the horse to the little creek. He had decided to call the horse Moonshine, because it had such a beautiful silver coat, and because it had spent the day carrying Charlie's jug of whiskey. Harrison wondered where Charlie had gotten such a pretty horse. He hadn't had it long, or it wouldn't be in such good shape. Charlie was hard on animals, as well as people.

When they reached the little creek, Harrison walked the horse right into the water, and it drank deeply. The cold water must have felt good to Moonshine, because after the horse finished drinking, it stood there, picking at grass that grew along the water's edge. Harrison looped the reins over a bush that stuck out over the creek, and then he turned and walked back to the cabin. To his surprise, Charlie had gone into the house for two more cans of food, and now he was opening them.

"Eat up," he said. "Got to keep up your strength."

"Why?" asked Harrison, wiping the spoon on his shirttail before he used it. It was the same spoon Charlie had used, but Harrison was starving. "What are we doing tomorrow?"

"That depends on Harry," answered Charlie. "And on you."

"Well, what's your plan?" asked Harrison, swallowing a mouthful of beans.

"Well, first of all, I think Harry will probably find us first thing in the morning, if not sooner. I don't think he'll try to track us in the dark, so it will probably be in the morning. By the way, I really appreciate how you left him those little signs you dropped along the way. That should help."

Harrison felt the food stop halfway down his throat, and he swallowed hard, afraid he might choke.

"Harry was never a very good tracker," said Charlie. "I don't know why. He could do most everything else. So I had to work pretty hard to leave a trail without it looking like I was trying to leave a trail. You helped me with that, and I appreciate it."

Charlie's eyes seemed to glow with satisfaction in the fading light. Harrison was sure now: the man was not just mean—he was crazy. And

The Captain Seeks the Lost

Harrison had helped him lead Harry into a trap. He put the can of beans down on the porch.

"I would advise you to eat that," said Charlie. "You might not get another meal for a long time. Eat it." His voice was threatening. Harrison was afraid Charlie would stuff the food into his mouth if he didn't cooperate, so he picked up the peaches and tried eating them. They were sweet and juicy and went down easier, but he still felt sick. He ate slowly and chewed carefully, trying to think what to do. He couldn't let Harry just walk into a trap.

"So, how does it depend on me?" he asked at last.

"Well, I've been thinking of giving you a little test. I'll ask a question, and you give me the answer, and if you give me the right answer, Harry gets to live. If you don't, I'll have to kill him."

"But you can't do that! What if I don't know the answer?"

"You seem like a pretty smart boy. I'm pretty sure you'll know the right answer."

"What's the question?"

"The question? You want the question now?" Charlie grinned, pleased with himself for taking the smirk off Harrison's face. The boy wasn't nearly as sarcastic now that he understood who was in control. "Okay, here it is. The question is, 'Who's your father?' So think real hard and tell me now, *Harrison*. Who's your father?"

Harrison blinked, seeing the impossibility of the situation and knowing that no matter what he said, things would go badly. Charlie would twist everything so that no matter what he said, it would be wrong. Then he lied quickly. "Well, you are. You've always been my father. A year ago, I didn't even know Harry. I knew about him, but I thought he had died in the war. There's no reason to wait for him at all. We can leave now if you want to, or first thing in the morning. We can go back to Dahlonega, and you never need to see Harry again. Things can be just like they used to be with you and me and Mama. Why don't we go right now?" Harrison asked desperately.

Charlie laughed bitterly and took a long swig from the jug. "It's always like this. People always love Harry. They always did, even when we were fifteen and in school. No matter what he did, everybody loved him. Your mother loved him from the first day she met him. She told me that. How could I compete with that? So here you are, willing to sacrifice yourself and go back with the horrible Charlie to save Harry's life."

"Well, wasn't it the right answer?" Harrison managed to ask. "What did you want me to say?" He hoped if he could keep Charlie talking and drinking, maybe Charlie would go to sleep, and he could get away.

Charlie shrugged. "That was the right answer, I guess, but you didn't really mean it, and you knew it was a trick question, anyway. The truth is, no matter what answer you gave me, I would have to kill Harry. But maybe I'll let you live, since you don't mind coming back with me and your mother. If she understands the rules, she'll come back, too. She always did before. She knew she had to if she wanted to keep you safe."

Harrison tried to placate him. "Nobody ever really appreciated you, did they? I never understood," he said. "I can see it, now."

Charlie took another drink. "And now you're just saying what you think I want to hear."

"No, I really can see it, Charlie. I'm older now, and I understand better. And I've been around Harry, so I know how he is." It was true. He knew how Harry was, and he admired him and loved him and wanted to keep him safe. Harrison looked at the jug. "Hey, Charlie, do you think I could have a taste of that? Harry won't let me try it."

The truth was, Harrison had had a small taste one day from their "medicine" jug, just to see what the big deal was. He thought it tasted horrible and hoped he never needed medicine.

"Sure, Harry. I'll give you a taste."

Harrison opened his mouth, and Charlie poured in more than enough. Harrison choked, sputtered, and spit most of it out. The liquor burned his throat and made his eyes water, and the more he choked on it, the harder Charlie laughed. Harrison choked again and had the stuff coming out his nose.

"So, how do you like it?" Charlie asked at last.

"It's good," croaked Harrison.

"Ha! You might be my son after all," laughed Charlie, and he took another long swallow. When he offered Harrison another drink, Harrison shook his head and held up his hands. Charlie laughed and drank again.

If Charlie kept this up, he'd get sleepy, and eventually he'd pass out. Harrison wiped his eyes and his mouth and prayed he could get away in

The Captain Seeks the Lost

time to warn Harry. Then he picked up the can of peaches and finished eating them. After that, he finished the can of beans. After all, there was no telling when he would get to eat again, and he had to be ready to go when the time came.

When Harrison had finished eating, Charlie remembered to tie his hands, but he never checked the boy's pockets, so he still had his knife and flint. Things were looking better than Harrison had hoped. "Tell me about this cabin," he asked, trying to keep Charlie talking and drinking. "Did you build it?"

"No, some poor fellow tried to farm up here after the land lottery," Charlie answered. "He cleared everything that was level enough to plow and built the cabin from the logs, but I guess it didn't work out for him, and the place ended up empty. There's a grave marker just behind the house, right up against the mountainside. My daddy used to stay here sometimes when he was prospecting." Then he started telling Harrison about his own childhood, when his father was one of the prospectors who really did find gold, back in the days of the big Georgia Gold Rush. Charlie's voice was already starting to slur.

"He told me he had a treasure of gold that he kept in a leather bag, and he hid it. He was afraid somebody would steal it, so he came way up into the mountains, and he buried it. He said it was near a waterfall, and I've looked and looked, but there are so many waterfalls, I don't think I'll ever find it."

"Do you think he really hid some gold?" asked Harrison, trying to sound impressed.

"Yeah, I know he did. I thought maybe it was near the cabin, but I can't find it." Charlie looked sadly at Harrison. "I was sure, you know, that Molly would love me if I found the gold, but the more time I spent looking, the longer I was gone, and the more I was gone, the more she learned to get along just fine without me."

Charlie was getting weepy now. Harrison had seen this before. It was okay if Charlie cried, but if he got angry, that would be a problem. Harrison tried to soothe him.

"It'll be all right. Maybe I can help you find it. Did he say anything else about where it was?"

"He said there was a disappearing waterfall, and the sun made it shine like a silver mirror, and he was on top of a mountain when he saw it, and that's where he buried it. That's all. I think he could have told me more, but either he didn't remember or he really didn't want to tell anybody where to find it. He eventually got to where he couldn't hardly remember his own name, and I think he just didn't know where he put it." Charlie looked around. "Say, it's getting dark. You better get that horse in."

Harrison agreed and quickly went to the horse and brought it close to the house. He tied it to the porch rail.

"There's some feed in there," Charlie said, pointing at the doorway.

When Harrison looked questioningly at him, wondering why he hadn't mentioned this before, he shrugged. "Food keeps a horse friendly," he said. Then added with a grin, "I stole it from Harry."

"I'll feed him," said Harrison. When he found the bag, he brought it out and poured some grain onto the step. The horse ate it eagerly, mouthing and licking at the board until every kernel was gone.

"Good boy," said Harrison, petting him awkwardly, wishing he could have kept his hands free. He watched until the horse had finished the grain. When he turned around, he saw that Charlie had put the corncob stopper in the jug, and using the saddle for a pillow, had sprawled out on the porch and gone to sleep. The gun was still beside him on the floor.

The light was fading fast. Harrison managed to fish his knife from his pocket, and he started cutting the cords around his wrists. It was harder to do than he'd expected. The blade was small, the rope was tough, and it was awkward to do it with his hands tied. He sawed back and forth on it, one strand at a time, being careful not to cut his wrists. That kind of accident would have been a disaster. He kept looking up to make sure Charlie wasn't awake, watching him. Harrison could probably outrun him now that Charlie was drunk, but he hoped he wouldn't have to run in the near-darkness with his wrists tied. At last the final cord was severed, and Harrison's hands were free.

He dropped the ropes, closed the knife and put it into his pocket, and very quietly picked up the gun. Here was his chance. He could kill Charlie and be done with it, then just wait here for Harry to find him. But he couldn't imagine sitting with Charlie's bloody body and waiting for Harry. And what if the first bullet didn't kill him?

He felt the cold weight of the pistol in his hands. He knew how to use a gun. Harry had taught him. It was a revolver, not quite as big as Harry's, but it worked the same way. Harrison checked the cylinder and found that it was fully loaded. All he had to do was aim it and squeeze the trigger.

Harrison's hands shook as he pointed the gun at Charlie. Then he remembered how pitiful Charlie had been when he talked about trying to make Molly love him. And he remembered how Charlie had opened the can of beans for him when he was hungry. He wanted to, but he couldn't shoot him. He thought of Charlie shooting Sparky and of the scars on his own back where Charlie had whipped him until he bled, and he wanted Charlie to be dead and gone, but he couldn't shoot him, not when he was lying there asleep. If Charlie had been trying to kill him, he was pretty sure he could do it—but not now.

Harrison lowered the shaking gun, almost crying with frustration, but he was pretty sure he was doing the right thing. He couldn't imagine Harry shooting a sleeping man. He backed slowly and quietly off the porch, afraid of waking him.

Harrison decided to keep the gun in case he needed it. He checked the cylinder again and remembered Harry's advice about carrying a revolver safely. He removed the cartridge that was in the firing position so that the gun wouldn't accidentally go off if he dropped it or bumped the hammer, and he put the extra cartridge into his pocket. After that, he put the gun under his belt, at his back. He got the saddle blanket from where he had hung it on the porch rail and threw it over the horse's back. Then he climbed up on the rail beside the horse, grasped the horse's mane and managed to mount him without benefit of saddle or stirrup. He watched Charlie closely to make sure he was still sleeping. Then, as quietly as he could, he signaled the horse with reins and heels and walked him slowly away from the house and into the deepening darkness of the wilderness.

What Charlie had said was true: when the sun went behind the ridge, it was suddenly dark. Harrison followed the stream and made it across the first meadow and into the woods before the light completely faded, and he knew he had to follow the stream farther, but not as far as the falls. Going too close to the falls could mean disaster.

Harrison remembered that after he left the stream there were other meadows to pass through and sections of woods where there would be no light at all. And the narrow trail they had followed to climb above the waterfall had zigzagged back and forth through steep and uneven terrain. It had been a hard path to follow in the daylight, but at night it would be impossible. He wondered if he had made a mistake leaving Charlie and the relative safety of the old cabin. Maybe that would have been better than this.

But Harry had to be warned before he came into Charlie's trap, so Harrison soldiered on. Both the boy and the horse were nervous, and neither could see very well. Harrison let the horse drink at the stream and crossed at the place where the branch met the larger stream and the trail turned. He recognized the long, smooth rock beside the creek that meant they were close to the waterfall. Both the horse and the boy jumped when they moved under the low branches of a hemlock tree and startled what sounded like a whole flock of mourning doves. The birds beat the air with their whistling wings as they escaped to the sky, and Harrison had to calm the horse to keep it from bolting.

He had just decided that it would be safer if he got down and led the horse, when the decision was taken out of his hands. The bright eyes of a mountain lion appeared in the dark woods on their left, and the cat screamed a loud warning. The horse reared back, terrified, then bolted. Harrison, who had never ridden without a saddle before, was completely unprepared and found himself sliding off the back of the horse, still clutching the blanket. The horse galloped off down the trail, but Harrison tried to run to the right, away from those glowing eyes. He knew immediately that he had made a mistake: he stepped into thin air and fell off the steep side of the mountain.

Harrison grabbed at the underbrush as he rolled and tumbled, and that slowed his descent, but it was solid rock that finally blocked his fall. He came to a stop entangled in thorny vines under a thick hedge of mountain laurel, still clinging to the horse blanket. Pain was shooting through one ankle that had twisted and cracked painfully when he hit the rock. He felt like a fly in a spider web, suspended in space, and to his horror, the sound that he heard very clearly on his right was the roar of a waterfall. He dared not move, because a fall from the top of the waterfall to the rocks below would mean certain injury, possibly death.

The mountain lion didn't make any more noise. It had probably been as startled as the horse and the boy and had gone on its way. Harrison reached for his gun, just in case the animal had followed him, and discovered that the gun was gone. Apparently he had lost it in the fall from the horse or the tumble down the slope.

Harrison felt carefully around him in the darkness. When his uninjured foot also touched solid rock he knew a sense of relief. He wasn't literally hanging in space; he was just caught in the underbrush, sitting on a steep slope near the waterfall with a rock at his feet. And he found that he could pull the horse blanket close around his back, which made him feel a little more protected from things that might bite, like snakes. Even if he could do it, he didn't dare make a fire, because that would bring Charlie. He made himself as comfortable as he could within his little nest of vines and laurel, leaned back against the hillside, and waited for daylight. He didn't dare move from this spot until he could see.

Day Three: Wednesday

CHAPTER 8

Sarah Speaks Her Mind

Dawn was just finding its way around the edges of a cloudy sky when Michael and Molly finally arrived at Ned and Winifred's house. Molly was so tired she could barely hold her head up, and she was sure she had slept part of the way. At some point in the night, Michael had tied a rope to her horse's bridle so that he could lead them. She didn't argue with him when he offered to lift her down from the saddle, and that was unusual for the independent Molly Baldwin, but right now she needed all the help she could get.

"Can you stand?" he asked.

"Yes, of course," she answered, swaying on her feet.

Michael responded by picking her up and carrying her to the house.

He set her on her feet and supported her while he knocked loudly at the door. Ned hurried to let them in.

"Ned, this is Molly. She hasn't had any sleep for a couple of days, and she needs to lie down."

Sarah stood in the doorway of her bedroom with a long multi-colored shawl covering her gown. "I'm just getting up. She can sleep in my room," she offered. "Your name is Molly?" she asked.

"She's Harrison's mother," said Michael.

"Oh," said Sarah. "Oh!" She mentally revised everything she thought she knew about Molly. "Well you must be exhausted, and so worried. Come in. We'll heat some water for your bath. Are you hungry?" Sarah walked quickly forward and took Molly's hands.

"A bath and some food would be good," Molly said.

"Come this way," Sarah said, and she showed her to the spare room. "Harrison's going to have some explaining to do when he gets home," she said, as if she and Molly were old friends and Harrison was off camping. "Did you know he told us you were dead?" She closed the door behind them. In a moment she opened the door and asked Michael, "Could you get Molly's saddlebags? And there's a medicine bag."

"Sure," said Michael, nodding slowly. He was as tired as Molly was.

"I'll heat some more water," said Ned. He already had a fire going in the stove and a kettle on for coffee.

Michael went out. Just then Winifred emerged from the bedroom she shared with Ned. "I heard voices," she said, tying the belt of her robe. "What's happening?"

"Nothing much," said Ned ironically. "The dead have arisen, that's all. Molly's here."

"Molly? Harrison's mother?"

"The very same."

"Well," said Winifred thoughtfully. "What about that. Won't Harry be surprised!" then after a moment, "How did Sarah take it?"

"Like a saint. The girl is a saint," said Ned. "She's in there making her comfortable. Molly hasn't slept for a couple of days, and she just rode all night with Michael."

"The poor thing. We'll need to fix her something to eat."

"Michael, too," Ned said, nodding.

Michael came back then with Molly's bags, and Winifred took them to the bedroom and tapped on the door, calling, "It's Winifred. I have your bags."

Sarah answered, "Come in!"

Winifred entered the bedroom and, once again, closed the door. Sarah was getting dressed behind a screen, Molly was sitting on the side of the bed, taking off her boots, and the women wanted a chance to talk.

Michael took a seat at the kitchen table near the stove, where Ned was beginning to cook breakfast. He pulled Mr. Whittaker's note from his pocket and waved it at Ned before putting it on the table. "From Mr. Whittaker," he said. Then he pulled the deputy's badge from his pocket and added that to the note.

"He deputized you?" asked Ned.

"He handed it to me. Told me to show it if anybody needed proof the note was from him. He said to give it to you when this is over."

"Well, in the meantime, just pin it on your shirt," said Ned.

"Are you serious?"

"Yep. We need your help. After you get some sleep, that is. You look like you could use it. We're on our own here. We sent someone for the sheriff over in Blairsville, but we haven't heard from him."

"He's probably tied up. I heard there was gonna be a raid on some stills up in Dooley," said Michael, offhand.

"You heard that, did you?"

"You know how it is. Word gets around."

"Sometime I'd love to hear exactly how word gets around. I'll bet there's nobody to arrest when the sheriff gets there. There might not even be a still. And nobody told me anything about this."

Michael didn't comment.

"So, while the sheriff is off on a wild goose chase, somebody who actually needs his help is out of luck." Ned shook his head and sighed. "Would you like some breakfast?"

"I'd love some."

"How did you find Whittaker?"

While Ned fried ham and eggs in a cast iron skillet, Michael described how agents had stopped him in the forest, and how—no surprise, of course—his load had been completely legal. He shared the interesting fact that it was Charlie who had set the revenuers on him. Then he recounted all that he and Raymond Whittaker had discussed, right up to his words of advice and his hint of a possible job.

"And what did you say to that?" Ned asked, watching him curiously.

"I told him I'd think about it."

"Good," said Ned. "Here, have some food."

Ned heaped country ham and two eggs onto a plate for Michael and added some cold cornbread that had been left over from the night before. While Michael ate, Ned measured ground coffee beans into an enamel coffee pot full of boiling water, then set it aside. He fixed a second plate, then tapped at the spare bedroom door, and Winifred answered.

"Do you want Molly's plate in here?" he asked her quietly. He waited while Winifred checked.

"Yes, that would be nice," she answered. "And just fill this with hot water." She handed him a pitcher.

After Winifred took the plate to Molly and Ned brought her the pitcher of hot water, he re-filled the kettle from a well in the back yard and set it back on the stove. Then he and Winifred joined Michael at the table for breakfast.

Ned spoke to Michael. "Harry said that if we hadn't heard from him in two days, I should get Liam and go find him," said Ned. "I don't want to wait another day. If you could stay here and look after the women, I could go on now."

"That's fine," said Michael. "But I'll need some sleep."

"Let me get a few things together, and then you can use our room," said Winifred. "Sarah and I are pretty good at fending for ourselves, but if we need you, we'll wake you up."

"Is this okay with you?" Ned asked Michael.

"Yeah, it's fine. I'll help however I can," said Michael.

"I'll be going, then," Ned said to Winifred.

She nodded, understanding, pushed back her chair, and went to her room to get dressed.

Ned finished his breakfast, then stood and turned to Michael. "You wear that badge. You're the person in charge here. If we don't come back by tomorrow, start organizing some of the men to help with the search, but you stay here with the women. I wouldn't put it past Charlie to get everybody riled up and wandering in the woods and then sneak back here and poison the well or something. You understand?"

Michael nodded.

"I'm depending on you. Don't let me down."

The two men shook hands.

"I appreciate your trust," said Michael.

"You're a good man, Michael. One day you'll figure that out."

Within a few minutes, Ned had gathered his rifle and other necessities, saddled his horse, and made ready to leave. He put the other two horses in the barn and fed them so that Michael wouldn't have to do it, said good-bye to Winifred, then rode off in the direction of Liam's cabin. He hadn't gone far when he met Liam coming toward him on his horse. Liam was dressed for battle, wearing a long duster and cowboy hat and packing a Sharps black powder rifle. It was the same gun he had carried during the war.

"Cap'n needs us," he said simply.

"Yes, he does," said Ned, wondering again how the news traveled so fast in the hills, apparently even to the hermits. But Liam wasn't big on conversation, so Ned let it go for now.

They followed Stink Creek just as the fishing party had done the day before, turning to cross the creek at the ford and following the path that led up into the mountains. When the trail turned at the second creek, Liam knew where they were going.

"Waterfall, c-c-cabin." He pointed ahead, and nodded. "It's where I'd go."

After that, they made good speed, making short work of the false trails and continuing along the creek. When the rain started, they kept going, and it was about noon when they came to Harry's camp. They decided to split up. Ned went toward the falls while Liam checked out the trail across the meadow.

* * *

Winifred made sure Michael had everything he needed and was settled in the bedroom, then poured a cup of coffee and sat down to drink it. Sarah came in carrying Molly's empty plate and fork. She put them to soak in a metal dishpan in the kitchen, poured coffee for herself, and joined Winifred.

"How is she?" asked Winifred.

"Absolutely exhausted, but I'd say she's doing pretty well, all things considered," said Sarah. She took a sip of coffee, then set down the cup. "She hasn't seen Harrison since September and now he's missing. She hasn't had any sleep for awhile, and she's just made that long trip through the mountains on horseback."

"That would be enough to do anyone in," said Winifred sympathetically.

Sarah went on. "She said that clouds covered the moon in the wee hours of the morning, and it was so dark she couldn't see her hand in front of her face. It's a good thing Michael was with her. He made a torch out of pine splinters and walked in front of both horses, leading them. On top

The Captain Seeks the Lost

of everything else, Molly is married to crazy Charlie and has had to deal with him for all these years. I feel sorry for her."

"Charlie must have been a different person back then, or why would she have married him?" said Winifred.

"Apparently, he can be whatever he needs to be to get what he wants. She said he was so kind to her, so sympathetic. All the while, he was lying to her. He's the one who told her Harry was dead. He manipulated her and took advantage of her grief. He knew the baby was Harry's from the start. She says he wanted her because he didn't want Harry to have her. Then after he got her, he lost all respect for her. It's all so sad."

"But last year, why did she let Harry think she was dead?" asked Winifred. "Did she explain that?"

"She read about our wedding in the papers, and that's the first time she found out Harry was alive. She said she was thrilled to learn that he was all right after all those years of believing he was gone, and she just wanted him to be happy. You remember that article—so dramatic, about people trying to kill us—and she said it sounded like we had enough troubles without her showing up and complicating things even further.

"When Charlie saw the newspaper, he went completely out of control and beat the boy so badly that she had to get him to safety, and so she sent him to Harry. She said that she and Harrison made up the story together, because she didn't want Harry to feel like he had to come running to her rescue. And she didn't want Charlie to know where she had sent Harrison. She was taking care of everyone but herself. I think she's amazing. She's been through so much, but she was thinking of our happiness. She's a very strong woman."

"Very strong," agreed Winifred. She was wondering if Harry had had a chance to say "no" when they were both young and afraid, the night before he left for war. Molly would have been a tragic figure and an almost irresistible force—but she didn't say that to Sarah. "What about you?" she asked. "How are you doing with all this?"

"I'm feeling a little intimidated, if you want the truth." She smiled ruefully. "Molly is beautiful and smart and perfect in every way, and Harry loved her once. And here I am looking like a giant—I don't know what. Cow? Turnip?"

"Oh, Sarah! Don't even think like that. Harry loves you more than life itself. And he's so excited about the baby! He thinks you're absolutely beautiful. Whatever happened in the past is past. It has nothing to do with you."

"I just wish he were here now. I wish things could be normal and everyone could be safe." Sarah said. Then she laughed softly, looking out the window as she heard a distant rumble of thunder. "And while I'm wishing, I wish I could go back to my own house and bring my clothes in off the line before it rains."

Winifred considered the clouds. "It does look pretty stormy. Well, I can get the clothes in if you don't mind me leaving you alone with two sleeping people for a little while. Do you think that's safe?"

"I think it would be fine. If Charlie shows up, I'll just shoot him."

"It would probably save us all a lot of grief if you did. I'll go get the clothes, and you can fold them and pretend everything is normal."

"Thanks, Winifred."

"Anything to help, sweetie." She pointed to the table. "While I'm gone, why don't you get some breakfast? Remember, you're eating for two."

"How could I forget?" said Sarah.

After Winifred left with the laundry basket, Sarah paced and fidgeted, feeling tired and anxious. She kept worrying about Harry. What would she do if something happened to him and he didn't come back? She would be completely lost; she knew it. She didn't think she would be as strong as Molly if she had to make it without him. Finally she sat down to eat some breakfast so that Winifred wouldn't fuss at her when she returned.

Sarah had finished her breakfast and was dozing on the couch when Sparky barked and a tap came at the front door. She carried Harry's pistol with her, but peeking through the curtains, she saw that it was Carlotta Payne outside the door. Of all the people she didn't want to see, Carlotta was at the top of the list. *Too bad*, she thought. *I'm not allowed to shoot her.* She put the gun down on a table near the door, put a smile on her face, and opened the door, pretending to be happy to see Carlotta.

Carlotta, who was about fifty-five years old, was dressed perfectly, as usual, in a ruffled dress made of black taffeta. She was a small person—in so many ways—with sharp, observant eyes and the quick, nervous movements of a bird. She had come in a smart little black surrey, and she would have been holding a parasol, but her hands were filled with a large basket holding covered dishes of food.

"I thought that with all that's going on, you might need some extra food," she said.

"How nice of you! Did you make all of this yourself? You must have been cooking all night," said Sarah. "Let me just take this inside, and then we can sit on the porch and visit," she said.

"Oh, no! I'll carry it in. I wouldn't think of making you do that in your condition," said Carlotta, practically pushing Sarah out of the way to get inside the house. Once inside, she looked around, collecting information, looking for anything that might make a good story to tell her friends. She peered around the living room, then bustled to the kitchen table, where she unloaded the basket, disappointed not to see anyone else. Both bedroom doors were closed.

"But where is Winifred? Where's Ned?" she asked loudly. "I hoped I could see them, too."

"Shhh!" Sarah held a finger to her lips, and then whispered, "People are sleeping. Let's go out on the porch."

"People? What people? Who's here, Sarah?" As Carlotta brushed past the table on her way out, a flounce on the back of her dress caught one of the crockery dishes and swept it off onto the floor. There was a crash of breaking pottery.

Carlotta cried out, "Oh dear! I'm so sorry! What a mess I've made!" but the noise brought the response she wanted. One bedroom door flew open, and there was a barefooted Michael Gibson in his long underwear, with a deputy's badge pinned on his shirt, which hung open, unbuttoned. Michael had a gun in his hand. He looked rough, with a two-day growth of stubble on his face and his hair sticking out in all directions.

"It's all right, Michael," Sarah assured him. "You can go back to bed."

The other door went wide, and there was Molly, who had taken time to throw Sarah's long striped shawl around her chemise and short bloomers. Her blonde hair was loose and wild, and she seemed completely unaware that her shapely bare legs and feet showed for all the world to see. "What's going on?" she asked groggily.

"Well, Michael!" exclaimed Carlotta. "What are you doing here? And what is that badge you're wearing? And who's this?" she asked, being quite friendly. "Are you Harrison's mother? Are you still friends with Harry? My goodness, but you're a pretty thing." She noticed that Michael was looking at Molly, too. "Isn't she, Michael?" She said coyly, then looked back at Molly. "Are you here with Michael? It looks like you've both had an interesting night. Do Harry and Ned know you're here?"

Both Michael and Molly stood silent beneath the barrage of questions, but something in Sarah snapped. She turned furiously to Carlotta. "How dare you question my guests? And I asked you to be quiet! Do you see what you've done? You've woken everybody up. Get out," she said. "Get out of this house."

"I'll just clean up the mess first," said Carlotta, reaching for a broom.

"No, you won't." Sarah took her by the arm, picked up the empty basket, and escorted her to the door. "Thank you for bringing the food. That was very kind. But I asked you not to wake people up, and you did it anyway. For your information, Michael is a deputy of the Secret Service and he escorted Mrs. Baldwin here, and their journey took all night. They are here to help us, and they need some sleep, which you've interrupted. Now get out of this house and don't come back."

"Well, I never!" said Carlotta, looking shocked. "What's the matter with you?"

"What's the matter with *you*?" asked Sarah, hurrying her out the door and slamming it behind them. "You always have to create a stir, don't you? You always have to find a story so you can go out and gossip. Well, take this one with you. You went to see the preacher's wife and she threw you out of the house. By the time you've told it three times, you'll be saying I threw the dishes at you and broke them over your head. You just go ahead and tell that. And while you're at it, tell everyone else that we don't need any more food right now. We're doing just fine. And if we need some of the men to help in the search, we'll let you know. Otherwise, everyone can just *stay away*!"

Sarah stomped back into the house and slammed the door behind her. "That horrible old *crow*!" she muttered, on the verge of tears.

She was embarrassed to see that Michael and Molly were still standing there. They were grinning and had heard every word.

"Whoo-ee!" said Michael, applauding. "Somebody has needed to tell her that for years! You're the first person with the courage."

Molly added her applause just as Winifred burst through the door, carrying a basket full of laundry and laughing out loud.

"Did you hear it, too?" asked Sarah, dismayed.

"Every word. I hid when I saw her surrey. I was behind the rose bush, listening."

"Well, shame on you! You should have helped me."

"Honey, you didn't need any help. You did just fine!"

Everyone continued to grin, and finally Sarah smiled, too. "Poor Harry. He'll come back and find out he doesn't have a job. Carlotta's husband is chairman of the deacons." Then she sat down on the couch, holding her stomach.

"I think I've woken the baby. It feels like she's sitting straight up in there poking her legs and arms out in all directions."

Molly came to her and knelt down. "May I?" she asked, and she put her hand on Sarah's stomach. It felt tight and hard.

"Has this been happening a lot?" she asked.

"Just every now and then."

"When did it start?" Molly asked.

"About the time I went to bed last night. It kept waking me up. Do you think something's wrong?" she asked with a frown.

Molly looked up at her and smiled sympathetically. "No, something is very right. You're in labor."

"Oh, but I can't be!" Sarah exclaimed. "It's too early. And I can't do this without Harry!"

"Trust me," Molly replied, still sympathetic. "You can."

There was a short silence while everyone remembered that Molly had managed to have a baby without him.

"I can help," Molly added. "That's why my son asked me to come. I'm a midwife."

"Well, then, thank goodness you're here!" Winifred said fervently.

"Okay, Molly." Michael took a deep breath and looked like he wanted to be very far away. "You just tell all of us what we need to do."

"For now, you can go back to bed. This will take some time, and you might as well get some sleep. Eventually, we may need you to go for the doctor."

"Nobody knows where the doctor is," said Winifred. "We couldn't find him for Pete."

"We should have asked Carlotta. I'll bet she knows, if anyone does," said Sarah.

"We'll be just fine," Molly assured them. "Delivering babies is what I do."

"Harrison asked you to come?" said Sarah.

"He sent the letter that got me here. It also got Charlie here, but that's beside the point." Molly looked around, gathering her thoughts. "Okay, Winifred. You could help me get the bed ready for Sarah and fix a pallet for me on the floor. We still need to get some sleep if we can. First babies usually take a while. This might be another long night." She looked at Sarah. "But then, you've been in labor for about ten hours, haven't you? It might not be all that long."

She squeezed Sarah's hand. "You just relax. Knit if you want to, or fold the clothes, or do whatever you want to do. You'll know when it's time to lie down." She smiled encouragingly. "We'll get the hard part done and surprise Harry with a baby when he comes home."

"Harry's going to have all kinds of surprises," said Winifred.

CHAPTER 9

Finding What Was Lost

Just before daybreak, Harry awoke to an overcast sky and the sound of two horses grazing near his head. One was Smokey and the other was a beautiful gray gelding. He sat up slowly, so as not to startle the second horse, but it seemed quite content to keep company with Smokey. Harry got to his feet, petted Smokey, then spoke softly to the gray and petted it, as well. The gray's bridle had apparently been caught in the brush, and it had pulled sideways, and the reins hung down, tangling in the horse's legs. Harry took the bridle off and put it on the ground near Smokey's tack, letting the horse roam freely. The horses were unlikely to leave this meadow where grass and fresh water were abundant, and Harry was confident that his horse would come if he whistled.

Harry took in his surroundings. A thunderstorm was brewing. Already there were some dim, rolling rumbles in the distance. He considered the horse. This had to be Charlie's horse. Had Charlie let it go because he was heading into steep territory and had no more use for it? It was possible, but unlikely. Harry thought Charlie would have wanted to keep the horse in case he needed it to make his escape. Could Harrison have tried to escape and failed? That was a frightening possibility.

Harry had had a lot of time to think before sleep came the night before. In the last fading light, when he had followed Charlie's trail until it reached the place where the path climbed the mountain, he had decided several things. For one, Charlie assumed he would follow. This was the same Charlie that Harry had dealt with in military school—always competing, always trying to prove he was better than Harry. The tracks he had left were a kind of challenge, and he thought Harry would rise to the bait in order to prove he could do it. He had never understood that Harry didn't care enough about him to compete with him. And Harry had gained a great deal of experience since those days. Charlie had underestimated him.

Charlie wanted Harry to follow him, and right now Harry would do it—he had no choice—but he would do it on his own terms. He had decided to climb the mountain near the waterfall on the little game trail he had found, not on the zigzag path where Charlie might be waiting in ambush, holding the high ground. And he had better do it soon, because a hard rain would not only destroy tracks, but would make the steep climb hazardous.

Harry wrapped some of the dried food and cornbread in a clean handkerchief and put it into his pockets, then filled his canteen with fresh water from the creek. He secured his campsite as well as he could, then started his own trek back to the waterfall on foot. He wished he had told Ned to come today. He had a feeling that the showdown would come somewhere above the falls.

* * *

It was only when the sun rose that Harrison knew how much trouble he was in. He was seated on a ledge that stuck out from an almost vertical wall of rock. Above him, there was some slope and enough soil to allow for the growth of mountain laurels and vines, and those had broken his fall, entangling him just before he reached the ledge. Had he gone over, nothing would have stopped his plunge to the rocks below. But even though the brush had slowed his fall, it had not prevented him from hitting the ledge with an awful crack and twist of his ankle. His ankle had throbbed and hurt all night, and the least movement caused excruciating pain. Harrison had sat as still as he could, both to protect the ankle and because he was afraid to move.

Looking down now, Harrison felt a wave of dizziness and fear. He wrapped a vine more securely around his arm. He had tried to dig up this kind of vine before. He didn't know the name of it, but it had shiny leaves and roots like potatoes, and it was extremely tough, somewhat thorny, and hard to break. When he had helped Harry dig them out of their garden spot, he had thought they were the most annoying plants on earth. Overnight, his opinion about the vines had changed dramatically.

Harrison looked for a way out. There was no hope of going straight down or to either side. To his right was the hard, wet rock that bordered the waterfall, and to his left was a steep drop from the rock cliff to the mountain slope. The only way out would be to go back up the same way he had come down.

Harrison carefully loosened the shoe on his injured foot. The ankle was black and blue and horribly swollen. He wondered if it might be broken. He was sure he couldn't put his weight on that foot. He looked up over his shoulder at the steep slope behind him. Even with the injured ankle, he might be able to pull himself through the plants above him, but he hesitated to move. One misstep or uprooted plant might allow him to slide, and the next time he might not be lucky enough to stop on the ledge. He hated to think how it would feel if he hit the ledge with that foot again, and falling off the ledge was unthinkable. So he stayed where he was. He wiggled the sore foot again to ease the pinch of the shoe, and to his horror, the shoe slipped off and dropped out of sight down the cliff below him.

Over time, the waterfall had cut its way into the rock formation, and water fell down between massive towers of rock. Harrison couldn't see it, although he heard it well enough. All the rock was wet and slippery. Attempting to climb the rock face would be suicidal, even without an injured ankle. So Harrison sat where he was, cold and wet from the damp spray of the falls and weary from a long night of little sleep, but thankful that he had not tried to move from the ledge in the dark. The weather had changed in the night, and a wind had come up. What with the cold mist, the wind, the loss of sleep, and the pain in his foot, he felt shaky and weak, and he was amazed at how cold he felt. He was shivering.

Harrison cringed when he suddenly heard a voice on the path above him. It was Charlie, talking to himself. Harrison drew his feet back and cowered under the bushes, hoping that Charlie couldn't see any part of him. He thought that his ledge was almost completely invisible from above. He prayed that it was. He held still, barely breathing. Thunder rumbled distantly, and then closer, and there was a sudden loud crash as lightning struck somewhere nearby. Harrison cowered silently on the ledge and pulled the horse blanket over his head when hail started falling. Charlie swore loudly and moved back up the trail.

* * *

On the trail above, Charlie stopped to pick up his gun, which he found in the middle of the path. There were mountain lion tracks here and a confusion of hoof prints. He guessed that the horse had reared and made a run down the trail. There were a few footprints, but they didn't seem to go anywhere, so the boy must have managed to get back on the horse. Or maybe the cat had gotten him. It didn't matter too much to Charlie. He had lost his hostage, either way. Charlie looked out over the precipice beside the waterfall. No chance the boy could have gone down there in the dark. If he had, good luck to him. He'd be lying at the bottom now.

A growing wind tossed limbs back and forth as large raindrops splatted on Charlie's face, and thunder echoed through the mountains. There was a sudden flash and a crash that seemed to shake the mountain as lightning struck nearby, and hail started falling, hitting his head like rocks. Charlie cursed and shoved the gun under his belt. At least he had a place to shelter in the storm. That was more than Harry and the kid could say. He turned and ran through the rain and hail back toward the shack.

* * *

Down below, Harry reached the foot of the cliff just after the loud clap of thunder reverberated through the hills. He stood for a moment studying the game trail as the wind picked up and rain and hail started to fall. He peered upward beneath the brim of his hat, watching for Charlie and for any sign of Harrison.

It was a long, steep, hazardous climb on a narrow clay path, but there were plenty of bushes and small trees to hold onto. With a little bit of luck he should be able to climb it and save some time. On the other hand, the longer trail would be safer. Harry decided that the risk was worth it if he could find his son faster. After a few minutes, the hail stopped, but icy rain came down heavily. Harry started up the cliff and climbed for some time in the rain. He thought he might be about halfway up the side of the waterfall when he caught a glimpse of something moving, high up on a ledge. It was too hard to see what it was from where he stood, and the rain didn't help. He climbed farther, holding carefully to the undergrowth and small trees. The path was growing slick, but he was closer now, and when he looked again, he was sure of it! What he saw was the sole of a shoe, and he thought it was Harrison's. It was moving back and forth.

Harry cupped his hands around his mouth and mimicked the call of a mourning dove. It was an old trick he had learned in the army, and he had taught it to Harrison. The mourning dove had a call that sounded like a wooden flute—a repeating song of a low note followed by a high one, then three tones in the middle. "Too-woo! Whoo, who-who."

At the sound, the foot stopped moving. Harry repeated it. Suddenly, he heard a return of the birdcall from up on the ledge. It didn't sound too much like a mourning dove, but it sounded like Harrison. Harry smiled. He had found his son. He did not dare shout to the boy, not knowing where Charlie was, but if he could get a little closer, he might be able to talk to him. Harrison's position was going to be hard to reach, and it appeared to Harry that it would be impossible to reach him from below. He'd have to climb to the top and come back down. Maybe the zigzag path was the best choice after all.

Harry climbed a little higher, but he still couldn't get close to Harrison. He braced his feet against the slender trunk of a gnarled mountain laurel and cupped his hands around his mouth to direct the sound. Rain came down harder than ever. Water dripped off the brim of Harry's hat.

"Harrison!" he called softly. There was no answer, only the combined roar of waterfall and rain. Harry called louder. "Harrison?"

"Dad! I knew you'd c-come." Harrison's teeth were chattering, and it was hard to talk.

"Are you hurt?"

"Just my ankle. It's pretty bad. I lost my shoe, and I'm really cold." The boy held branches aside and peered down through the leaves. He had the horse blanket over his head to keep the rain off.

In spite of the boy's injured ankle, Harry could have wept for joy. His son was all right. "You'll have to hold on awhile longer. Can you do that?"

"Yeah. If the r-rain doesn't wash me off the c-cliff."

"Just hang on. Don't move from there, whatever you do. I'll come back for you, but it might take a little while."

"Okay. But, Dad?"

"What?"

"There's a cabin up there. That's probably where Charlie is. He means to kill you."

"I know—but he won't. Wait where you are. I'll be back!" said Harry.

"Okay." Then, in a good imitation of Ollie Collins, Harrison drawled in a low voice, "I'll be *rite cheer* when ya git back!"

The conversation suddenly ended when the thin tree trunk Harry was standing on gave way. He slid a short distance before he could regain his footing, and he ended up on his hands and knees in the mud. Rain was still pouring down, and he had red clay all over him, but Harry was exuberant. Harrison was safe, and he still had his sense of humor. He was all right. Now, if Harry could just keep him that way.

* * *

Charlie stood on the front porch of the prospector's hut brooding and looking out at the rain, which was pouring off the roof in a solid curtain. His head hurt from the excess of liquor he had drunk the night before. That had been a foolish mistake. He had made it easy for the kid to run away, and he'd almost lost his gun as well. Lucky the boy hadn't shot him.

But the kid was not the kind to commit cold-blooded murder. That was the thing about good people: they made it easy on bad ones by following all those rules. But the kid was one thing; Harry was another matter altogether. Charlie was pretty sure Harry wouldn't hesitate if he got the opportunity to kill him. But then, you could say Harry had reason. Charlie had always tried his best to bring Harry down during their days at the academy, but somehow Harry had always risen above it, whatever it was. Charlie had stolen Molly and the kid from him, and Harry had never even *known* it. What a waste that was! But Harry knew about it now.

After Charlie married Molly, Harry had disappeared off the face of the earth for fourteen years. According to the newspaper story last fall, he had fought in the war, been captured and taken to prison in the North, and had finally been released to go out West and join the cavalry. When he had eventually come back, he'd gone to college. Charlie would have been miserable doing all those things, but Harry had apparently just sailed right through. He became everyone's hero and went on having a good life, no matter what happened to him. How Charlie envied him for that!

Harry always came out on top. He was the one who was happy with his life, not Charlie, even though Harry followed the rules. Rules didn't apply to Charlie. He just did whatever he had to do to get what he wanted. Unfortunately, once he got what he wanted, he usually didn't want it any more. There was just no lasting satisfaction in things. Charlie wished that just once in his life, something would make him happy. But if that couldn't happen, he would do what he had always done. If he couldn't make his own life better, he would try to make Harry's worse. That would even things up a bit.

The rain was easing off. At that moment, there was a break in the clouds, and sunlight beamed onto the bare face of the mountain, off to the right of where Charlie was standing on the porch. And there it was: a waterfall where one had not existed five minutes earlier. A sheet of rainwater poured off the face of the mountain, shining like a mirror in the sunlight, overflowing the little stream that rolled through the meadow toward the bigger stream and the waterfall. Not long after that, the rain stopped completely, and within just a few minutes the new flow of water dwindled back to nothing. It was a disappearing waterfall, just like his father had described.

Charlie could picture his father sitting on this very porch on a rainy summer day long ago, seeing the same unexpected vision. He had probably been drinking, and maybe that was why the memory was clouded. But the treasure would be somewhere close by.

Charlie had spent years of his life searching the mountains for the stupid disappearing waterfall, and it had been in front of his nose all this time. He didn't know whether to be happy or angry, but being Charlie, he was angry. He was angry with his father for being confused, and for not telling him what he needed to know before it was too late. He wanted that treasure now, before Harry came barging in, spoiling things for him once again. He wanted to wave it in Harry's face before he killed him. And then he would take off for California, where no one knew him, and he would be somebody important there, with his pouch full of gold. It was his turn to be the hero—the one everybody loved.

Charlie kept a rusty, broken pick under the house near the back steps. He went to find it. He was pretty sure he knew where to dig. If the disappearing waterfall was this obvious, the burying place would be obvious, too. And what could be more obvious for a burial place than a grave?

Charlie retrieved the pick and walked to the little gravestone that lay flat on the ground behind the house, up against the mountain. It was a smooth slab of rock, no doubt picked up from the ground somewhere close by. There was no name or date, but someone had scratched the location of a Bible verse on it: Acts 3:6. Charlie thought now that it must be some kind of a clue or a message from his father, but he didn't know what it meant. His father had become very religious in his later years before he got senile, and the verse must have meant something to him. All this time, he had assumed this was the grave of the original owner of the house.

The ground was soaked from the brief, heavy rain. Charlie used the pick to pry up the edge of the stone and turn it over. Then he scraped away the dirt underneath it. It didn't take much digging to find the box. It was almost too easy. Maybe he wouldn't even need to see Harry. Maybe he could take his money and get away from here and forget this place once and for all.

He dug and scraped until he finally managed to pull the old metal box out of the hole, and he carried it over to the back steps. The box wasn't locked, but the lid was rusted shut. Charlie tapped it with the edge of the pick and finally felt the lid loosen. He lifted it, and sure enough, there was a leather pouch inside. It wasn't heavy enough to be full of gold, though, and he felt a moment of panic, thinking someone might have beaten him to his treasure. He opened the pouch and found a folded sheet of paper.

He unfolded the paper to find a letter, undated. In painstakingly neat handwriting, it read:

Dear Charlie,

You found the treasure box! I hope you had fun looking for it, and I hope your life is happy now.

Times have been hard. I have not been the perfect father, and I know that, and I am sorry. Your mother has had to work hard all of her life to keep us going. I want your life to be different from ours. I think that if only I could of had a better education, I could of made something of myself, and I could of made life easier for you and your ma. So I took the gold I saved and paid for your schooling. This was the deal I made with the sheriff. It was school or jail for you. I wanted to give you a chance to make a better life for yourself.

I know you'll make us proud.

Acts 3:6.

Your father,
Hub Baldwin

Charlie wadded the letter up and screamed, "No!" Then he looked frantically into the pouch to see what else there was. There was one five-dollar gold coin from the Dahlonega mint. His father had been so proud that some of the gold he had found had been turned into beautiful coins like that. Charlie left it in the pouch. Compared to the treasure he had expected, five dollars was nothing!

There was one thing left at the bottom of the box. It was a New Testament. The passage from Acts had been bookmarked and underlined. Charlie read the verse.

> "Then Peter said, Silver and gold have I none; but such as I have give I thee: In the name of Jesus Christ of Nazareth rise up and walk."

"No!" Charlie screamed. "You stupid old man. You useless piece of filth. You've *ruined my life*!"

There would be no happy ending here. No chance to move to California and start over. He was stuck with the life he had always known, stuck with the choices he had made and the people he hated. He had lost whatever chance he had to make a life with Molly and the boy. Worse than that, Harry Richardson was still there, being successful, being loved, always making the right choices. He hated his life, and he hated Harry. It wasn't fair, and he wouldn't put up with it any longer.

He'd go to California anyway. But first, he'd do his best to ruin Harry's life, and then he'd find Harry and let him know what he had done.

Then he would kill him. The boy, too, if he could. The boy looked just like Harry, anyway. What a waste.

Right now, Charlie had an advantage over Harry. He had been following trails in these woods for most of his life, always looking for that disappearing waterfall, whereas Harry was new to this part of the world. Right now, for example, Charlie knew that there was a shorter way back to Harry's house. Following the stream to the waterfall had brought them in a wide circle east and south of Harry's house. If he followed the ridge trail to the west, he could go back by a closer route. Then, while Harry was still catching up with him, Charlie could pay a call on Harry's wife. He left the cabin and strode off in the direction that would lead him to the old Indian trail that followed the ridgeline. The rain started in again as he walked, but he didn't care. He had a purpose now.

CHAPTER 10

Annie?

By midmorning, the thunderstorm had passed through with heavy rain and wind, and now the clouds were dissipating, and a refreshing coolness filled the air. Sarah's labor had intensified rapidly, and she had not needed to pass the time folding clothes or knitting, but had almost immediately dressed in a gown and taken to her bed. Molly, who had examined Sarah and was timing the pains, said that the baby would come soon. Everyone had given up on the idea of getting any sleep.

Now that the rain had stopped, Michael was keeping watch outside the house, on call if he was needed, but fervently hoping his services would not be required. He was wearing his badge and his pistol and carrying a rifle propped against his shoulder, and he felt about as useful as a toy soldier. The only thing he had accomplished was to keep the stove going and a kettle filled, so that there was plenty of hot water. He'd rather catch murderers or run from revenuers all day long than be on hand for a birth.

A few neighbors had stopped by to learn the news and to bring dishes of food, and the message had rapidly gone throughout the valley that there was no word about the boy, but the preacher's wife was in labor. Michael sent Albert Jones in search of the doctor again and told him to let the men know that if the Captain did not return tonight, a search party would leave at dawn. When Albert returned, he said there would be plenty of volunteers to help the Captain, but no one had seen the doctor. People were beginning to worry about him, because he always left word at the store about where he was going, and this time he hadn't.

Through it all, Sarah had remained calm, but now that the baby was almost here she was worried, because all the blankets, diapers, and baby clothes she had so painstakingly prepared were at home. She had nothing to wrap the baby in!

"Winifred, could you go up to my house and get some of the baby's things? They're all right there in a basket next to the cradle. And the cradle! Could you get that, too? Oh!" She stopped talking to moan in pain as another contraction—the strongest yet—wracked her body.

Molly squeezed her hand reassuringly and consulted her watch. She looked solemnly at Winifred and nodded. "If you're going, best go soon," she said.

"Right," said Winifred wide-eyed. She grabbed up Sarah's striped shawl and wrapped it around her shoulders as she made a dash for the door. Meeting Michael, she explained where she was going.

"You're planning to carry all that stuff by yourself? You don't need to do that!" protested Michael. "I'll get the wagon and take you."

"There's no time. I think the baby's coming!" said Winifred. When the dog Sparky tried to follow her, limping on his bandaged leg, she turned back and said firmly, "Stay here! Stay! Good boy!" The dog returned to its rug-lined box, and Winifred hurried up the path toward the preacher's house, pulling the shawl up around her head and tying it together in front to protect herself from rain that still dripped from the trees.

Michael looked at the forlorn dog and shook his head. "*Stay! Good boy!*" he muttered. "I don't know if she was talking to you or me." He decided that he wouldn't be a good boy and he wouldn't stay. He would help Ned's wife whether she liked it or not. He poked his head in the front door. "Molly?" he called.

Molly opened the bedroom door.

"How much time do we have?"

Molly shrugged. "Less than an hour, I think. It may be soon."

"If you don't need me for a few minutes, I'm going to help Winifred."

"That'll be fine," she answered. "Just don't be too long."

Michael nodded, then he followed after Winifred.

* * *

Within a few minutes, Winifred had reached the other house. The small cabin seemed forlorn amid the mist and sodden trees, with no one at home. A large oak limb had fallen in the yard, and a rocker lay on its side on the front porch. Winifred paused long enough to straighten the chair, thinking how quickly things would fall apart if people didn't keep working all the time. She opened the front door and walked quickly inside.

* * *

Back in the doorway of Harry's little shed, Charlie watched the woman in the shawl go into the house. Good. He had been afraid he wouldn't have a chance to see Harry's sweet wife again. He couldn't see her face, but that had to be Sarah straightening the porch furniture, not knocking, but hurrying in the door as if she owned the place. He remembered seeing the pretty shawl thrown casually over a chair the day he had visited her. It had been a bright splash of color in a cozy little room, and he had hated Harry for his happy wife and his perfect cabin.

Today, Charlie had been disappointed when he had found the cabin empty, but things had brightened for him when he discovered the big tin of lamp oil so conveniently left by the lamp, which was still lit. He had splashed it on the curtains and on the basket of dry corncobs and kindling by the wood stove, and he had pushed the box of kindling right up against a wall beneath a curtain where it would do the most good. After that, he had wedged the back door shut. All he had to do was to add a little spark of fire and then block the front door after he got out. Then he'd let the perfect little wife see how it felt to be roasted alive in a fire. That would be something to tell Harry about! He couldn't wait to see Harry's face when he heard the news.

Charlie hurried to the front door and looked inside. The woman had gone to the bedroom. He opened the door wide and tiptoed quickly across the room to the wood stove, striking a match as he went. He dropped the match into the oil-soaked kindling, and a fire surged up. He picked up a sliver of fat pine, held it over the flame to light it, then went from one gauzy curtain to the next, setting them all on fire. Black smoke billowed up from the box of kindling and the curtains.

"Michael, is that you? I smell smo—" called Winifred, but her voice stopped suddenly and she slammed the bedroom door when she caught sight of Charlie. She heard Charlie drag something large and heavy across the floor, and then the front door slammed, and there was the sound of hammering. She felt a cold chill when she realized Charlie wasn't trying to get to her. He was making sure she couldn't get out.

Smoke was already coming under the bedroom door. Winifred opened the door, but a heavy wooden cabinet blocked her way, and she couldn't move it. She quickly shut the door to block the smoke, ran to the window and yanked the curtains wide. It was a little window, and even when it was wide open it was too small for a grown person to climb through. The other window in the room was just like it. Winifred put her face out the window and screamed for help, taking a deep breath of the fresh air. Smoke was filling the bedroom, even with the door closed. She heard shouts and gunfire. Then someone was wrenching open the front door and pushing the cabinet away, and there was Michael, filling the doorway with his welcome presence.

"Come on, Winifred. We've got to run for it."

"Here," she commanded, lifting the cradle filled with the basket of baby clothes and blankets. "Take this. And we need to take the trunk, too. It has all of Harry's treasures. And grab the spinning wheel! It's by the fireplace."

Michael shook his head in exasperation and quickly followed orders, muttering something under his breath about bossy women who don't even know when they're being rescued. But he dragged all the things away from the house and hurried back for more. Winifred covered her nose and mouth with the shawl and scanned the two rooms to see what else needed to be taken. The last things she rescued were Harry's Bible, which was on the table by his chair, and his fiddle case that was propped in the corner beside the front door. Then she was overcome by a fit of coughing, and Michael hurried her out of the house.

Michael tossed the porch rockers out into the yard, then he ran around to the back porch to see if he could get enough water to put out the fire. Even using the pump and a bucket, he and Winifred couldn't draw water fast enough to make a difference. The lamp oil and kindling had made too hot a blaze, and the old log cabin was becoming fully engaged. When it became too dangerous to stay on the back porch, they finally gave up and hurried around to the front.

"Where is Charlie?" asked Winifred, coughing, looking cautiously around.

"He shot at me, but he took off through the woods when he found out I was armed and could shoot back. I think I nicked him on one arm, but it wasn't enough to slow him down. I wish I had aimed better, but I was afraid to kill him, in case we can't find the boy." Michael scowled fiercely. "You know that he tried to trap you in the house, don't you? He meant to burn you alive."

Winifred shivered and nodded, removing the shawl. The air was still damp and cool, but now it was a welcome change after the scorching heat of the fire. "I'd be dead by now if you hadn't come," she said, and then, looking at the shawl, she made the connection. "He thought I was Sarah."

"We need to get back to her," said Michael urgently.

They hurriedly loaded the cradle, trunk and other things onto a two-wheeled wooden cart that Harry kept in the shed and started pulling it down the path to Winifred's house. Winifred set the shawl on top of the load, then walked ahead, helping Michael pull the cart. Neither of them noticed when the shawl caught on a bramble, slipped off the load onto the ground, and was left behind. Behind them, the fire roared, eating away at the little old cabin that had once belonged to Harry's grandparents. All the hard work that the young couple had done to make the cabin a home disappeared with the black smoke that rose into the sky.

* * *

After the cart rolled out of sight, Charlie came out of hiding, clutching his arm. Then, stooping and moving cautiously, he went to the place where the shawl had fallen, picked it up, and hurried back behind the house. He hadn't killed the preacher's wife after all, but Harry didn't have to know that. This was his wife's shawl, all covered with soot and smelling like the fires of hell. And maybe a little blood would look good on it, too. He rubbed it across his bleeding arm. Harry would think his wife was dead, anyway; he'd believe Charlie's story. Charlie ran back up the hill. He had to hurry back to the prospector's hut. Had to find Harry and the boy.

* * *

"I should have posted a guard on the house," Michael said bitterly.

"It isn't your fault. You haven't exactly had the time," said Winifred. "Besides, if you had listened to me, you wouldn't have come to help at all. But you did come, and you saved my life." Winifred frowned. "Not only that, but you got Molly here in time to help Sarah. Don't be too hard on yourself."

"Thank you," said Michael humbly, as they approached Winifred's house. Michael raised one hand in warning. Everything seemed peaceful around the house, but he drew his gun anyway, and went through the door first, just in case. There was no sound.

"Molly? Is everything okay?" he called.

Just then there was a thin cry that sounded a little like a kitten mewing, the sound of a slap, and then a louder wail that was definitely a baby's cry.

"Everything is just fine," Molly said at last.

"Thank God," said Winifred. Then she hurried to the bedroom to see if she could help.

Michael walked away from the house and fired three shots into the air. Then he put his hands around his mouth and made three loud, yipping, rebel yells. If any of his friends were close enough to hear, they would spread the word, and they would come.

Within a few minutes, men began arriving on horseback or on foot. Some were former soldiers, some farmers straight from their fields, and some were moonshiners—rough looking, bearded, and tough.

Most of them had been Winifred's students, and they respected her. Michael reminded them who she was and of how fair her husband Ned had been since he took the job of revenuer. "He's a good man doing an honest job," said Michael. "You can't ask more than that."

Then he told them about Charlie, who was not from around here, who beat up Pete and nearly killed him, stole his money, and then took the Captain's boy. Everyone listened respectfully as Michael told the story. "Just a little while ago, while Harry and Ned were gone to try to get the boy back, Charlie snuck back and burned Harry's house with Miss Winifred inside," said Michael. "He knew she was there. He probably thought she was Sarah, the preacher's wife, who was just about to have a baby, and he meant to murder the mother and the child." The men were murmuring about the cravenness of a man who would kill a pregnant woman that way. "He saw Miss Winifred go into the house and then set the fire and blocked the doors so she couldn't get out. If I hadn't come along, Miss Winifred would have burned to death."

There was a general murmur of outrage among the listeners.

"I need some men to stand guard around this house in case he comes back. I need it guarded day and night until this is over. He's burned one house. He may try to burn the other one. Others need to watch for him in the woods around about. Do you think you can help me with this?"

All agreed.

Michael continued. "Some of you might have issues with Ned, but this is not the time to fight about those. This is the time to help a neighbor who's in trouble. Be careful you don't accidentally shoot anybody. If you catch Charlie, try to take him alive and bring him to me. He might be wounded. I think I nicked him on the arm. But watch out for him and don't trust him. He's mean and he's crazy, and he's out to kill the preacher and his family, and he almost killed Pete and Winifred. I wouldn't care if you killed him, but we may need him to find Harrison, so we need to take him alive. Ned and Liam have gone to try to help the Captain find the boy. Don't be shootin' one of them by mistake."

"Now Michael, you know none of us would *accidentally* shoot the revenuer," drawled one moonshiner whose name was Luther. There was low laughter.

"Very funny! But I'm serious about this. Ned is my friend and Miss Winifred's husband, and I want you to be careful how you treat him."

"You know I was only kiddin'," said Luther. "We're gonna help out here. But don't get too used to wearing that badge now, ya hear? Next time we might not be so agreeable."

"I'll be sure and give that some thought, Luther," Michael said dryly. "You know how much I value your opinion." There was more laughter.

Another man spoke up. "You say Liam's with Ned? Liam Banks?"

"Yep. They're old friends."

"Well, whaddaya know," said the man. "Ned might be all right, after all."

After that the group spent some time deciding who would stand guard and when. Shifts were set up, and the first group agreed to start immediately. Several of the men went up to the burning cabin to see if anything could be saved, and to make sure the fire didn't spread. The recent heavy rain should help. Finally, Michael was satisfied that Winifred's house was as secure as it could be under the circumstances, and he had done all he could do.

* * *

Inside the house, a tiny baby girl named Annie had made her appearance. Sarah held her in her arms, marveling at how perfect she was in every detail, and how little her fingernails were. Molly was there, teaching her how to hold the baby to her breast, and while Sarah was happy to be helped, the baby didn't seem to need any instruction. She had latched on and was nursing eagerly. When another contraction caused Sarah to gasp, Molly returned to the business end of the bed, while Winifred stayed beside Sarah and the baby, watching the infant and mother with joyful, tearful, eyes.

"I thought the hard part was over," said Sarah.

"It is. You just have to pass the afterbirth. Another push should do it," said Molly calmly. She didn't tell Sarah that there was more blood than there should have been, and that the force of the contraction alarmed her. She wanted everything to be perfect for Sarah and Harry. *Please, God, don't let anything go wrong now.* Sarah cried out again and pushed because she could do nothing else. Her body had taken charge. Winifred took the baby from her and rocked it gently when it cried.

"There, now! Don't cry, baby girl," said Winifred. "She'll take you back in just a minute."

Suddenly Molly was smiling. "You're doing great, Sarah, and boy, is Harry going to be surprised! You're having twins!"

When the second child was born, Molly held it by the feet and lifted it into the air. "It's a boy!" she said. The baby cried loudly, and Molly laid it on the bed, wiped it off, and tied off the cord before cutting it. "He's beautiful, Sarah. You've got two beautiful, healthy babies!"

Now all three women had tears in their eyes, and both babies were crying. Michael knocked timidly at the door.

"Everything okay?" he asked.

"Everything is fine," Molly told him. "Harry and Sarah have twins—a girl and a boy!"

"Well, I'll be!" said Michael. "I'll be."

CHAPTER 11
Saving Harrison

As Harry descended the cliff on the game trail, he considered his options. He was tempted to let Harrison sit right where he was, find Charlie and end this feud once and for all, and then go and get the boy. The boy was probably safe from Charlie on that ledge. But there were problems with that plan. Suppose, for example, Harry got hurt or killed, and wasn't able to go back for Harrison? Even if Charlie didn't find him, that would leave the boy at the mercy of the elements. Ned and Liam should be here eventually, but how many hours would that leave Harrison clinging to the ledge, chilled and unprotected, in danger of falling or of falling prey to wild animals? And what if Ned and Liam didn't come?

Ned had warned him to *be the Captain*, and not to let his emotions color his judgment, but Harry knew that even as the Captain, he had never worked in an emotional vacuum. He had always needed to assess the situation before making a decision. Which was more pressing: the boy's immediate safety or the need to destroy the enemy who had placed him in this danger? And which emotion was more likely to destroy his good judgment—worry over his son, or his growing fury with Charlie? He had to admit it. Right now, if he gave in to his emotions, he would hunt Charlie down, capture or kill him, and end his threat once and for all. That was his emotional response, but he decided that the boy's safety had to take priority.

Harry scrabbled to the bottom of the cliff, sliding, grasping at small trees when he went too fast. He needed to get Harrison off that ledge before Charlie found out where he was. He was also worried, because despite Harrison's bravado, there had been a tremor in his voice, and Harry thought the boy's teeth were chattering. Yesterday his son had been forced to ride for hours, and he might not have been given anything to eat. His ankle was injured—possibly broken—and he had been exposed to the cold spray of the falls overnight. Now he was caught in pouring rain and hail. He was wet, cold, injured, and exhausted. People sometimes went into shock or died of exposure under those conditions. Harry's first priority was taking care of his son. Until the boy was safe, nothing else mattered.

Harry reached his camp just as the sun broke through the clouds. More dark clouds were blowing across the sky, so the storm wasn't over, but even a temporary break from the rain was a relief. He had hung his saddle and saddlebags on a low branch of a hemlock tree with his cape on top and his folded coat and the horse's blanket under everything else. The cape was soaked, but it had offered some protection to the other things, and the thick hemlock branches had diverted some of the rain. The clothes in the saddlebags and the blue cavalry coat were still pretty dry. That was important. Harrison would need some dry clothes.

Harry called Smokey, and both of the horses came to him, expecting food. Harry took a handful of feed from the nosebag and offered it to the gray. Then he slid the bag onto Smokey's nose and let him eat the rest. He put the gray's bridle on and tied a rope to it so he could lead him. Harrison would need a horse for the ride home. Then he used his folded cape to wipe the water off Smokey's back the best he could before saddling him. At least the horse's blanket wasn't very wet. After he cinched the saddle firmly in place, he strapped on saddlebags, bedroll, and rope, and he put the rifle in its scabbard. Then he removed the feedbag and led both horses to the creek for water.

While the horses drank, Harry checked his rifle to make sure no mud had gotten into the barrel. It still seemed to be fine. He put extra ammunition into his pockets so that it would be handy. He studied the clouds. This was just a brief respite from the rain. No telling how much more would fall before the storm passed through. He ate a few pieces of beef jerky and dried apple and drank some water. He refilled the canteen for Harrison and made sure he had food for him. Harry was preparing for battle.

Harry shook the water from his hat, pulled it firmly back onto his head, then mounted up and headed across the meadow toward the long, meandering trail that the horses could traverse up the mountainside. Harrison was hurt, and Charlie might be on the prowl. There was no time to waste. There was also no way of knowing if this was a trap.

It was almost noon when Harry reached the summit of the cliff. He tied the horses in the woods some distance from the top, bringing only the rope and his rifle with him. He moved quickly and cautiously, watching for Charlie, but there was no sign of him. He could hear the waterfall before he reached it, and he looked over the cliff to his left. Because he knew where to look, he could make out the outline of the ledge where Harrison was hiding, but he could see how Charlie would have missed it. Even though it was precarious, it was a perfect hiding place. He moved on up the trail, scouting it out, watching for an ambush. He crossed the stream above the falls and followed it until he came to the little hut that backed up against the mountainside. He quickly searched the area. There was no sign of life. Charlie was gone. Then he hurried back down to take care of Harrison.

He reached the place where Harrison had gone over the edge and marveled that the boy had survived such a fall in the dark. Surely God had protected him.

"Harrison!" he called.

"Dad?" answered the boy.

"I'm going to lower a rope to you. Can you tie it around your chest, under your arms?"

There was no answer. Harry felt a moment of panic. Could he have come too late, after all?

"Harrison! Can you hear me?"

"Dad?" the boy replied weakly.

"Are you all right?"

"I'm so c-cold!" the boy answered. "My hands are numb, and I can't quit shaking."

"You just sit right where you are. I'm coming! Do you hear me?"

There was no answer.

Harry set down the rifle and hurriedly tied the end of the rope around a sturdy tree at the side of the path. He tested it to make sure the knot was strong enough to hold his weight. Then he started climbing carefully down the cliff among the laurel bushes and vines. He reached the ledge very quickly. The ledge was solid rock and plenty strong, but there wasn't much room on it. It was wide enough for Harrison, but narrowed to nothing within just a few feet on either side of him. Harry managed to kneel beside him, feeling momentarily breathless with dizziness when he looked over the edge at the great distance to the bottom of the cliff. He had always been scared of heights.

"Harrison! I'm so proud of you!" Harry cried, taking the boy into his arms to warm him. "I'm going to get you out of here. You're going to be fine. Do you hear me?" Harrison, pale and shaking, nodded at his father.

"I knew you'd come," he said.

Harry offered the boy water from his canteen, and he drank it. Then he took dried apples and cornbread from his pocket, and handed those over. Harrison made short work of them. Maybe it was Harry's imagination, but he thought Harrison already looked stronger.

Harry took the rope and tied it around the boy's chest. "I've got some dry clothes in my saddle bags, and we can go up to the shack and build a fire to warm you up."

"What about Ch-charlie?"

"I didn't see any sign of him," Harry answered.

"He's c-crazy, Dad. He hates you. He'll be back."

"Well, we'll just take this one thing at a time. First we get you off this ledge. How's your ankle?" Harry pulled the boy's pants leg up to take a look, and cringed inwardly when he saw it. The ankle and foot were painfully bruised and swollen.

Harrison seemed confused. "I know it hurts, but I can't feel it anymore," he said.

Harry had planned to climb back up the cliff and then pull Harrison up after him, but he knew now that Harrison wouldn't be able to make that climb. He'd have to carry the boy up on his back. And that meant that somehow he had to get him onto his back. The trouble was there just wasn't enough room on the ledge. If there was one bright spot in the situation, it was that the sun was now shining. Maybe the storm had passed.

"Now listen to me," Harry said seriously to his son. "Even if it hurts your ankle, we've got to get you back on solid ground. I'm going to stand up just as close to the cliff as I can, and then I want you to hold onto me and stand up behind me. Don't be scared. You can't fall far with this rope around you. Then I'm going to pull you up onto my back and carry you up the cliff. Got it?"

Harrison nodded. Harry gripped the rope and pulled himself to a standing position. As soon as Harry was upright, Harrison held onto his father's belt and pulled himself up behind him. His legs were stiff from sitting in a cramped position all night. He gasped when he accidentally put weight on the sore ankle, and he leaned into Harry's back, holding onto him. Harry immediately grabbed the boy's arms. "You doing okay?" he asked. He could feel Harrison shaking.

"I just got a little dizzy when I put my foot down," said Harrison. He took a deep, ragged breath. "I'm sorry to be so much trouble."

"You're doing great. Now I'm going to try to get you up onto my back. Are you ready?"

"Yeah."

"When I do, just don't lean backwards or I might fall off this ledge and leave you swinging on the rope by yourself!"

"That would be bad," said Harrison. "Really bad. I'll lean forward."

Harry leaned into the cliff, then stooping and reaching behind him, grasped Harrison behind the legs and hoisted him onto his back. He pulled Harrison's arms around his neck, worried by how cold and clammy the boy's skin felt, then hitched him a little higher and made sure he was secure. Then he held firmly to the rope and began climbing the steep slope again with Harrison clinging to his back. It occurred to Harry that at the age of thirty-three he was not as young as he used to be, and that Harrison was heavier than he looked. He hoped that his knees and the rope could take the strain.

Harrison felt his father's warmth and his strength and the heat of the sun on the back of his head, and for the first time since Charlie had taken him, he knew things would be all right. At last they reached the top, and Harry moved a little way past the tree where he had tied the rope, toward the creek. He stopped at the smooth, flat slab of rock that bordered the creek above the waterfall. There he knelt and let Harrison get down.

"Sit right here in the sun while I get the horse," said Harry. "I'll just be a few minutes."

Harrison pulled the loop of rope off over his head and dropped it onto the rock beside him. He stretched his arms, feeling his circulation returning and his body warming in the noonday sun. The long, cold night was over, and it was still July after all! Harrison pulled his wet shirt off and stretched full out on his back on the rock, using the shirt for a pillow. If not for the increased throbbing in his ankle, he would have felt wonderful. He understood for the first time why snakes and lizards liked to sun themselves on rocks and thought that if Harry didn't hurry, he'd fall asleep. He folded his arms over his eyes and allowed himself to relax. At last he heard footsteps approaching.

"You have no idea how good it feels to be able to stretch out in the sun," said Harrison.

"I have a pretty good idea," said a low voice that was not Harry's. It was Charlie.

Alarmed, Harrison sat up quickly, gasping at the pain in his foot.

"So, where's my old friend Harry?" asked Charlie, looking around. His pistol was in his hand, and a sodden shawl was slung over one shoulder. The man looked terrible. There were dark smudges on his face, and his arm had been bleeding.

Harrison didn't say anything. He dropped his eyes as he always did with Charlie and saw that Charlie was standing in the loop of rope he had left coiled like a snake on the rock. Too bad it wasn't a real snake. Harrison knew that Charlie was deathly afraid of snakes.

Charlie repeated angrily. "Look at me, boy! Where's Harry?"

From the trees beyond the path, Harry replied. "I'm right here." He emerged from the woods leading the horse, his Winchester in one hand.

Charlie, who was standing on the rock with his back to the creek, aimed his own gun at Harrison's head and nodded toward Harry's rifle. "You'll want to drop that."

"We need to talk," Harry said, raising his hands. "We don't need guns. Let the boy go. I'll just put my gun in the scabbard."

"You do that," said Charlie, his own gun still pointed unwaveringly at Harrison's head.

Harry put his gun away. "Come on, Charlie." He slowly walked closer to Charlie, his hands raised. You don't need to hide behind a kid. We can talk this out. Put your gun down, too."

"Not likely," said Charlie.

Harrison knew that Charlie meant to kill Harry, and he couldn't let that happen. Suddenly he had an idea. He pointed at Charlie's feet and yelled, "Snake!" then rolled abruptly to one side and yanked hard on the rope. Charlie's foot slipped on the wet rock, and he threw his arms up to try to regain his balance. Harry moved in, knocking him onto his back in the shallow water of the creek. Then the two men were slugging it out, rolling and punching, with Harry trying to dislodge the revolver from Charlie's hand. The gun went off twice, the bullets flying harmlessly into the air. Finally Harry slammed Charlie's hand against a rock until he let the gun go. After that, Harry delivered one more solid punch, and Charlie said, "Enough! I give up!" Then he grinned. "The gun was empty, anyway."

Harry eased back, not trusting him, and only then did it register in his mind that there was a shawl on the rocks beside them. It was a dirty, smoke-scented, bloody shawl, and it was his wife's. There was only one shawl like it: he had watched Sarah knit it from odds and ends of different-colored yarn right after they were married.

He looked coldly at Charlie. "Where did you get this?"

"What, that old thing?"

Harry bent down, grabbed Charlie by the shirt collar and lifted him out of the water. "I said where did you get this?"

Charlie shrugged. "I rescued it from a burning building." He looked out at the distant view of rolling hills. "Over there, see?" There was a narrow plume of smoke spreading over the sky. "That's your house. By the way, Harry, you can get there a lot faster if you go by the ridge trail, back thataway, instead of following the creeks. I know, because I went to visit your wife this morning."

Harry spoke through gritted teeth. "You're a liar. You've always been a liar. I don't believe a word of it. If you know what's good for you, you'll tell me the truth. If you've hurt my wife, I'll kill you with my bare hands."

"Well, Harry, that puts me in a tough position. If I know what's good for me, I'll tell you the truth, but if I tell you the truth, you'll kill me." Harry drew back his fist. "Actually, I don't think she was in pain when she died. I'm pretty sure the smoke would have killed her before the fire did."

Harry let out a roar and punched Charlie so hard that he fell backward into the water, landing right beside the revolver. Charlie grabbed the gun just as Harry reached him. Once again they struggled for possession of the gun, fighting and rolling until they were almost at the top of the falls. The creek had narrowed and deepened where it had eaten its way into the rock cliff, and the water was now a torrent around them. The two of them grappled for control. It looked as if both of them would be swept to their deaths.

From somewhere in the distance, Harry heard Harrison shout over the roar of the falls, "Let him go, Dad, or you'll both die. Let him go!"

The two snakes had swallowed and swallowed until both snakes were gone. *One of them should have let go,* Harrison had said. Instead of punching Charlie again, Harry let go and stepped back, grabbing a gnarled root that grew out of the rocky bank on the opposite side of the narrowed creek to brace himself against the force of the water. Charlie lifted the gun and held it in front of him, aiming it straight at Harry.

"I lied about the gun: there's one more round. You know I never forget how many rounds I've shot. So I win, Harry, and you lose." He fired the gun straight into Harry's face, but the cylinder only clicked harmlessly. Charlie stared at the gun, bewildered. A split second later, he jerked backward and grabbed his own chest. Then he fell to his knees and looked down to see blood leaking through his fingers as the sound of a gunshot finally reached them. Water rushed around him, carrying his blood toward the falls.

"What was that?" he asked Harry, dazed.

Harry knew the sound of the gun and he knew the one person who could make a shot from that distance. "That was Liam," he answered. He knew that Charlie was finished, and he was surprised that he felt no joy in the man's destruction. He reached out to him.

"Give me your hand. You can still make it."

"What? Let you save me?" Charlie shook his head.

"Why not? Let me help you! There's still hope for you!" Harry leaned out as far as he could while holding onto the tree root. "Take my hand!"

Charlie shook his head, still dazed, still astounded that it was his own blood that was leaking into the water and not Harry's. He sneered at Harry. "I wouldn't give you the pleasure."

Harry lowered his hand, defeated. "I've never understood it, Charlie. What did I do to you? What could I have done to make things different?" he asked, frustrated.

"You mean, besides dying?" Charlie laughed and coughed, holding himself against the pain and the force of the water. "You could have been me. And I could have been you."

Charlie struggled to his feet and faced outward as if to see who had shot him, or to take one more look at the world before he died. Then he walked purposefully toward the edge, holding onto branches, staggering when his feet slipped on the sloping rocks, still struggling, not quite ready to go. When he was almost there, he threw his arms out in a grand gesture. "Here I am, Liam! Take your best shot!" he yelled.

If Liam heard him, he ignored him. "I can't even get myself killed," Charlie exclaimed, looking at Harry with frustration. Then a floating limb that had fallen in the storm swept down the stream and crashed against Charlie's legs. His feet slipped out from under him, and the water swept him over the edge. He was gone without another sound.

Harry sighed and let himself sink lower into the water, leaning close to the bank, hanging onto the root. His thoughts were bleak. When it came to helping this man, he had failed utterly, and even though he had refused to compete with Charlie, Harry felt he had lost. Harry had not only failed to save Charlie, he had failed Molly and lost her, and now, if Charlie had told the truth, he had lost Sarah, too. He couldn't face that. Harry felt a rush of weariness sweep over him. He was growing numb from the cold water, and for just the briefest moment he thought how easy it would be to slip over the edge with Charlie, to give in to despair and disappointment and take the easy way out. Then in his mind he heard the mighty voice of the old preacher in the desert who had forbidden him to give in to those feelings: *You can't live like that!* the old man had said. *You know better, for you are a man in whom the Spirit of God dwells!*

"Dad?" came a voice from above him. Harry straightened, pulled himself together, and looked up. There was Harrison, clinging to the trunk of a tree, lowering the rope with its loop still fixed.

"Put this around yourself, Dad. Hurry!" he said with some urgency. The boy was afraid.

Harry grabbed the rope and slid it over his head and one arm, still holding firmly to the root with the other hand.

"Put it all the way around you!" insisted Harrison.

The rope was a little snug, but Harry managed it.

Harrison smiled. "Don't worry, you won't fall far. It's still tied to the tree."

Harry's look of devotion belied his words as he muttered, "Smart aleck. I'd still drown!" and he knew that Harrison was living proof that God could take his worst mistakes and turn them into something good.

"We need to get home, Dad. Mother will be worried about us," said Harrison.

Harry nodded and, pulling the rope, hand over hand, began walking against the flow of the water to the wider, shallower part of the creek where he could get out. When he got there, Ned was there to help him. He was still out of breath from his desperate climb up the cliff.

"Harry, I couldn't see from down there. I couldn't see if Charlie had shot you or not."

"Well, he did try, but he was out of ammunition. It's okay, Ned. I'm okay." Harry pulled the rope off over his head. "How about helping Harrison." He gestured toward the boy, who was slowly hobbling back across the rock, awkwardly using a stick for a crutch.

Harry waded back out into the creek and found Sarah's shawl where it still clung wetly to a rock. He lifted it carefully trying not to snag it, then dipped it into the cold, clear water and rinsed the bloodstains out of it. He knew better than to rub it or wring it. Sarah had taught him that wool was precious and easily spoiled. He remembered watching her sort the colored yarn while they were on the train when they were newly married. She had explained how the wool had been sheared, carded, spun and dyed. Then she had taken the time to knit it into something warm and useful, and she had been lovely in it.

Harry gathered the sodden shawl in his hands and carefully squeezed the water out of it, then hugged it to his chest and fought the tears that had been building in him since Charlie had told him about the smoke and the fire. In spite of his efforts, the shawl was still stained, and he could still smell the smoke in it, and he feared that whatever Charlie had done, he would not be able to undo it.

Ned's hand clasped his shoulder. "Come on, Harry. Your son needs you to be strong."

Harry nodded and looked back to where Harrison was seated on the smooth rock again with his head in his hands.

"Thanks, Ned," said Harry, wiping his eyes. "Listen, we need to get some dry clothes on Harrison. There are some in my saddlebags. If you could get Smokey, we'll let him ride the horse and we'll go up to the little cabin and get him cleaned up."

Ned nodded, satisfied that Harry was back in control, and went to get the horse where it was grazing beside the creek.

"There's a gray horse down in the woods, too," Harry called to him.

"You got Moonshine?" Harrison said, looking up.

"Moonshine! What kind of name is that for a horse?" asked Ned.

"That's a great name!" said Harry. "You like that horse?" he asked, sitting down by Harrison on the rocks.

"Yeah, he's a beauty."

"Well, if we don't find out that he belongs to someone else, I guess he's yours," said Harry. "Anyway, he'll need somebody to care for him while we check into it."

"I'll take care of him!" said Harrison, nodding.

Harry looked his son in the eye. "Thank you for the rope."

Harrison nodded again, still crying a little.

"I'm sorry about what happened to Charlie," Harry said.

"I know."

"You gonna be okay?" Harry asked gently.

"Yeah. There was nothing you could do. Charlie brought everything on himself." Harrison sobbed quietly. "But I always felt sorry for him, even when I hated him. Does that make sense?"

"Yes," said Harry, wondering at the wisdom of a child. The boy wasn't really a child any more. He was almost a man. "I understand exactly what you mean."

"I had a chance to shoot him while he was asleep, but I couldn't," Harrison said.

"I'm glad you couldn't," said Harry. "So glad."

"But what if he had killed you? What then?"

"You still would have done what was right. It wouldn't have been your fault," Harry insisted.

Harrison reached into his pocket and pulled out the cartridge he had taken from Charlie's gun. "I had the gun for awhile, and I made the gun safe, like you taught me, but then I lost it, so it didn't matter."

Harry took the cartridge and looked curiously at it, then back at his son. "It mattered, Harrison. It mattered!" Harry bowed his head and covered his eyes, overwhelmed.

Ned came back, leading both horses. "Which one do you want to ride, Harrison?" he asked.

"The one with the saddle," Harrison said. "The last time I rode bareback I ended up on that ledge."

"Ha! Wise choice," said Harry, helping the injured boy up and giving him a shoulder to lean on, then giving him a lift into the saddle.

"I'll bet that ankle's sore," said Ned. "By the way, I found your shoe down at the foot of the cliff, along with a horse blanket and Harry's hat. I thought it was your way of leaving bread crumbs so we could find the trail."

"It worked, didn't it?" asked Harry. He was rummaging in his saddlebags to find a shirt for Harrison.

"Yeah, it worked. That and the sound of gunfire. That got my attention in a hurry."

Harry helped the boy into a dry shirt and his blue cavalry coat, rolling up the sleeves to make it fit. Then he and Ned walked ahead, leading the horses while Harrison rode.

"Thanks, Ned," said Harry.

"Any time," said Ned, looking at Harry with concern. Harry looked desperately sad, and he was still holding the shawl. "Sarah was fine when I left this morning."

"That was before Charlie burned the house," replied Harry.

"He burned your house?" Ned asked.

"That's what he said."

"Well, nobody was home. They were all at my house," said Ned. "I moved Sarah right after you left. Winifred and Michael were with her at my house."

"Michael was there, too?"

"Yep."

"That explains why Charlie was wounded. Michael must have caught him setting the fire. Maybe she's all right."

"I'll bet she's fine."

"I've got to go as soon as I can, though. I've got to know," said Harry. "Can you and Liam take care of Harrison and deal with Charlie's body?"

"Yes, Harry. But there's something else you need to know."

"What?" Harry frowned, hoping there wasn't more bad news.

"Michael brought someone back from Dahlonega. A midwife. She's there with Winifred and Sarah." Ned hesitated. He couldn't just spring it on him, the news that Molly was still alive.

"Is the baby coming? Is that what you aren't telling me?"

When Ned hesitated again Harry didn't wait for an answer. He turned to Harrison. "Sorry, son, but I need this horse. You'll have to take your chances on Moonshine. Ned will help you." While they were transferring Harrison to the other horse, they saw Liam approaching, riding his horse and leading Ned's.

"Here, take the saddlebags," Harry said to Ned. "There are more dry clothes in there and some food and bandages." Then he turned to Harrison. "Are you all right, Harrison?"

The boy nodded. He looked very happy to be on the gray horse again.

Harry patted the horse, then looked gravely at Harrison. "You saved my life. Do you know that? When you took one cartridge out of the pistol, you saved my life." He shook the boy's hand. "Be careful on that horse, now. You don't want to fall off and hurt that foot."

"Moonshine knows how it feels to have a sore foot," said Harrison. "He'll look after me."

"I wouldn't count on that, but Ned will look after you, anyway," said Harry. He looked at Ned. "You take as much time as you need. Keep Harrison safe. Get him into some dry pants and bandage up that ankle. Get him warm and give him food—something hot, if you can. Let him rest tonight."

"Yes sir, Cap'n Richardson," Ned muttered good-naturedly, giving a sloppy salute. Harry ignored him, mounted Smokey, and rode to meet Liam as he approached them. Liam handed Harry his hat. He couldn't remember when he had lost it.

The Captain Seeks the Lost

"That was a good shot, Liam. I thank you." Harry put on the hat. "What about Charlie?" he asked quietly.

"He's dead," Liam assured him.

"Charlie said there's a trail along the ridges. He said it's the quickest way to my house," said Harry. "Is that true? Where is it?"

Liam didn't seem surprised by Harry's brusqueness, and he didn't stutter much, nor did he waste words. He pointed with his hand as he gave directions. "Indian trail. There are steep places. Follow the branch to the creek; turn up the creek. At the headwaters, follow the ridge. Then follow the smoke."

Harry frowned at "the smoke," then nodded. Somehow Liam knew about the fire. He had to have talked with Charlie. "Did Charlie say anything to you before he died?"

"He said he was sorry. I'll tell you the rest later," he said, as Ned and Harrison approached.

"Ned? Are we set?" Harry asked.

"We're fine," Ned said. "Go to her."

Harry turned the horse and rode—still muddy, wet, and exhausted, and still holding tightly to a soggy shawl—but a man with a mission.

As the other three watched him ride away, Harrison asked Ned, "Mama's there?"

"Yep," said Ned. "I couldn't tell him about her. I just told him there was a midwife."

"I couldn't either," said Harrison, sympathizing. "Mother's okay, then. Mama won't let anything happen to her."

"I hope you're right, son," said Ned. "I sure hope you're right."

Liam looked at Ned. "This midwife. Is she the girl Harry left behind?"

Ned nodded. "Yep. Charlie's wife."

Harrison added, "My mother."

Liam thought it through. "That explains it."

The three rode slowly to the cabin with Ned leading Moonshine while Liam rode alongside, both men keeping Harrison safe. And Harrison was pretty sure the horse was walking carefully, mindful that he was on his back without a saddle.

"What did he say at the end?" Ned asked quietly, when the two adults rode temporarily side-by-side.

"He said to tell Harry he was sorry," said Liam. "He was dying. I helped him."

Ned nodded, not sure what Liam meant, exactly, but satisfied that no more questions were necessary at the moment. The boy was catching up with them. They rode on toward the cabin without further conversation.

CHAPTER 12

A Ghost from the Past

It was late in the afternoon, and although the sun wouldn't set for several hours, visibility was poor. Thick clouds had draped themselves around the peaks and shoulders of the mountains and closed in around Harry as he rode his horse toward home. It occurred to him—not for the first time—that he should have asked Liam to come with him and show him the way. The path had been pretty easy to follow in most places, but now fog obscured the view of the world around him. He could only watch the ground in front of him, taking one step at a time, not knowing what was ahead or to either side. It seemed like a metaphor for his life, and to be honest, Harry was pretty tired of it. He was ready for a little clarity. As usual, there was no real choice in the matter. There was no turning back. He could only persevere, and so he did. He was glad that Smokey was a good, steady horse, and when he doubted himself, he relied on Smokey to find the path.

Hours had passed. Harry smelled the smoke before he saw it, and the horse caught the scent at the same time. Smokey had a terrible fear of fire, and he shied and snorted his alarm.

"Easy, boy. We're almost home," said Harry, and he urged him forward.

Just then, a wild-looking bearded man stepped out in front of them holding a gun.

"Stop where you are!" he commanded. Then he called out, "I've got him, Luther!"

Harry reacted quickly, thinking these were Charlie's henchmen lying in wait. No wonder he had told him to take this path. He kicked the horse and rode directly at the man in front of him, yelling "Get out of my way!" and he reached for his Winchester as he rode.

Before Harry could retrieve the rifle, the man fired a warning shot into the air then leaped out of the way, but another man grabbed Harry from the side, pulling him out of the saddle and punching him as he fell. Harry hit the ground hard and lay there, stunned. Then the two men seized him, pulled his arms behind him, and forced him to stand.

A third man emerged from the fog, took in the scene, and called out in disgust. "That's the Captain, you idiots. Let him go!"

Michael Gibson hurried to Harry and looked anxiously at him. "Are you okay, Harry? I'm sorry! They thought you were Charlie."

Harry brushed some fresh dirt off his sleeve while he regained his composure. "Charlie's dead, and if I'd had my Colt, these men probably would be, too." Harry used the back of his hand to wipe some blood from his nose, let out a long breath, and looked at the two sheepish guards. "So, you're guarding my house?"

"Yeah," Luther admitted.

"Then I should be grateful to you, I guess," Harry said.

"I'm sorry I punched you," said Luther. "You didn't look like a preacher."

Harry regarded himself briefly. He had to admit he looked pretty bad. His face was covered with stubble and dirt, his clothes were filthy, and his boots were caked with mud. He couldn't remember the last time he had combed his hair.

"You're right," he admitted.

"How's your boy?" asked Michael.

"He's safe, and he'll be okay. Ned and Liam will bring him tomorrow. You should probably call off your guards before they come," suggested Harry, smiling slightly. He wasn't feeling quite right. Maybe the punch or the landing on the ground had rattled his brain a little. He blinked and swayed.

"Harry?" said Michael, alarmed. He reached to steady him.

"I'm a little dizzy," Harry admitted. "Luther's got a good, strong right."

"Come on. Let me walk you the rest of the way," said Michael, then he turned to his men and gave them instructions. Luther was to bring the horse while the other man told the rest of the guards that they could go home.

"Thank the men for me," said Harry. The first man hurried away, and Luther took Harry's horse by the bridle and started to follow them.

"Wait," said Harry. "I'll take that," he said, pointing at the shawl that was draped over the saddle horn. It was still damp, but he folded it carefully and hung it over his shoulder.

Michael thought it was amazing that Harry was still polite to these men after they had attacked him. He definitely had a different perspective than most people. He took Harry firmly by the arm, steadying him as they walked toward what was left of the cabin.

The smell of smoke was pungent here, and eerie wisps of fog trailed around the blackened ruins of the cabin. Harry felt he had walked into one of his nightmares. They ducked under the clotheslines, where ghostly rags and sheets hung dripping in the fog. There in the little washhouse beside the scorched back porch, a fire was burning under the iron wash pot, and someone was using a scrub board at one of the washtubs. She looked up at him as they approached, and it was Molly—but Harry knew Molly was dead. His mind spun. "Molly?" he asked, frowning. She lifted her hands from the water, and in the dim light, the water appeared to be red with blood. He blanched and turned to Michael. "What nightmare is this?"

He turned, trembling, back to Molly, and his face twisted. "I lost you, Molly. Have I lost Sarah, too?" then he felt his knees buckle, and everything went dark.

* * *

Harry opened his eyes to see Michael's concerned face above him. "He's awake," he said.

Then Molly came back into view, also frowning. "Harry?" she asked, kneeling beside him. She laid a cool, wet cloth on his forehead and started wiping the dirt off his face. "Sarah's fine. Do you hear me? Sarah's fine, and the babies are fine, too. You didn't expect to see me here. I'm sorry I shocked you."

Michael thought Harry and Molly deserved a little privacy for this meeting, so he spoke up. "I'll help Luther with the horse," and they walked off toward the barn, leading Smokey.

Harry sat up, and the motion made his head spin again. He felt sure he wasn't absorbing everything that was being said. He smiled slightly, still amazed to see Molly.

"Harry? Are you listening to me?" she asked, still concerned about him, looking at his pupils. His eyes weren't quite focused. She was the vigilant nurse, wringing out the cloth and reapplying it to Harry's head.

"Molly!" he whispered. "You're alive!" His mind was beginning to clear.

"Yes, Harry, and you've had a bump on the head. I'm sorry I lied, but we can talk about that later. You don't have time now."

Harry nodded, wondering how to tell her about Charlie. "Stop that," he said, taking the cloth from her. "My face is fine. There are things I need to tell you," he said.

"Is my son all right?" she asked anxiously, sitting back on her heels.

"He'll be fine. He's twisted his ankle, but Ned is going to bandage it and let him rest overnight before they come home tomorrow."

Molly nodded, waiting for the rest. "And Charlie?"

Harry sighed. He knew there was no way to soften it. "He's dead."

She nodded, not surprised.

"I tried to save him, but I couldn't. He wouldn't let me help him," said Harry.

"I doubt if anyone could have helped him."

"I should have known you were alive," Harry said, as things became clearer. He rubbed his eyes. "I should have guessed from Harrison's hints. He told me you were a midwife, and wouldn't it have been nice if you could have come to help Sarah? If only you weren't dead, of course!" he added ironically. "Ned knew today, didn't he, but he didn't have the courage to tell me, either. Some friend he is."

"So when you saw me, you thought your were having a nightmare?" she asked ruefully. "Really, Harry! I wasn't all that bad."

Harry dabbed at his sore nose with the cloth. "It's your own fault. If you'd told the truth from the beginning, things might have been a little easier, all the way around. You have no idea how Harrison has agonized over lying to me! You shouldn't have made him do that," he said.

"I'm sorry, Harry. It seemed like the right thing to do at the time." Molly stood as Michael came toward them.

"Here, Michael, help me up." Harry reached up, and Michael gave him a hand. He stood for a moment, getting his balance and studying Molly, still amazed to see her. "My old friend!" he said, offering her his hands. And with those three words, he defined their relationship in no uncertain terms. "I'd hug you, but I'm too filthy," he said, embarrassed.

"Don't be silly," she said, putting her arms around his neck and pulling his face to hers. Then he put his arms around her for a strong, brotherly hug. "I'm glad you're alive!" he said fervently, then he backed away and looked intently into her eyes. "And I'm sorry for everything that went wrong. I'm sorry I was never there for you. You've done an amazing job with Harrison. He's a great kid."

Molly was blinking fast, controlling tears, and nodding. "We'll have time to talk about all this later," she said. "Right now, you need to see Sarah and the babies."

Harry frowned and stared. "Has Sarah already had the—did you say *babies?*"

"Yes, Harry." Molly said, smiling. "You have twins—a girl and a boy."

"Twins! And they're okay, and Sarah's okay?"

"Everyone's fine."

"Thank God," he murmured. "Thank God." He turned then and set off at a rather crooked jog down the hill toward Winifred's house. Looking back, he called to Molly, "You won't go away, will you? We'll talk more later! Thank you!"

Molly sighed and turned back to her scrub board. *When you don't know what to do next, do the thing that's nearest,* she told herself.

"Are we about done here?" asked Michael.

"There are just a few things to wring out and hang on the line. Maybe you'd better follow him and make sure he's all right."

"Okay. Then I'll come back and help you," he said, and he hurried after Harry.

CHAPTER 13

"You're Not Alone"

It was after midnight, and silence had finally settled on the household. Winifred had gone to her room. She had offered to share the space with Molly, but Molly preferred to stay in the living room, just in case Sarah needed help during the night. Harry and Sarah were behind their closed bedroom door with the twins, and for the moment, both babies were asleep. From her place on the couch, Molly had been able to hear the soft voices of Harry and Sarah, who had talked for a long time. She couldn't hear what they were saying, and she was glad. It was enough to know that they had been overjoyed to see each other and that everything was all right between them. The babies were a beautiful miracle, and even though both Harry and Sarah were exhausted, they were walking on air.

Molly had been trying without success to go to sleep. Her mind raced with the events of the day, not least of which was seeing Harry again after so many years. Harry was no longer the nineteen-year-old cadet marching bravely off to war. She had heard enough to know that the years had not been kind to him, but he wore them well: he was more handsome than ever. Molly thought she would always love him, but not in the way she once had. Her youthful hero worship seemed a lifetime away, and she had long ago accepted the truth that they would never be together. She had made that decision when she married Charlie.

Now that she knew he was alive and well, but happily married, Molly had decided to pretend to herself that Harry was an adopted brother. It was all right to love a brother. She liked Sarah and wanted only good things for her, including a long and happy life with Harry. It would have been a terrible thing if something had gone wrong for Sarah and the babies on her watch, but things had gone well. All things considered, this should be a happy day.

So why did she feel so sad? There was Charlie's death, of course. His destruction had been in progress for years and came as no surprise, but it was still a crushing defeat, an overwhelming personal tragedy. For Charlie, today was the end of a long, disastrous descent into insanity. She had tried to help him; had tried to have a normal life with him; had tried to save Harrison from him; but nothing had worked. She had been on the verge of leaving him when his final break had come. His belief that she had left him for Harry was probably the thing that had driven him over the edge.

Harrison was safe now, thanks to Harry, and Molly would see him tomorrow. And now, after all the years of that terrible marriage, Molly was free of Charlie and surprised that she didn't feel free. Instead, she felt wounded, empty, lost, and alone.

Molly turned and tried to find a comfortable position on the couch as her thoughts continued to churn. She and Harry had not talked much during the evening; there had not been time. Harry had offered to conduct the funeral for Charlie, and she had agreed. His kindness and solicitude had almost been her undoing. There, in front of Sarah, he had held her hands and prayed for her. She reminded herself that he was her "adopted brother" now, her old friend, and—for the moment, at least—her pastor. And that was all.

Molly would need to go back to Dahlonega soon. She wondered if Harrison would want to stay here with Harry or come back home with her. She was surprised at how easy it had become to call the boy "Harrison" after all those years of calling him "Harry." She understood why Harry had insisted that the boy come up with another name. There could never be two Harrys. It would be far too confusing.

If Harry didn't mind, she would let the boy make the decision about whether to go back home with her or stay in the mountains. And what would Harry and Sarah do, now that they had two babies and a burned house? Would they want Harrison to stay, or would their lives be too full, their space too crowded? Would Harrison be sad if he had to leave them and go home with her?

One of the babies cried in the next room, and Molly gave up on sleep. She sat up and then stood and put on the robe that Winifred had loaned her. Winifred—now, there was a kind soul if ever there was one. Molly had known about Harry's Aunt Winifred since she and Harry had been kids, but she had never imagined she would get to know her. Now she was happy to have her as a friend. Harry seemed to attract kind people. He was the strong center they orbited around. Maybe he held them together by the force of his goodness.

It was stuffy in the house, and Molly decided to get some air. She went quietly to the front door and stepped out onto the porch. The fog had cleared, blown away by the last remnants of the storm. Now there was a bright moon, and she could see the outline of the chairs on the porch, but shadows obscured the darker corners close to the house. The dog was quiet in his box and only wagged his tail half-heartedly as she passed, then went back to sleep.

Molly sat down on the edge of the porch with her feet on the steps and pulled the heavy robe closer, and in the stillness, she put her face in her hands and quietly gave in to tears. She cried for Charlie and his miserable, misspent life and wondered if she could have done more to save him. There was always room for guilt. She cried because Harry was more lost to her than ever. Theirs was a love that should never have been, and yet it had given her a son. How could that be wrong? And she cried for her son, who was still far away from her and injured and might not want to go home with her again. She cried for herself because she was tired and lonely.

A deep, slow voice spoke quietly from the wicker loveseat beneath the windows. "You're not alone, Molly."

Startled, Molly jumped and wiped her eyes, dismayed at being caught with her defenses down. It was Michael, of course. "What? Are you some kind of spiritual advisor, now?"

"No, I was just letting you know you're not the only person on the porch," said Michael apologetically. "I'm sorry. I didn't mean to scare you. If you need to be alone, I can leave."

Molly almost laughed. It seemed she and Michael had a talent for talking at cross-purposes. "I'm glad to have the company. I thought you'd gone home."

"No. I promised Ned I'd stay until he gets back. And I promised Agent Whittaker I'd look after you."

"You're a good man," said Molly.

"That's what people keep telling me, but I'm not so sure," said Michael. "We should keep our voices down. Why don't you come and sit with me?"

"All right."

Molly joined Michael, and it felt perfectly natural when he put his arm around her and gave her shoulder a squeeze. It felt like friendship—nothing alarming.

"I'm sorry for your loss," he said quietly.

"Thank you."

"And I can't tell you how glad I am that you came with me, and that you were here to deliver the babies. I don't know what we would have done without you. It all happened so fast, we could never have gotten another midwife here in time."

"I was glad to be able to help," said Molly. "They're beautiful babies, aren't they?"

"They're amazing. And so are you."

"Well, thank you!" Molly was taken aback by his praise. "It's hard to believe how much has happened in twenty-four hours."

"It's true. The funniest thing was the look on Carlotta Payne's face this morning, when you came out one door in that shawl, and I came out the other in my long underwear and badge, like two birds poppin' out of a cuckoo clock."

Molly smiled, remembering. "That was funny. She actually stopped talking for just a second to stare at us. You looked more like a really bad sheriff than a bird, though—or maybe a pirate."

"And you looked like an angry fairy with your wings hidden under that shawl."

"An angry fairy!" she said, surprised. "That's different."

"Yeah. Your hair was all wild and curly, and your legs were—well, absolutely gorgeous, to be honest—and the expression on your face! I wasn't sure if you'd fly away or stay and put a spell on Carlotta that would make her sleep for a hundred years."

"A hundred years would have been about right. I would have done it if I could. Right now I wish I could sleep a little bit, myself." There was a pause. Finally Molly asked, "Are you a big reader of fairy tales? That seems strange for a bootlegger."

"I haven't always been a bootlegger. I used to be a little boy."

Molly laughed softly. "I don't believe it!"

"It's true!" Michael said solemnly. "One of my grandmothers was Cherokee. The other one was Irish, and they both told stories about little people. And my mother read fairy tales to me until I was old enough to read them for myself. I still have the book. I'll have to show you the picture of yourself someday. I still like to read, but now I read other things."

"Like the Bible?"

"Sometimes." said Michael. "Maybe not as much as I should. Why?"

"Because you knew the story about Paul on the road to Damascus."

"Ahh, yes. Well, I did have the feeling I'd been blinded by the light. Sometime I'll explain that, too." Michael covered his mouth and yawned.

It was a nice thought, that there would be a "sometime" when she and Michael would be friends and would talk about things.

"There's no telling what Carlotta's saying about us. Does that bother you?" she asked.

"Not a bit. It could be worse. If she's gossipin' about you and me, she'll have less time to gossip about you and Harry. That might be a good thing."

"That's true, I guess," said Molly, also yawning. "In this situation, the possibilities for gossip are practically endless. Do you think we'll ever sleep again?" she asked.

"Nah, I doubt it!" he answered. "Not around here, anyway," but there was a smile in his voice, and he squeezed her shoulder again. She felt remarkably comforted and no longer alone. She leaned her head back against his arm and closed her eyes.

And they did sleep—until the sun rose and the sound of a horse and surrey roused them. Molly awoke to find herself leaning into Michael's side with her legs curled up beside her. His arm was still around her, and she was cuddled up to his chest, as if sleeping with him were the most natural thing in the world. Sometime during the night someone had thrown a blanket over them both.

And there was Carlotta Payne with her husband, the chairman of the deacons, driving the black surrey into the yard. Michael groaned, then whispered, "Don't those people ever sleep? Leave this to me." They quickly separated from each other. Molly pulled her robe snugly around her and tightened the sash, dreading the smug look she expected to see on Carlotta's face.

Day Four: Thursday

CHAPTER 14

What They Found in the Smokehouse

As the surrey circled through the yard and drew up by the porch, Molly and Michael became aware that something was wrong. Carlotta's face seemed frozen with fear, and her husband's expression was grim.

Michael hurried to the porch rail. "What's the matter?" he asked.

"We need you, Michael. Get the preacher, too," said Mr. Payne. Carlotta was staring straight ahead, seemingly in shock, unaware of her surroundings.

Harry came out of the house, then, carrying one of the babies securely wrapped in a blanket. He had seen the surrey and was prepared to divert Carlotta's attention from the couple on the porch. He looked completely different from the way he had looked the afternoon before. He had bathed and shaved and put on clean clothes, and he seemed happy and fairly well rested. Winifred had followed him to the door. When he saw that something was wrong, Harry handed the baby to Winifred. She took the infant without question.

"What is it, Eldridge?" he asked. "What's the problem?"

"We've found the doctor," he answered slowly. At this, his wife moaned and covered her face with her hands.

"He's hanging in my smokehouse," said Eldridge in a choked voice. "He's dead."

Again, Carlotta cried out softly.

"He killed himself?" asked Harry, frowning.

"Apparently," answered Eldridge. "Can you come with us?"

"Of course," said Harry.

"Michael, too," added Eldridge. "We need someone from the law."

"But…" Michael started to argue that he wasn't really "the law," but Harry interrupted him, shaking his head.

"Michael will come, too, won't you?" he said, looking questioningly at Michael, who nodded. "Don't touch anything, Eldridge. We'll take care of everything," said Harry. He turned back to Michael.

"Can you go with me? Help me take the body down?"

Michael nodded.

Harry turned back to the Paynes. "Carlotta, would you like to stay here with the women?"

Carlotta shook her head, and she hunched over, tightening clenched fists against her chest, but she still didn't speak.

Molly spoke up. "I'll go with her."

Carlotta looked up at Molly to see if she really meant what she said. "Thank you," she whispered. Then she spoke to Harry, alarmed. "Bring your gun! Whoever did it might still be there."

"But surely this was a suicide," Winifred objected softly from the doorway.

"Bring your gun!" Carlotta insisted.

Harry studied Carlotta's panicked face and took her seriously.

"Carlotta's right. We don't know what happened. It's best to be prepared," he said.

"I'll need a minute to get dressed," said Molly.

Molly went into the house and came out again in a short time wearing her riding clothes. Her hair was tied back out of the way, and she was carrying her medicine bag, back in her role of nurse. She stopped to speak briefly with Carlotta, then got into the seat behind her. Michael was standing by Eldridge, talking quietly. He was wearing his holster and sidearm. Molly heard enough of their conversation to gather that Carlotta had been the one to find the body. She had gone out to the smokehouse to bring in a ham and had run back to the house screaming. She had hardly spoken since.

Eldridge was talking. "We've got a man that helps on the farm—Rafe Ledford. I sent him to bring the sheriff. I just don't know how long that will take."

"We'll stay with you until he comes," said Michael.

Then Harry came riding on Smokey, Michael got into the surrey beside Molly, and they all left for the Payne farm.

The farm was spread across a rich piece of bottomland that bordered the Nottely River. The house stood on a hill in the center of the farm. The lane they followed forded the river and then led up the long hill and around to the back of the house, which was a large, frame building painted white. Its bare clay yard had been swept clean before the recent rain; only freshly fallen leaves marred its surface. Molly had the impression that nothing would dare grow in this yard without permission. Along the outer edges of the yard, just inside the rail fence, wild roses were as carefully pruned as the apple trees that were ranked in rows outside the fence, and a double row of severely trimmed hedges marched along each side of a fieldstone walkway that curved from the front door to the back of the house, ending at the driveway. The house, which was divided by a dogtrot, had wide porches on the front and the back, and there were rooms upstairs with windows in the gable ends.

The farm seemed unusually prosperous for the area. In the front, between the house and the road, cows grazed in a pasture that sloped down toward the river. In the back there were several outbuildings, including a tobacco barn, a small barn for livestock, and a corncrib, in addition to the smokehouse, which was not far from the house, and, of course, an outhouse. The view from the back porch was of rolling cornfields, wooded hills, and beyond that, blue mountains fading into the distance. It seemed too peaceful and pretty to be the site of a violent death.

Eldridge stopped at the back door so that Molly could help Carlotta get out and walk with her into the house. Michael got out from the other side and walked straight to the smokehouse, and Harry followed close behind. Eldridge stayed in his seat, apparently unwilling to look at the body again.

The smokehouse was a small, unpainted building without windows. The only light came in through the open doorway, narrow cracks between the gray siding boards, and small, square vents at each gable. A series of beams extended across the room about eight feet off the floor, and when cold weather came, there would be rows of hams and sausages hanging from them. Right now the smokehouse was almost empty. There was a workbench across the far end of the room, and the body was suspended from the beam closest to it. One end of the rope was tied around a wooden brace below the workbench; the end with the noose had been stretched across the beam. Beneath the body, an apple crate had toppled over. Apparently the doctor had stood on it, then kicked it out of the way when he hanged himself.

Harry and Michael stood in the doorway, not wanting to disturb the scene before the sheriff came. In the dim light they could see that the man was clearly dead and had been for some time. His face and his tongue looked blue. A few flies were buzzing around, and dust motes floated in a beam of light that came through the gable vent, but there was no smell of decay. Harry guessed he had been there one day at the most.

"We should wait for the sheriff," he said quietly.

"We can probably learn more without him, and there's no telling when he'll come," said Michael.

"You don't like him, do you?" asked Harry. "Why is that?"

"Let's just say that I know he can be bought. And he expects to be bought. I don't trust him." They were both keeping their voices low, not only out of respect for the dead man, but so that Mr. Payne wouldn't overhear them. They studied the scene for a moment without talking.

"Carlotta might be right. I don't believe this was a suicide," Harry said at last. "I don't think a man could do this without help. Look how high he is and how close his head is to the beam. I don't think he could get his head through the noose that high. I think somebody else had to pull him up."

"I agree," said Michael. "And look at the rope." He pointed without moving from the doorway. "It's made a groove in the beam. It wouldn't do that unless somebody dragged it across the beam bearing the man's weight. And the rope is black from being pulled through the soot and dust on the top of the beam."

Harry nodded. "It looks like somebody put the noose around his neck and then threw the loose end of the rope over the beam, pulled it down, and tied it."

"It had to be somebody pretty strong, then. Or more than one person," said Michael. He knelt to examine the dirt floor of the building, looking for footprints or signs of a struggle. "The floor is too clean. There aren't prints of any kind. Looks like the place has been swept."

"There should be tracks—at least the doctor's. And didn't Carlotta walk in here to find him?" asked Harry. "And wouldn't Eldridge have come in to see if he was dead?" Harry looked around. "We need to ask him. And I need a lantern."

Michael stepped back and called to Eldridge Payne. "Eldridge. Can you help us? Where do you keep a lantern?"

Eldridge got down from the surrey and walked over to the porch to retrieve a lantern and some matches. Michael met him there. "I know this is hard on you, Eldridge, but we need to ask you a few questions. Tell us what happened one more time. Carlotta came out here to get a ham. Then what?"

"When she opened the door to the smokehouse, she saw the doctor's body hanging, and she started screaming. She ran into the house, still screaming, and I came out with her."

"All right. Go on. Exactly where did you stand to look at the body?"

"I stood right where Harry's standing, right there in the doorway."

"Did you go inside at all?"

"No, I could see plain as day that he was dead."

"And then what happened?"

"Then Rafe came running up, wanting to know what all the screaming was about, and I showed him the doc and told him to go and get the sheriff."

"Did any of you go into the smokehouse at all?"

"No, we didn't need to. We didn't want to. It made me sick at my stomach. I just couldn't believe it. I still can't bear to look at it."

"That's fine. You just sit here on the porch in case we need to ask you anything else, okay?"

A buggy was rolling up the long driveway. Michael didn't recognize who it was and wanted to see what else he could learn before anyone else came. He walked back to the smokehouse, scraped a match against the wall to ignite it, lit the lantern, and then handed it to Harry. Harry went in, holding the lantern low, examining the dirt floor as he went. Michael followed him.

Harry talked softly. "You're right. There are no scuffmarks or footprints. And the dirt is not packed so hard that you wouldn't make footprints. See?" He pointed at the marks his own boots were making on the ground. "In fact, it almost seems like the dirt has been raked. It's less packed than it should be. I don't see how the doc could have walked in here without leaving footprints." The two men examined the entire dirt floor. The only prints were their own.

A shadow blocked the light from the doorway, and a man spoke. "Well, Harry. What have you gotten yourself into now?"

Harry recognized the voice. "Walt?" He hurried to the door to greet his old friend. Walt Drake was the doctor that Harry had telegrammed in Atlanta. He was shorter than Harry, and slender, wearing spectacles and a three-piece suit. He had answered Harry's request and come as quickly as he could. "You've come at just the right time."

"That's not what Sarah said!" Walt answered.

"Well, you're too late to deliver the babies, but in time to help us figure out this death."

Harry looked beyond Walt to see that two other men had arrived by horseback. They had stopped at the porch and were talking with Mr. Payne.

"We'd best hurry. I believe that's the sheriff," he said softly.

Walt stepped into the smokehouse and took the lantern from Harry, then moved closer to the body. After a moment of study, he said, "He may have been dead before he was hanged."

"Why do you say that?" asked Harry.

"It's hard to tell until we get him down from there, but I think his heart had stopped beating before his throat was constricted. There's no sign of the congestion you'd expect if arteries were suddenly blocked while the heart was still beating. He looks like he was already dead, and then someone just hauled him up there."

Michael stepped forward and offered his hand to Walt. "I'm Michael Gibson."

"Walt Drake, up from Atlanta," the doctor responded. "I believe we met last fall."

Michael nodded, remembering, then turned back to Harry, "Can we move that apple crate and see if he could have used it?"

"I don't see why not. Let's just mark where it is right now so we can put it back." Harry knelt and, using a small rock he found, drew an outline around the box. Then he picked the box up and moved it under the man's body. The feet did not touch the box, even when Harry set the box on its end.

"Well, there you have it," said Harry. "Unless Dr. Carter stood here and jumped up high enough to pull his head through the loop, he did not stand on this box to commit suicide. I don't think a young, athletic man could do that, much less the old doctor."

All the men stood silently, looking up at the knot.

"What kind of a knot is that?" asked Michael. He moved the box and turned it on its side again to make a larger surface to stand on, then reached for the lantern. Then he stepped up to examine the loop around the doctor's neck. "This is not just a slipknot or a regular noose. I've never seen one like it before." Michael got down, handed off the lantern, and Walt took his place.

"I've seen it, but I'm not sure where. It might be something that fishermen use. Something for tying up a boat, maybe." Walt looked closely at the man's neck. "I don't see any scratches on the neck. No indication that this man fought to remove the rope. And his hands are clean. There's no sign of a struggle."

There was a sudden outburst at the door. "What do you think you're doing?" sputtered an angry voice. It was the sheriff. "Who are you?"

Before Walt could answer, Michael spoke up. "Well, hello, Warren," he drawled. "Took you awhile to remember that Choestoe is part of your territory."

"Michael Gibson! Come out of there. What kind of a badge are you wearin'?"

All the men walked out of the smokehouse, led by Michael, who was not about to be out-maneuvered by a sheriff he had no respect for. His country-boy accent was more pronounced than usual. "I'm workin' with the Secret Service. This mornin' I was guardin' the Captain's house while he got some sleep. By the way, he managed to rescue his son without any help from you. I know you've been real worried about that." Warren Oaks was furious. It occurred to Michael that the sheriff was bluer in the face than the corpse, and he made an effort not to smile. "Mr. and Miz Payne asked me and the Captain to come here after they found the doc's body. They weren't sure how long it would take you to get here."

Michael continued with introductions. "You know the preacher, don't you? This other man is Dr. Drake from Atlanta. I think he could be real helpful to you in figurin' out the cause of death. We haven't touched the body, by the way. All we've moved is the apple crate, and we can put it back exactly where it was. We drew a line around it before we moved it. Before we went in there, we looked, and there were no footprints or marks of any kind in the dirt."

"I've been watching," said Mr. Payne from behind the sheriff. "They're telling you the truth."

Something in Mr. Payne's voice got the sheriff's attention, and he bit back whatever he had planned to say. "All right. Let's get this man down, then." He scowled at Michael. "I think it's pretty obvious what the cause of death is," he muttered. "Don't think we need any expert from Atlanta to tell us that." He looked toward the barn, where Rafe was emerging after putting up the horses. "Rafe," he called. "Give us a hand here."

While they waited for the hired man to come back, the sheriff called Michael aside. "I need a word with you," he said, walking away from the group at the smokehouse.

Michael followed, and they stopped a short distance away. The sheriff got right in his face and spoke bluntly. "You need to make sure your friends understand that this was a suicide."

"You haven't even looked at the body yet."

"But I know Eldridge Payne, and I believe what he's told me."

"So, what, then? Did Eldridge watch while the doctor committed suicide? He's a witness?"

"Don't be an idiot. He knew the doctor's mood. He wasn't surprised by it."

"Well, maybe the doc was surprised by it. He couldn't have done it without help."

"That's just your opinion. Listen to me!" The sheriff bristled in frustration. His hands clinched and seemed to inch closer to his guns. "There could be a whole lot of trouble if you don't let this go."

Michael shook his head in disbelief. "Are you threatening me?"

"I'm just telling you how it is. You need to let this lie. Just let me do my job. There are things here that you don't understand."

Michael studied him, considering the best way to answer. The sheriff didn't want the truth; he wanted compliance. It wasn't just because he wanted to prove he was in charge. There was something at stake here—something that scared the sheriff. He felt that he had to control the situation.

"Do you plan on explainin' what it is that I don't understand?"

"No, I can't. But you need to trust me on this one: innocent people will get hurt if you stir up trouble. You need to convince your friends to leave it alone."

They were out of time. Rafe was almost there. Big-shouldered, strong-armed Rafe was frowning and walking in their direction.

Right now, compliance seemed like the safest response. "I'll do what I can."

Sheriff Oaks nodded at Michael, and then he nodded almost imperceptibly at Eldridge Payne as they walked back to the smokehouse.

Eldridge mumbled something about checking on his wife and went into the house, while the other men began the grisly job of removing the body.

* * *

After Molly and Carlotta reached the house, Molly added sticks to the fire in the kitchen stove. There was a kettle of hot water there, and it wouldn't take long to bring it back to a boil. Molly wanted to make some herbal tea for Carlotta. She always carried a variety of herbs with her in her medicine bag, and the tea she mixed for Carlotta was known to have a calming effect, containing, among other things, chamomile, lemon balm, and mint. She tied the herbs in a square of cheesecloth and dropped it into a teapot.

After a few minutes, when the kettle was ready, she poured boiling water over the tea, then put the lid on and allowed the herbs to steep. When the tea was done, she added a dollop of honey and a generous splash of whiskey that she found in Carlotta's pantry, stirred it well, and used a spoon to taste it. She nodded, satisfied, and then got two cups that were hanging from hooks under the cupboard. She put the cups and the teapot on a wooden tray and brought them to Carlotta, who was slumped in a wing-backed chair in the living room, staring into space. Molly put the tray on a low table, then moved another chair close to Carlotta's so they could sit together.

Molly poured her a cup of tea. "Here, take a sip of this. It's medicine. Drink it slow; it's hot," she said gently, pressing the cup into Carlotta's hands and helping her to drink. Carlotta took a sip, sighed, and then wrapped her hands around the warm cup as she studied Molly, finally seeming to focus.

"You're kind," she said. "Not what I thought you'd be."

"Thank you," answered Molly, not responding to the implied insult, but allowing silence to envelop them as they drank their tea. Carlotta sipped thirstily at the hot tea, as if she needed it desperately. Molly thought that if the woman could get over her shock, she would want to talk about the doctor, so what she finally said came as a surprise.

"I wish you could be there when my daughter has her baby," whispered Carlotta, eyes brimming with tears.

"Where is your daughter? Maybe I can come," answered Molly.

"We sent her up to stay with my sister in North Carolina. Nobody here knows about it."

"I see," nodded Molly. "She's not married?"

"No," answered Carlotta, sniffing. "And she won't tell who the father is, but it has to be Albert Jones's boy, Caleb. That's who was sweet on her."

"Has anybody told Caleb she's expecting?"

"No. He's not here. He's gone off to college in Athens. He's studying to be a farmer. I ask you, who needs to go to college to be a farmer? I don't understand it."

"Well, he sounds like the perfect one to marry your daughter. He could help with this big farm, and you could have your grandchild close by. I think you should find out if he's the father."

"I think Eldridge would kill him if he saw him right now. He's so mad he won't even talk about it, and he forbids me to talk about it, and I haven't told anybody, but you're not from around here, and, being a midwife, I thought you would understand if anybody would. What should I do?"

Molly gave it some thought. "I think you and your husband should talk. If you can't, maybe you should talk to the pastor. See if he would counsel your husband and your daughter. What's her name?"

"Abigail," answered Carlotta.

"If your husband won't help, maybe Harry could talk to Abigail, and if she tells him who the father is, maybe he could go and talk to the boy. People can't make good decisions if they don't know what the facts are. You should give the boy a chance to do the right thing. Give your daughter a chance to have a normal life." Molly paused, refilled Carlotta's cup and poured a little more into her own, then went on.

"Does Abigail plan to give the baby up for adoption?"

"No, she won't."

There was a short silence, then Molly spoke again. "You asked my opinion, so here it is. If your daughter is determined to keep the child, even if you never find out who the father is, you should bring her home and welcome that baby into your house. It's your grandchild. You're only hurting yourself if you cast them out. And you can help them more by having them here than by sending them away. Surely that's the Christian thing to do."

"But what would people say?" Carlotta asked, horrified.

"What difference does it make?" answered Molly. "Maybe they'll say what a kind, forgiving woman you are and how you're willing to take care of your own family no matter what. Or maybe they won't. Maybe they'll be nasty and vicious. You can't control what others say. You can only control what you do, how you react. You should just do what you think is right and tell others if they don't like it, they can go jump in a lake."

"Oh, I wish I was as brave as you are!" said Carlotta.

"I'm not that brave. But I know how much I needed my mother's help when my boy was born—and I was married. I would have needed her all the more if I'd been alone. Your daughter will need you. You need to help her if you can."

Carlotta nodded, refilling her cup.

"Is Abigail your only child?" asked Molly.

Carlotta nodded sadly. "She is now. I had four children. The oldest two were sons. They both went off to war. One fought for the North and one for the South. Neither one of them ever came home again."

"I'm so sorry!" exclaimed Molly. "They both died?"

"We don't know. They just never came home."

"Well, that is one of the saddest things I ever heard," said Molly.

"And there was another baby girl. She died of the croup."

"You poor thing. I'm so sorry!" murmured Molly.

"Abigail is all I have left, and she's gone. And now there's this," said Carlotta, helplessly, waving in the general direction of the smokehouse.

There was a brief silence.

"What did you mean when you told Harry to bring his gun?" asked Molly. "You said, 'Whoever did it might still be there.'"

"Did I?" said Carlotta, looking a little sleepy, a little nervous. "I don't know what I meant."

"Tell me about what happened. What did you do when you went into the smokehouse?" asked Molly.

"Well, I walked in like usual. I was lookin' down, because one time there was a snake in there, and I always watch where I step. It's dark in there out of the glare of the sun, and I was lookin' down, so I didn't see him at first. I walked right in to get the ham. The ham was about halfway back in the smokehouse. I always stand on an apple crate to get things down, and I keep the crate by the door, so I picked it up and brought it with me. And then I saw the body, and I couldn't believe it. I've known Doc Carter for years, and I just couldn't believe it."

Molly looked at Carlotta in concern. She was looking dazed again and lost. Maybe the tea had not been a good idea after all.

"I still can't believe it. And now I know the truth, and I don't know what I'm supposed to do. He was tied up there just like one of our hams! Just the same way! I'll be next, you know! I'll be next."

Carlotta looked desperate. "Could you stay here with me? We have lots of room. You can stay as long as you want to. You can wear Abigail's clothes if you need to. She won't mind."

For some reason, the idea of wearing Abigail's clothes made Molly feel strange, but she could see that Carlotta needed support. "I'll stay here if Michael can stay, too. He can protect you."

"And he's supposed to be guarding you." Carlotta's words were just a bit slurred. Molly was alarmed. Could she be drunk, or was she just reacting to the shock?

"That's right," Molly said. "Michael is guarding me, and he can guard you, too. Come on, Carlotta, I think you need to go and lie down," said Molly, helping her to stand.

"All right," said Carlotta.

"Which room is yours?" asked Molly.

"Follow me," said Carlotta. And she opened a door onto bedroom, sat on the edge of the bed, and then lay down. Molly pulled a quilt over her, and Carlotta immediately closed her eyes. Then she opened them again and spoke calmly, as if they had just finished a social engagement. "You must remember to give me the recipe for that tea. That was just the thing."

Then Carlotta closed her eyes and seemed to go to sleep.

Molly checked Carlotta's pulse, and it was strong and steady. Maybe she just needed some rest.

When Molly turned, she came face to face with Eldridge Payne, who was standing just inside the doorway.

"Oh!" she said, startled. Then she whispered, so as not to waken Carlotta. "I didn't hear you come in."

"What has my wife been telling you?" he asked guardedly.

"She's worried about Abigail," said Molly. "I suggested some things. Let's go out." Molly motioned to the door.

Eldridge seemed to relax slightly. Molly knew she had said the right thing and wondered what he would have done if she had mentioned anything else. He turned to lead her back to the living room.

"Anything else?" he asked.

"Mostly that. You know, woman-to-woman talk. I suggested that the two of you should talk to Abigail—maybe get Harry to help—find out who the father is, see if he's willing to marry her. Also, she told me that you had lost two sons in the war. I'm so sorry to hear about that."

"Did she mention the baby that died of the croup?"

"Yes," said Molly, not knowing what to say. They took seats in the living room, Eldridge in the wing-backed chair, and Molly back in her place beside it. "I'm sorry for all your loss."

"Carlotta hasn't had an easy life," he said. "And now this."

"Was the doctor a close friend?"

"As close as any, I guess. I don't know why he chose to end his life in *my* smokehouse," said Eldridge bitterly.

"There's still a little tea," said Molly. "Why don't you finish it?"

"Which cup is Carlotta's?" he asked. When Molly pointed at it, Eldridge poured the rest of the tea into his wife's cup and took a taste.

He didn't seem to like it. "Now I know why she got sleepy."

"Alcohol has medicinal uses," said Molly.

"So it does," he said, putting the cup back down without drinking any more.

He studied Molly solemnly. "I want you to know that people will talk about this death. They'll find other explanations because they won't want to believe the old doctor would take his own life."

"But you feel sure that he did."

"Yes. I know how it feels to get that low in your spirit. And the doc hasn't been well. People thought he was drinking, but it wasn't drink. He's been taking laudanum."

"For pain?" asked Molly.

"Who knows?" He shrugged. "There's more than one kind of pain."

"Yes," agreed Molly.

"So you should be careful what you say to people when they ask about what happened here. They'll think you know, because you were here. People could get hurt if the story is wrong."

"Surely Carlotta will tell people what they need to hear," said Molly. "They won't need to ask me." That was apparently the way news was delivered in this area. Carlotta found out everything, then told people what she felt they needed to know. Molly wondered what part Eldridge played in the control of information. Maybe he told her what to say or what to think. It was an interesting idea.

"This has been hard on her," said Eldridge. "After the funeral, I think maybe we'll take your advice and go see Abigail for a few days. Maybe we can settle some things with her and stay away until this dies down." Eldridge stood. "Of course, with all the extra people in town, and the preacher's house burned, you'll need a place to stay. You're welcome to stay here. We have plenty of room. The young doctor and Michael can stay, too, if they need to, and if Doc Carter has family from out of town, they can stay. It will be like a rooming house. Women can stay on this side, men in the rooms across the breezeway. Or some upstairs and some down. Would that be proper enough?"

"If you said it was, I think people would believe it," suggested Molly, ironically.

Eldridge considered her intently. "Maybe they would."

Molly stood, and they walked toward the door. There was the sound of footsteps on the back porch. Harry knocked just as they reached the open door. Behind him stood Michael.

"Let's talk outside," said Molly. "Carlotta's asleep."

CHAPTER 15

Making Arrangements

Everyone gathered on the porch. Molly sat down in a rocker, and Michael leaned against the wall behind her. Harry and the deacon sat on a bench, while the sheriff and Walt propped against the porch rail. Rafe came last and sat on the steps. The men seemed unusually quiet—not just solemn about the fate of the doctor, but somehow wary.

Harry needed to talk to the deacon about funeral arrangements. There would be two bodies for burial—Charlie's and the doctor's. Both men had already been dead at least one day, and both had died violently. The bodies might be disfigured, and they wouldn't hold up long. The men agreed that funeral services should be held the next morning as soon as graves could be dug. No one suggested that the graves be dug immediately: it was considered bad luck to dig the graves the day before the burial and leave them open throughout the night. Whether or not they would leave the caskets open would depend on the condition of the bodies, but they would probably be open for the wake, at least. Ollie Collins usually had a few caskets available at his store. If he didn't have any already made, Eb would build them. Someone would need to see him, and neighbors needed to be notified about digging the graves. Eldridge said he would take care of all of that.

Molly had remained quiet during the discussion, but she spoke up now. "I can pay for my husband's casket," she said.

"You won't need to," insisted Eldridge. "Eb doesn't charge for that."

"I'll take care of preparing the bodies," offered Walt Drake. When the men looked surprised, he explained, "Better me than close friends of the dead."

"They've dealt with worse, I imagine," said the deacon. "You underestimate the strength of the mountain people." It was traditional in the community for men to "lay out" the bodies of men, while women provided that service for women and children.

"All the same, I would spare them," said Walt.

"That's good of you," Harry said quickly. "I'll help. We'll need the women to prepare their clothes. Carlotta will know who to ask about that." Before anyone could speak, he went on. "Now, what about the wake? Can we have a joint wake? The doc doesn't have any family here as far as I know, but everyone in the county will want to come to his wake and his funeral. No one knows Charlie or Molly except us, but people will still want to show their concern."

"A joint wake would make it easier on everyone," said Michael. "Would that be all right with you?" he asked Molly.

"Whatever is convenient," she answered softly. She had no home to offer and was happy to have someone else making the decisions.

A voice spoke up from the doorway. It was Carlotta. "We can have the wake here for both of them," she said. "One casket can be in the parlor, and one in the living room."

"But, Carlotta, are you strong enough?" asked Molly.

"I'll be fine. You helped me a lot." Carlotta was determined, now. "You men can lay out the bodies in the barn, then bring the caskets into the house, and people will come for the settin' up tonight. All the women will bring food, and we'll light lamps all over the house. Poor old Doc. We'll show the world how much we appreciated him." Carlotta started to cry. "He was a good man. He shouldn't have died this way." She looked angrily at her husband. "Eldridge, bring me that wretched ham. I've got to get started with the cooking. Rafe, you kill some chickens and pluck them. And see if there's still enough blackberries for a cobbler."

"You don't have to do it all yourself," said Molly, as Carlotta went back into the house. She got up, intending to follow her.

"Just let her go. The work will be good for her," said Eldridge, as the door slammed behind his wife. He seemed kind and patient. He stood, then, indicating that the meeting was over. "I'll just take the wagon in to get the caskets and spread the word about the wake. We'll toll the bell so everyone will hear it. The word will spread."

"What will you say about how he died?" asked Michael.

"Well, I don't guess there's any reason to keep it a secret. The doc hanged himself in my smokehouse." Eldridge looked to the sheriff. "Is there any reason we can't just tell people like it is?"

"No reason I can think of. It's the truth. There was nothing you could have done. The doc hanged himself."

Michael turned to Eldridge. "Can you drop me and Molly off at Winifred's house? We need to be there when her boy comes home. And they'll be bringing her husband's body."

"Of course," said Eldridge. "Forgive me, Mrs. Baldwin. What with all of this, I've completely ignored your loss. I'm very sorry."

Eldridge reached out to her and took her hands in both of his. His voice was kind, but his hands were cold and dry, and his pale blue eyes were steely, assessing. A chill went through her. She knew in that instant that the deacon had killed the doctor, and that he would kill her, too, if she said a word.

"Thank you for your kindness," she whispered, then she pulled her hands out of his and covered her eyes, pretending to be overcome by grief. She stepped quickly back, bumping against Michael. He held her shoulders, steadying her. At that, she turned and threw herself into his arms. Michael gathered her to himself and gently patted her back.

"It's okay, Molly. We'll take care of everything. It's okay," he murmured. She was shaking, but when she looked up at him, it was fear, not grief in her eyes. He gently pulled her closer and stroked her hair. "Shh, shh. We'll take care of everything," he repeated softly.

"Take my buggy," offered Walt. "Then Mr. Payne can go on and get the caskets. We'll be here to help Carlotta if she needs us."

"Thanks," said Michael, "We'll do that." Molly clung tightly to his arm as he walked her past Rafe and out to Walt's buggy, and they rode slowly away, past the barren yard with its repressed rosebushes and marching shrubs, down the long driveway, across the river at the ford, and out into the free world. Only then did Molly take a deep, sobbing breath and loosen her grip on Michael's arm.

He squeezed her hand briefly, looking at her with concern. "Are you okay?"

"He killed the doctor," she said.

"Maybe. If he didn't do it, he knows who did."

"You know that? But—?"

"After Eldridge leaves, Walt and Harry are going to examine the body and see if they can figure out the cause of death. Walt believes the doctor was dead before he was hanged. That doesn't necessarily mean he was murdered. It might mean that he died, and for some reason, somebody wanted it to look like he killed himself."

"I see," said Molly. "Do you think Harry and Walt are safe?"

"They're aware of the situation, and Harry's armed. As long as Eldridge thinks we've accepted his story, we think he'll just play along. Harry asked me to get you back home."

"Good old Harry!" she said fervently. "But if everyone knows something's not right, why didn't the sheriff ask questions? Why didn't he arrest Eldridge?"

"Either he can't or he won't. He's chosen to back Eldridge's story. He's saying it was suicide. He warned me not to stir things up. Said innocent people would be hurt."

"Maybe he's talking about Carlotta. Whatever happened, I don't think she was in on it. She's scared to death, and I can understand why," said Molly. "When the deacon took my hand, his eyes bored right into me. I felt threatened. I can't imagine how it would feel to live in that house with him. Carlotta asked me to stay with her, and I told her I would if you would," said Molly, "—and then we both left her."

Michael took a long breath. "Harry and Walt are there, and you need to be here when your family comes home."

Molly's face twisted, and she sobbed aloud.

Michael pulled the buggy to the side of the dirt road. There was no one in sight. He turned to face her. "What's wrong?"

Molly seemed speechless. "Everything?" she said sadly, with a gesture that included the whole universe.

He sighed. "I know this is the wrong time for this." He brushed his fingertips across her cheek, wiping away her tears. Then he touched his lips to her cheek, tasting the saltiness. "Molly?" he asked hesitantly.

He felt her quick intake of breath, and then her response answered his question. Her lips found his, and they kissed long and deeply.

"You're not alone," he reminded her at last. "I will help you get through this."

"Oh, Michael!" she answered, burying her face in his chest.

Just then, a wagon pulled noisily around them. It was Eldridge Payne, of course.

Michael continued to hold Molly as the wagon went past. "Let him get an eye full. Maybe it will keep you safe."

"Do you think he'd hurt me?" Molly asked.

"If he's done one murder already, and he thought you knew something, who knows? He'll have to go through me to get to you. He might as well know that."

Molly looked gravely at him. "It's too soon, you know. I can't rush into anything."

"I know. I'll wait. I just wanted you to know how I feel."

Molly smiled gratefully. "I'm not alone?"

"That's right."

"Thank you, Michael. It means everything." She didn't say it, but Molly felt that she had been alone for a long time.

Michael gave the reins a shake, and they started back down the road. They rode the rest of the way in silence, keeping their thoughts to themselves.

* * *

Eldridge watched the couple curiously as he passed. They looked guilty to him—so much guiltier than he did. The handsome rogue was kissing the merry widow while on the way to claim her husband's body, not even waiting until the man was in his grave. And this was the same woman who had once been the preacher's lover. That was before he was a preacher, of course, but it showed a distinct lack of character. It was a bad example. He could definitely make that case.

The woman had seemed intelligent, but she was obviously a fickle little Jezebel. The preacher, the woman, and the bootlegger—they could all be tarred with the same brush. That was a good thing. And if these two stayed busy with each other, they wouldn't have time to worry about him.

Maybe the girl was not as shrewd as he'd thought. And if it came down to it, whose word would people believe? His or hers?

Michael didn't have a great reputation, either. He had always been pretty casual about obeying the law. Sheriff Oaks, who had benefitted from Eldridge's tutelage (and his money) for all these years, thought he could control the bootlegger, and Michael was apparently willing to use his influence to keep the preacher and the young doctor in line, as well. It was all about controlling the tide of public opinion. If this group went along, so would everyone else.

Eldridge had gone to get the preacher and Michael because his wife had insisted, and he had needed to keep her calm. He had underestimated her, thinking she would believe the death was a suicide, but she hadn't, and by telling the men to bring their guns she had raised their suspicions, too. He had underestimated the two men, as well. He had thought they would rush straight in, take down the body, and never think about footprints or the length of the rope. And who could have guessed that this young doctor would show up?

This had all happened fast, and it wasn't as if he had planned anything. When the old doctor had started asking questions about his red-haired daughter Abigail, the conversation had gotten out of hand, and he had said too much. It had been a mistake to let the doctor make the connection between Eldridge's unfaithful wife and Liam's red-haired father. Nobody had ever suspected that Eldridge had killed Fred Banks all those years ago, because Eldridge had never said a word—not even to Carlotta. He had never even told her that he knew what the two of them had been up to, but he had taken care of the situation.

Doc Carter had been there when they took Banks's body down from where Eldridge had strung it up in the barn. If he had suspected that the death was anything but a suicide, he'd never said a word. And Eldridge had assumed that nobody would question the doctor's death, either. Eldridge had not planned it, but last night when the doc had started asking questions—well, he really hadn't had a choice. The doctor had to go. The old secrets had to stay buried. That was the only way. If one secret came to light, others would follow.

For all these years people had believed everything the deacon had said. They had accepted him. They had praised him for his generosity, depended upon his contributions to the church and to every other worthy cause that arose in the community. Even his stupid, unfaithful wife had never questioned him. He had to carry on, rise above this, and assume that people would go right on believing in him. If he didn't, it would all unravel. If people had to die or their reputations had to be ruined, so be it. They should never have questioned him in the first place. He had worked too hard and given up too much to back down now.

That annoying preacher had already ruined so many plans. He would have to be handled very carefully, and if he didn't cooperate, he'd have to go too.

CHAPTER 16

A Homecoming

As the buggy turned up the road to Winifred's house, a church bell began tolling slowly: one ring for every year of Dr. Carter's life. It seemed as if the tolling would go on forever. Then, after a brief pause, the bell started tolling again, this time for Charlie.

Harrison was the first person Molly and Michael saw when they arrived. He was sitting on the steps with Sparky, wearing his father's blue cavalry coat. Michael pulled the buggy to a stop.

"He's changed in the past year. He's grown up," Molly said softly, looking at her son. "He looks so much like Harry!"

Michael squeezed her hand sympathetically as he helped her down from the buggy, then she led the way to the steps.

"Hey, Mama!" Harrison said, smiling, but he didn't try to stand up. There were crutches beside him, and his ankle was still bandaged. Molly sat down beside him and hugged him hard.

"I'm so glad you're all right!" she said.

Sparky stayed by Harrison's other side, vying for his attention. Reunited with Harrison, it was no longer the mopey, pitiful dog of last night, but a happy, wagging pet. Harrison had removed the dog's bandages, and Michael took a look at the dog's leg.

"You've been misnamed, Sparky! He should have called you 'Lucky'!" he said, roughing the fur of the happy dog. The bullet had only injured flesh, not bone, and the wound was healing nicely. He turned to the boy. "How's that ankle?"

"It's pretty sore. Uncle Ned gave me his old crutches, though, so I can get around."

Molly was kneeling in front of the boy now, unwrapping the bandages and trying not to let anyone see the tears in her eyes. Michael touched her shoulder briefly as he walked past them to meet Winifred, who was coming out onto the porch carrying a quilt and some clothes.

Winifred spoke softly. "Ned and Liam have taken Charlie's body to the barn. Would you take these out there and give them to Ned? They're for Charlie." He nodded and took the items, understanding that she was giving a handmade quilt and some of Ned's clothes to dress Charlie's corpse.

Michael looked at the quilt. He saw the fine stitches and the carefully pieced fabric, thought of the hours of labor that had gone into its making, and marveled that Winifred was willing to give it away to bury a man who had tried to kill her.

"He doesn't deserve it," he said.

"But Molly does," said Winifred.

Michael nodded. "Could you look after her?" he asked in return. "She hides it well, but she's pretty shaken up. She should eat something, and she'll need some rest. It will be a long night tonight."

Winifred smiled kindly at him. "You're a good man, Michael."

"I wish people would stop staying that." He shook his head, unhappy with what he thought was an unearned compliment. "Coming from you, that's high praise, Miss Winifred." He turned and took the quilt and clothes to the barn.

There he found Ned and Liam loading Charlie's shrouded body into the back of a small covered wagon. When Michael handed him the clothes, Ned put the clean items carefully under the seat, away from the body in the back. "She's giving away my clothes. What about that! I guess I should be glad I'm not the one that needs them."

"I'll say," said Michael. "Must be tough on you, though."

"What's that?" asked Ned.

"Bein' married to such a hard woman."

Ned laughed. "You have no idea! No idea." Then he offered his hand to Michael. "Winifred told me what you did for her. I would have lost her, if not for you. I can never repay you for that."

"No need," Michael said simply. "You'd have done the same." He nodded toward Charlie's body. "Harry and Walt said they'd lay out the body over at the Paynes' house. The Paynes have offered to hold the wake there. Eldridge Payne is getting the caskets."

"That's a relief. I was wondering how we'd manage everything here," said Ned.

"There's more. A lot more," Michael said. "We should go inside so the women can hear, too. This affects us all."

The men stopped on the back stoop to wash their hands in a basin, while the others gathered in the living room. Sarah insisted on joining them, even though custom demanded that she "lie in" for at least two weeks. She was wearing a loose blue dress, and, although tired, she looked like the picture of health. So far her only job was to recuperate and to nurse the babies on demand. Winifred was taking care of everything else.

"I appreciate all the help, but if I stay in bed for two weeks, I'll be as weak as a kitten," she had argued, but Molly had encouraged her to rest while she had the chance. Now Molly suggested she lie down on the couch, and the women helped her get situated. She was propped up on pillows and covered with a quilt when the men came in.

Michael asked Harrison to stay on the front porch and be the lookout, and to let them know if anyone came. He wanted to spare the boy the gruesome details of the hanging. Harrison agreed, but after the door was closed, he sat down just outside it so that he could hear every word.

When everyone else was seated, Michael pulled a straight chair from the dining table and sat down next to Molly. He started talking first, describing what the men had seen in the smokehouse—the smooth, trackless dirt floor; the soot-stained rope and the grooved beam; how short the rope had been and how high the corpse had hung; the impossibility of standing on the box to accomplish such a feat. He told what Walt had said about the possibility that the doctor had already been dead when he was hanged. He mentioned the unusual knot that had been used for the hanging. It was the first time Molly had heard some of the details. She frowned and shook her head.

"What is it, Molly?" he asked.

"Carlotta's story is different."

"Molly stayed with Carlotta while we were in the smokehouse," Michael explained. "Tell us," he said.

Molly described how she had made the tea for Carlotta to ease her shock, and she admitted that she might have used too much alcohol. Carlotta had talked freely about some other things. She looked uncertainly around at the faces that were looking gravely back at her. "Some of the things she said were in confidence. I don't want to be guilty of gossiping."

Ned shook his head. "You can trust all of us to keep our mouths shut. We need to know everything that might explain the situation there." Michael and Liam nodded their agreement.

Molly continued. "Carlotta is worried about her daughter. They've sent her away to Carlotta's sister in North Carolina because she is pregnant. She also told me about the sons that went off to war and never came back and the baby that died of the croup."

At that, Sarah whispered, "Oh, how awful."

"She's had a hard life, and on top of all that, she'd just found the doctor dead in her smokehouse. Then she told about how she went out to get the ham, and the way she told it is completely different from what Eldridge told Michael."

"Go on," Michael said.

"She didn't stand in the doorway, she walked right in. She said it's dark in there, and she always looks down because she almost stepped on a snake one time, so she was looking down, and she always keeps the apple crate just inside the door, because she uses it as a step when she gets anything down. She carried the crate in. And then she looked up and saw the body and started screaming, and she ran out."

"There would have been tracks," said Michael.

"Somebody's lying, that's for sure," muttered Ned.

"Poor Carlotta!" said Winifred.

"We need to hear every detail, Molly," said Michael. "What happened next?"

Molly stopped to think for a minute. "Well, I kept refilling her cup of tea."

"That was brilliant," said Ned, nodding his approval.

"I remember exactly what she said, because it seemed odd to me. She said, 'Now I know the truth, and I don't know what I'm supposed to do.

He was tied up there just like one of our hams! Just the same way! I'll be next, you know! I'll be next.' And she asked me if I could stay with her. She didn't feel safe. I told her I would stay if Michael could stay, too. I told her Michael could protect her. She said if I stayed, I could use her daughter's clothes." Molly stopped talking, seeming chilled by the story. Michael reached out and took her hand.

"Now tell them about Eldridge," he said. And so Molly told how she had put Carlotta to bed and had turned to find Eldridge behind her. How, when he asked what they had said, she only told about Abigail, and the sons and the baby. She was afraid to let him know that Carlotta had talked about the smokehouse. She told how he had warned her about gossiping about the hanging, and in a roundabout way had told her what she should say—how the doctor had been unhappy and taking laudanum, and how it was not a surprise that he would take his own life.

"I felt like he was putting words into my mouth, controlling the message he wanted everyone to hear, and I wondered if he did that to Carlotta all the time. Then we went out on the porch to talk to Harry about funeral arrangements, and everyone acted like everything was just fine, only they were all real quiet. The sheriff and Eldridge seemed to be watching us all to see if we had learned our parts or not."

"And how did you feel when Eldridge took your hands?" Michael asked.

Molly took a deep, ragged breath. "I've never been more frightened in my life."

"And, after all of that, you're still going to have the wake at Eldridge's house?" asked Ned gruffly.

Michael and Molly looked at each other and shrugged.

"It seemed like the right thing to do," Michael said. "It seems safest to go along and pretend things are normal, at least for the time being." Michael stood and looked toward the door, as if he had heard something. He held up his hands for silence, then walked to the door and opened it suddenly.

"Why don't you come in?" he said to Harrison, as the boy fell in on the floor.

Everyone laughed, and it was a good feeling, to laugh again.

"Come on in, son. You need to know about this, too," said Michael, helping him up. "I shouldn't have made you stay outside."

Molly watched Michael, grateful that he hadn't yelled at the boy, hadn't belittled him the way Charlie would have done. No wonder Harrison had become so grown up and confident in this place, with so much male approval and support. It was a good place for him. Maybe it could be a good place for her, too, in spite of everything. She felt a lump growing in her throat and knew she was going to cry and there was nothing she could do about it. She covered her face with her hands.

Suddenly Winifred was there. "Come on, honey, let's go to the kitchen. I don't have any tea like you fixed for Carlotta, but I can make some fresh coffee. Would you like that?" Molly nodded, crying harder because of her kindness, and the two walked into the adjoining room.

"Michael?" It was Sarah who called softly to him. Michael walked over to her and knelt down beside her. "Where's Harry?" she asked, concerned.

"He and Walt are at Carlotta's house. They're going to prepare the bodies and help her however they can," he answered.

Ned and Liam had been talking with each other on the other side of the room. They walked over. "We'll take Charlie's body over there now," said Ned. "But, listen, Michael, there's something else. Liam wants to know more about the knot you saw."

"Was it like this?" Liam asked. He had borrowed a tieback cord from Winifred's curtains, and now he used it to demonstrate. He quickly tied a special form of slipknot that had a loop that turned back through the noose.

"I think that's it," said Michael. "Where did you learn to do that?"

Liam swallowed, then he formed the words carefully, trying not to stutter. "That's the same k-kind of knot that was used to hang my father."

"He thinks that whoever killed the doctor killed his father, too," Ned said.

A stunned silence fell on the room. Finally, from the bedroom, a baby's cry broke the stillness.

Sarah sat up and put her feet to the floor. Winifred was standing in the doorway. "Winifred?" said Sarah, quietly. "I think I could use some help going back to my room." Then she turned to Ned. "Could you go and see about Harry and Walt? Maybe Harry could come home for a while.

I know he'll want to stay there all night, and I'd like to see him first, if that's possible."

Ned smiled sympathetically and offered his hand to help Sarah up. "Liam and I'll both go. Don't worry, Sarah, we'll look after Harry."

Molly spoke up from the kitchen doorway. "Whoever comes back first could bring my medicine bag. I think we might all want some tea," she said.

CHAPTER 17

Laying Out the Bodies

Harry and Walt had finished washing the old doctor's body and arranging it on a plank when Ned and Liam arrived with the second body. Walt had managed to close the doc's mouth and had tied his jaw shut with a bandana. It made him look as though he had died of a toothache, but that was better than having his jaw hanging open and his tongue sticking out. They had arranged the arms with hands folded across the chest, and they had placed coins on the man's eyelids to keep them closed. They had brushed the doc's clothes and made them presentable, then cut the shirt and coat down the back so that they could dress him easily. Now they only needed the casket.

While they waited, Walt walked up to the house to see if Carlotta needed anything.

Then Liam and Ned came—Liam bringing Charlie's body in the wagon, and Ned returning Walt's buggy—and it was time to do the whole job over again. Liam drove the wagon straight into the barn, hoping to avoid attention from visitors who were coming and going from the Payne house. Harry closed the barn doors behind him. As he was pulling the second door closed, Rafe approached, and Harry motioned for him to come in.

"Preacher, is there anything I can do to help?" he asked.

Harry looked around. "There is," he said, pointing at a couple of buckets. "You could bring us some more water."

"All right," said the young man, and he picked up two buckets and headed back out into the yard toward the well. Liam got a third bucket and followed him, leaving just Ned and Harry.

Harry motioned to the prepared body that was laid out on a table Harry had built out of boards and sawhorses. "Let's just move the good doctor out of the way and make room for Charlie," he said.

Each man took one end of the plank that held the body, and they moved it carefully to one side, setting it down on a row of stacked apple crates. Then the two men pulled the plank bearing Charlie's body out of the wagon and set it on the improvised table.

Harry looked sadly at the remains of the man who could have been his friend, but never had. "What a bloody, awful shame," he said. "Has Molly seen him?"

"No. We thought it best if she waited."

"Good. Well, let's see if we can clean him up. Walt loaned us his razor and scissors," said Harry.

"You mean to shave him?" asked Ned. "I don't think I'd ever use that razor again, if it belonged to me."

"Walt's a doctor. He knows how to sterilize things," Harry said, smiling. Then he got to work on Charlie. He'd make him look like a decent human being if it was the last thing he did—for Molly's sake and for Harrison's. He started by cutting his hair, and he worked without speaking for a few minutes while Ned watched.

Finally Ned spoke. "Have you talked to Rafe yet?"

"No. He's been busy running errands for Carlotta."

"Is he trustworthy?" asked Ned.

"I think so. As far as I can tell, he's an honest, hardworking young man."

"Liam knows him. Says he's okay. We need to know what he knows," said Ned.

"Yes," said Harry. He paused in his work of cutting hair to look up at Ned. "I take it Michael filled you in."

"Molly, too," said Ned. "She got Carlotta's version."

"Different?" asked Harry, back at work.

"Very different," said Ned, then he told Harry what Molly had learned and what Liam had said about the knot.

"That's interesting," said Harry. "If Liam's right and the same person killed them both, it would have to be someone as old as Eldridge. Rafe wouldn't have been old enough to be involved in Fred Banks's death." Harry walked around to reach the other side of Charlie's head. "I have news, too. Walt says the doctor died from head injuries, not from hanging. Somebody hit him on the back of the head and cracked his skull."

Someone rattled the door, and Ned went over to open it. Liam, Walt, and Rafe came in, each carrying a bucket of water. "Ahh, the bucket brigade," said Ned. "Come right in." He looked out to see if anyone else was around, and then closed the doors.

Walt spoke quickly. "Rafe has things to say. We should hurry."

"Well, come over here," said Harry. "Bring the water."

Walt helped Harry wash the body while the others mostly looked away. They dragged up more apple crates for seats.

"Go ahead, Rafe," said Harry.

"I saw it all," the young man said.

Ned looked sharply at him. "Exactly what did you see?"

"Mr. Payne and Doc Carter had an awful argument. I didn't understand at first what they were fightin' about, but it had to do with Abigail, so I listened."

"Are you close to Abigail?" asked Harry, not looking up.

"I want to marry her," said Rafe. "She's everything to me."

"I see," said Harry, considering the young man.

"So what did they say about her?" asked Ned.

"It was about her red hair. And about how old Mr. Banks—Liam's father—had red hair, and how Mr. Payne has been thinking all these years that Abigail wasn't his child. He thought Miss Carlotta—" The young man was embarrassed; he couldn't find the words.

"We get it," said Ned. "He thought his wife had been unfaithful because she had a red-haired child." Ned had reddish hair himself.

"But that's ridiculous," said Walt. "Everyone knows it happens all the time. Plenty of redheaded babies are born to parents who don't have red hair. Usually there's a grandparent or an aunt or someone in the family that's red-haired, but not always."

"But why would they be fighting about that now?" asked Ned.

"Because Abigail is expecting a baby. My baby," said Rafe. "I didn't even know it until I heard them fighting. They sent her away, and I didn't even have a chance to say good-bye, and they don't know I'm the father. Mr. Payne wouldn't have approved of Abigail seeing the hired man, so we never told them. We kept it secret. The doc asked Mr. Payne why he would want to send away his only child and his grandchild when he's lost so many of his children, and Mr. Payne said, *You know why. She's as faithless as her mother.* But the doc didn't know what he was talking about, so he told him, and Mr. Payne was so mad he was gritting his teeth and cussing. The deacon *cussed.*"

"All right," said Harry, encouraging the boy to keeping talking. He found it interesting that Rafe seemed more shocked that the deacon had cursed than that he might have committed murder.

Rafe went on. "And he said it was that red-headed Fred Banks, and how he had come around smiling at his wife and helping her out when he—Mr. Payne—had to be gone, and she said how nice he was and how helpful. *He was helpful all right*, he said. The doc just laughed at him and shook his head and told him he was a poor fool for believing that nonsense all these years—that Carlotta had never strayed from him, not once in all those years. He said that being redheaded didn't mean anything! But Mr. Payne said, *It did mean something. It meant that Fred Banks had to die.* And then the doc just stared at him, because all of a sudden he knew what had happened. 'You murdered him!' the doc said. 'You said it was suicide, and I believed you, even though poor Ivalee knew it couldn't be. You just patted her on the shoulder, and said how hard it must be to believe something like this about someone you love. I believed you,' he said. And Mr. Payne said, *People will believe me when I tell them about you, too.* And he picked up an ax handle that was propped against the smokehouse and swung it as hard as he could and hit him right on the back of the head."

"Where were you?" asked Ned.

"I'd been coming from the barn, but I hid behind the corn crib. He thought I'd already gone home, but I'd stayed late. I was waitin' to talk to him about Abigail. I wanted to ask him if I could marry her."

"So, he doesn't have any idea about what you saw?" asked Harry.

"No. Today I just went on like always and acted like I never saw a thing. Mr. Payne doesn't really see me. He thinks I'm stupid, like one of the farm animals or a piece of furniture, so I just keep my mouth shut and let him think what he wants to."

Liam coughed at that, and shrugged innocently when Harry looked sharply at him. Maybe this explained why the severity of Liam's stutter came and went. Sometimes it was more useful than others.

"You're obviously not stupid," Ned said to Rafe. "So after he hit the doc, then what happened?"

"Then he dragged his body into the smokehouse, and as soon as he was out of sight, I ran home."

"Where is home?" asked Harry. He had started soaping up Charlie's face.

"I have a little cabin just down the road. I live by myself. My parents used to own this land."

"Really!" said Harry. "What happened to your parents?"

"Just bad luck. My mother died when I was born. My older sister had to look after me. Then our father got thrown off a horse and hurt his back, and he couldn't do the work any more. He couldn't make enough money to pay the taxes. The Paynes came to town about then and had plenty of money, and they bought the farm. My father eventually died. I've worked for the Paynes since I was about ten. That's when the war broke out and both of their boys left. I helped Miss Carlotta with simple things like carrying in firewood and fetching water, and over the years I've gradually taken on more of the work on the farm. When I got old enough to take care of myself, my sister got married and moved away, and since then I've lived alone."

"Well, we need to get you somewhere safe," said Harry. "You're the only witness."

"I'll t-take him to my house. I need to let my mother know what's going on, anyway," said Liam.

"That's a good idea, Liam," said Harry.

"Better do it now, before Eldridge gets back with the caskets," said Ned.

Harry agreed. "You can take the wagon."

"Maybe Rafe should hide in the back, in case they meet Eldridge coming back," said Walt.

And that's what they decided to do. Rafe lay down behind the seat in the back of the wagon, and they covered him with the clean quilt that Winifred had sent, bunching it up to make it look like someone had just thrown it in there. "If Eldridge stops you and looks in, tell him I wouldn't let Winifred use her pretty quilt on the likes of Charlie," said Ned. "That's not far from the truth."

Liam nodded and started to drive the wagon away.

"One more thing!" said Harry. He walked to the back of the wagon so that Rafe could hear him. "Rafe?"

"Yes, Captain?" came a voice from under the quilt.

"You don't have to have Eldridge's permission to get married if you're both old enough," he said. "You and Abigail can go to the nearest courthouse, or I can marry you when you bring her home."

"Thanks, Captain. As soon as I can, I'll talk to Abigail."

Harry gave Liam the go-ahead, and the wagon pulled out of the shelter of the barn. Then Harry and Walt went back to work.

Ned watched silently while they arranged Charlie's body. Finally he commented. "If preachin' and doctorin' don't work out for the two of you, you could open up a funeral parlor."

Harry looked up, pretending to take him seriously. "You think there's money in it?"

"Probably. And I could supply you with bodies," said Ned.

"We'll keep that in mind," said Walt.

"I can't believe she donated my good shirt," muttered Ned, as they dressed the body.

"That's not the only shirt you lost today," said Harry. "What do you think I'm wearing?"

Ned frowned, looking at Harry's clothes.

"Well, I thought your taste had improved. That explains it."

All three men laughed.

Suddenly, the door opened, and there was Eldridge Payne, and they all stopped laughing.

"What's so funny?" asked Mr. Payne.

"Well, Ned, here, is handing out shirts today," joked Harry. "Do you need one?"

"Don't think we'd wear the same size," said Eldridge, and he walked over and extended his arm next to Ned's. "I passed your wagon coming in, and I agree with you about the quilt. Winifred shouldn't have given that pretty one for the likes of this fellow. Good that you're keeping her straight." Although Eldridge had made the remark lightly, Harry was pretty sure that he had a low opinion of women, and he enjoyed being "one of the boys." He was also being cautious. Apparently he had taken the time to talk to Liam and had looked into the back of the wagon, but hadn't looked closely enough to spot Rafe. That was lucky.

"Well, how do you like my shirt?" Ned asked, pointing at the one the corpse was wearing.

"You want the truth?" asked Eldridge, his eyes glinting.

"That would be nice," said Ned.

"I think the corpse looks better in that shirt than you ever did!"

All four men laughed heartily, and Eldridge walked back out, satisfied that nobody in the whole place suspected him. He was one of the boys. Everything was just fine. "I'll see if Carlotta can come up with an older quilt that will do for Charlie—and one for the doc," he said.

Nobody said anything else until Ned walked over to a crack between the logs in the wall and saw that Mr. Payne had returned to his house. "He's back at the house," Ned reported.

Then Walt said, "That's the scariest man I've ever seen. He seems so normal, but his smile doesn't make it to his eyes. He's being friendly, but all the while he's watching everyone like some kind of predator."

"Like a snake with a rabbit," Harry said grimly. "And if we stir up trouble without having the evidence to convict him, it will be our word against his, and innocents really will suffer. He could accuse Rafe—or even Liam. Liam knows how to tie the knot—and it would be his word against theirs. One of them might hang for it while he walked away a free man."

"We'll just take our time. He didn't turn evil overnight. There have to be other secrets in his past, and we'll find out what they are," said Ned. "I wonder where he lived before he came to this part of the world."

"Carlotta knows, but we can't all ask her at once," said Harry. "I'll try to talk with her this evening, or I'll get Molly to do it. We can't let anyone think we suspect anything, not even Carlotta. We need to talk to

Harrison and the women. Make sure they know how important it is to keep quiet," he said.

"Carlotta's in danger too, if Eldridge gets spooked," said Walt.

"He's coming back, and Carlotta's with him," Ned warned, still watching through the crack in the wall. "He's carrying two quilts."

"All right," said Harry. "Let's get this job done, and then we can go home for awhile and talk to the others. I need to get cleaned up. Then I want to hug my wife and hold my babies! And I need to see what can be salvaged from my house. I hope my suit isn't burned to a crisp."

"Maybe it's just smoked," said Ned. "That could be to your advantage. It will give you credibility when you preach about hell. People will think you've looked right into the flames."

Harry sometimes felt that he *had* looked into the flames, but he didn't say it. "Or I could just borrow more clothes from you," he suggested.

"I'll help you dig through the ashes," said Ned.

"I thought you would."

It turned out that Carlotta had a talent for lining a coffin with a quilt and wrapping it just so around the bodies. Both bodies appeared quite respectable when she was done. Everyone agreed that the shave and haircut had improved Charlie's appearance, but Harry was somber when he looked at him in the coffin. Charlie looked more like he had when they had gone to school together. The burden of his own failures lay heavy on Harry's shoulders.

Ned noticed. "Come on, Harry," he said. "Let's get these caskets moved into the house, and we'll go home."

CHAPTER 18

A Visitor Comes Forward

When they reached the house, Harry asked Walt to stay behind and talk with Molly and see if any medical advice was needed for Sarah or the babies or Harrison. He and Ned would see what could be salvaged from the burned house before time for the wake. So, after a brief visit, armed with shovels, hoes, and work gloves, Ned and Harry walked up the hill to the burned house. Walt called out as they left, "Be careful where you step. There'll still be hot coals down in the ashes!"

As they approached the blackened ruins, Harry stopped to stare. This was the house where his mother, Annie, and his Aunt Winifred had grown up. It was tiny but it had been sufficient. It was also where Harry had come to live when he was ten and Winifred was eighteen. Winifred had driven a wagon all the way to Marietta to get him after his mother died, and he had spent two happy years there. During the past year the old cabin had been a home to Harry, Sarah, and Harrison. Now it was destroyed, and Winifred was giving him shelter again.

"I had begun to feel sorry for Charlie. I take it all back," said Harry bitterly.

"He trapped Winifred in there," said Ned. "I wish I'd killed him myself."

Without further conversation, they got to work, piling trash in one place and things that might be salvaged in another, carefully lifting aside fallen timbers and watching where they walked to avoid hidden, smoldering coals. The combined living room, kitchen and loft were completely burned, with only a blackened shell of log walls remaining, but the big cabinet that had been pushed partly across the bedroom doorway had apparently served as a kind of firebreak. The cabinet and wall were charred, but standing, and the bedroom beyond was not a total loss. The wardrobe that stood against the far wall was intact, and the clothes inside were smoky, but still usable.

"That's good news, anyway," said Harry. "Sarah has some dresses, and I've still got my suit. I'm not left with just the shirt on my back."

"Which is my shirt, don't forget," said Ned.

"I'm not likely to."

Harry used an undamaged dresser drawer to pack some clothes for his and Sarah's immediate use. They would come back the next day to remove the rest. Finally, he and Ned walked around to the back of the ruin, where the washtubs were still standing and water was still available.

"You know what?" said Harry.

"You're going to have a hot bath," said Ned.

"That's exactly what I'm going to do."

"I can't say that I blame you. Not after watching you wash those two bodies. I'll just carry this load of stuff down to the house while you're at it."

Harry filled the big iron kettle with fresh water and made a fire under it. While the water was heating, he went back inside the cabin to get clean clothes and a towel. When the water was hot enough, he put out the fire and scattered the charred sticks that remained. "No sense cooking myself," he muttered. He looked quickly around to make sure he was alone, then stripped off his clothes and stood beside the kettle to bathe, using lots of homemade soap to make lather. Then he poured buckets of hot water over himself to rinse. It was a pleasure to wash away the soot and grime of the day.

He had dried off and started getting dressed when Ned came back.

"You've got company. Are you decent?" Ned called before he came around to the back of the cabin.

"Decent enough," Harry replied. He had his pants on and was reaching for the shirt he had hung over a bush when Ned came into sight with another man following him. Ned stared at Harry's back and shoulders, which were covered with old scars and new bruises he'd gotten when he fought Charlie on the rocks in the creek and when he was knocked from his horse.

"Harry! You're all beat up. You need to take better care of yourself."

"Right," Harry agreed. "Who would have thought that the ministry could be as hazardous as the war?" Harry looked curiously at the other man as he came closer. "Jimmy?" he asked.

"Yep. We met at the store the other day."

"I remember. The writer. You were letting Eb beat you at checkers and listening to old Ollie tell his stories." Harry finished buttoning his shirt, then offered his hand. "What can I do for you?"

"I came to give you a warning," said Jimmy.

"Really!" Harry looked down at his bare feet. "Can it wait until I put my shoes on?"

"Sure."

"Let's go around to the front yard and see if there's somewhere to sit," Ned suggested.

"I'll be just a minute," said Harry.

After the other two walked away, Harry tucked his shirt in and strapped his gun back on. He put his coat on over that, then quickly put on his shoes and socks before following.

By the time Harry reached the front yard, Ned had straightened the two rocking chairs that Michael had left in the yard and set them near the fallen log. He sat down on the log, leaving the chairs for Harry and Jimmy.

"What's happening?" Harry asked. Jimmy's demeanor had changed now that he was no longer playing the gullible visitor. His expression was serious.

"I was at the store when Eldridge Payne came for the caskets," he said, "and I know some things about him that you need to know."

Harry studied him. "First, maybe you should tell us who you really are."

Jimmy looked cautiously around, then spoke quietly. "My name is Jimmy McClanahan. I'm a journalist from Memphis. I work for the *Memphis Daily Appeal*, and I'm following a story about Eldridge Payne. I want to make sure you know what kind of a man you're dealing with."

Then Jimmy told them about the sinking of a steamboat on the Mississippi River some years before the Civil War. Recently, when a drought lowered the water level and the wreck was recovered, some interesting discoveries were made among the wreckage. Gold that should have been in a safe aboard the ship was missing. People who were thought to have drowned appeared to have been murdered. He gave details of the deaths of the owner of the boat, who was Carlotta's father, and members of the crew. He described how Eldridge Payne might have done the whole thing, and how he had made money off of it. Not just the gold, but insurance money, too.

"How did you track him down?" Harry asked.

"It wasn't easy. For one thing, he's going by his middle name now. His first name is Wilbert, and he used to go by Bert. I found Carlotta's sister in North Carolina, and she sent me to Choestoe. But once I arrived, I didn't know who to talk to. I wasn't sure who could be trusted in Choestoe. The sheriff seemed unreliable, and Eldridge appeared to be everyone's friend, including yours," he said to Harry. "I was afraid that if I talked to the wrong people, I might end up dead."

"But you've decided we can be trusted," said Harry.

"I've heard nothing but good things about you. The people here love and respect you."

"They respect Eldridge Payne, too," said Harry. "He's the chairman of deacons at my church."

"That's what worries me. I want to make sure you know what you're up against. You can't trust Eldridge Payne. I don't know what he's been up to since the war, but I don't think he's changed his character. When I heard that the doctor was found hanged in Eldridge's smokehouse, I figured the doctor must have stumbled onto something, and he killed him."

Harry sat back in the rocker, studying the man. "So you wanted to warn us. Is that all?"

Jimmy nodded. "And I thought we might be able to help each other by pooling our information."

Harry looked at Ned. "Tell him what we have, Ned."

Ned looked surprised that Harry wanted him to speak up. "Well, we have Dr. Walt Drake's expert opinion that Doc Carter didn't die from hanging. He died from a blow to the back of the head."

"That's typical," said the reporter. "That's how the crewmen on the paddleboat died. They were locked in a hold, and they all had fractured skulls."

"Really!" Harry said thoughtfully. Then he turned back to Ned. "What else?"

"Rafe, who works for the Paynes, witnessed Eldridge knocking out the doctor and dragging him into the smokehouse. But he's the only witness, and it would be his word against Eldridge's, and Eldridge could as easily accuse him of doing the same thing."

Harry spoke up. "And Michael Gibson and I examined the scene in the smokehouse. We can testify that the rope was too short, and the step the doctor was supposed to have used was too low. His feet didn't reach it. We're convinced the man couldn't have hanged himself. And there were no footprints of any kind in the smokehouse. Someone had to have cleaned up. It was all wrong. I guess someone could claim that the doctor had committed suicide, then later someone else moved the boxes he stood on and swept out the room, but why would they do that? And that still wouldn't explain the fractured skull."

"If we had a sheriff who wasn't working for Eldridge, I think we'd have enough to get him arrested," said Ned. "Do you have any proof of what happened in Memphis?"

"No proof, but I have a file of information: reports from the time of the accident, newspaper articles. And the Marshals Service is looking into it because of the suspicion of murder and the theft of the gold. It was a shipment from the New Orleans mint to a bank in Memphis, so the Treasury Department is interested," said Jimmy. "And the insurance company will want to know if they've paid out a fraudulent claim to a murderer."

"Are you certain that Eldridge and Wilbert are the same person?" asked Harry.

"Carlotta's sister says he is. Carlotta could verify it," said Jimmy.

"We've hesitated to ask Carlotta much. If Eldridge thought she suspected anything, he might kill her. And I think he might be getting nervous," said Harry. "The sooner we get him locked up, the better."

"I sent a telegram to the marshal in Atlanta," said Jimmy. "Seth Collins was going to send it from Gainesville."

"Marshal Joel Underwood?" asked Harry.

"Yes. You know him?"

"Yes. He's an excellent man," said Harry. "And he'd have the authority to do something."

"I haven't heard anything back yet, of course. Choestoe isn't exactly on the beaten path, is it?" he asked. "I'm hoping for a message from him when Seth comes back with the wagons on Saturday."

"Meanwhile, what do we do?" asked Ned.

"I think we have to try not to let him know we suspect him," said Harry. "He could either make a run for it or do what he threatened: make sure innocent people pay the price."

"I agree. If we can wait for a few more days, maybe the marshal will come," said Jimmy.

"I'd love to see Joel Underwood. He'd be a tremendous help." Harry stood up. "Right now I want to go down and spend a little time with my family. Why don't you come and join us?" he said.

"No, I'll just go back to the store and hang around there. People are used to seeing me there, and I do hear the gossip."

"Well, thanks," said Ned, standing and offering his hand. "If you hear anything useful, let us know."

"I'll do my best. Anything I can do to help." Jimmy shook hands with both men. "I'm also on the lookout for stories. I have a feeling you two could give me some good ones."

"Everyone who lived through the Civil War has stories," said Harry.

"Just the same. I'd like to keep in touch with you after this is over."

"Sure thing," said Harry. "Here! You want to help? Carry something."

Harry went back into the house to salvage more clothes, and they carried them down the hill to Ned's house. Then Jimmy mounted his horse and rode away.

As he rode off, Ned and Harry shared a glance.

"You think Joel will come?" Ned asked.

"I hope so. But will he come in time? That's the question."

CHAPTER 19

The Wake

There are so many good things about a wake, Harry thought. *Why do we wait until someone dies to do this?*

He was standing in his slightly smoky black suit outside the Payne house where the curved walkway approached the front door. That was the door that looked out over sloping pastures toward the road and the grand view of mountains beyond. From where he stood, Harry could see the tallest mountain in the state. The Cherokee had called it Enotah. White settlers had renamed it Brasstown Bald. It was part of a long, blue ridge, and it made for a beautiful view in the soft glow of late afternoon.

Usually people entered the house from the back door, through the kitchen, but tonight was a more formal occasion, and most would be coming to the front door. Long lines of people were beginning to gather at the bottom of the hill, walking in groups up the long driveway, or riding in wagons or on horseback. Harry was ready to greet people as they arrived.

Sarah would have been standing beside him if she had not been at home with the new babies. He missed her but was happy she was safe at home. This afternoon, after he and Ned had returned from the ruined cabin, they had spent some time talking about what Jimmy had told them and informing the others of what they had learned. Harrison was there, too, with his foot propped up at Walt's orders, listening to every word. They were all amazed at the extent of Eldridge's criminal behavior, and Harrison asked a question that troubled them all.

"Wonder what he's been up to since he's lived in Choestoe?"

Harry had spent the rest of the time with his family, marveling at the beauty of his wife and babies, reveling in the joy of life. He had never realized how much love the human heart could hold; had never fully understood the feelings of a parent for a newborn child.

From the first day he had met Sarah, Harry had felt protective of her, and the love he felt for her had been instant and overwhelming, but the immediate connection he felt with the babies went beyond anything he had imagined. He loved feeling the tiny hand of his child clutching his finger and was amazed to discover that barely brushing the baby's cheek caused it to turn and search with open mouth for its mother's breast. "Sorry, baby. Papa can't help you there," he had said tenderly, feeling a little embarrassed and somewhat inadequate. Being with his family eclipsed everything else that had happened in this momentous week—possibly everything else that had happened in his life. He wasn't sure he had adequately expressed those feelings to Sarah. He planned to spend the rest of his life trying to do that.

He was happy to have a little girl to name for his mother, and just as happy with his little boy. Sarah was trying to dress them differently so people could tell at a glance which baby was which. She had finished the yellow and white granny square blanket, and that one was Annie's. The little boy had a blue knitted blanket. The babies were so tiny that Harry could hold both babies at once, and he had done that this afternoon, marveling at how beautiful and perfect they were.

Harry had missed this experience when Harrison was born, but he didn't want to let his thoughts go there. Letting his mind dwell on the things he had lost and mistakes he had made might diminish the joy of the moment. And, in recent days, some of the lost things had been restored.

They had named the babies Annie and Daniel. *Daniel*, not Danny—Harry had insisted on that. "Danny" was all right, but Daniel in the lion's den—now that was a strong name. Sarah had nodded and smiled, knowing full well that people would still call the children Annie and Danny. Harry was never called Henry, either, but no one suggested his name was weak.

Harry heard footsteps on the porch behind him and turned to see Eldridge Payne coming down the steps.

"Eldridge," he greeted him, just as if nothing was wrong. He didn't know how things would eventually work out, but he felt pretty certain that nothing bad would happen tonight, with all these people around. "I want to thank you for opening your home to us tonight," he said, offering his hand and then looking down the driveway. "They're almost here."

Eldridge shook his hand heartily. "That's one of the nice things about a long entrance road. You can see people coming."

"Indeed," said Harry, finding Eldridge's words interesting. "You can fire off a few warning shots from here if you don't want to see them," he joked.

"I've thought of that," said Eldridge. "Actually paced the distance off one time."

"Really! I didn't know you were a marksman."

"I'm not, not at all. Fortunately, I've never needed that skill."

Just an ax handle to the back of the head, thought Harry, wondering where this conversation was going.

"Harry, I know you've been through a lot this week, losing your home and all. I want you to know that I'm going to call a special meeting of the deacons, and I'm going to propose that we build a parsonage for the church. All we've ever had is a little hut for the circuit rider. You were lucky enough to have a cabin that belonged to your family, but now that's gone. I'd like to see us build a real house, not far from the main church here in Choestoe. Whoever the current pastor is, he and his family will live in the house." Eldridge paused, waiting to see Harry's reaction. Harry was thinking how welcome this conversation would have been if he hadn't known he was being bought off.

"I don't know what to say, Eldridge," he finally answered honestly.

"I know how hard it is for you. We don't pay the preacher well enough that he can afford to build a house of his own, and since he has to be elected every year, there's usually no point in the man getting too settled, anyway. But you're special."

Harry felt his hackles rise at the obvious flattery, but he didn't let on.

Not hearing any negative response from the preacher, Eldridge continued, sweetening the offer. "Your family is from the area, and you get along well with the people. I think we'll want to hold onto you as long as we can. You've done an outstanding job this year. After you're elected again this fall, I plan to propose a raise in your pay."

Harry remembered Michael's words about the sheriff. *He's a man who can be bought. In fact, he expects to be bought.* Harry wanted to tell Eldridge that, unlike the sheriff, he was not for sale, but this was not the time for that conversation. *Innocent people will suffer.*

"I'll have to pray about it, Eldridge," he said at last.

"You do that," the man said, smiling the smile that never quite reached his eyes. "And here they come," he added, motioning toward the people who were just reaching the top of the hill.

"I'll go and tell the others," said Harry, and he made a quick retreat into the house.

The doors at each end of the dogtrot had been opened wide, so there was an open hallway right through the house from front to back. Within that hallway there was a staircase on the right that led to the upstairs bedrooms, and opposite the stairway a long plank table had been set up against the wall to hold the food the neighbors would bring. Harry walked into the first doorway on the right. That was the living room, where Charlie's casket was standing against one wall. Molly was seated in the wing-backed chair close by, and Michael stood beside the door behind her, guarding her and keeping her company. That door led to the kitchen, and another one led into Carlotta's room, where Molly had taken her after their tea. Harry nodded at Michael, and then walked over to speak to Molly. "Are you doing okay?" he asked.

"Fine," she answered. She looked down at Charlie's body. "Thank you, Harry," she said, indicating the corpse. He nodded, understanding.

"I am *so* sorry," he said, feeling that his words were inadequate. "About everything." His condolences extended to more than just her husband's death, and she knew it.

"I'm all right, Harry," she answered. "I'm gonna be all right."

He nodded. "People are coming."

"Okay," she said. "I'm ready."

Next, Harry went across the hall to give the message to Carlotta, who was with the doctor's casket in the parlor. In that room, Walt was standing guard, greeting people who were beginning to arrive and keeping an eye on Carlotta. He had removed the bandanna and the coins from the corpse and had been relieved to see that the body was behaving itself and looking very solemn.

It was traditional in the mountains for neighbors to come and pay their respects, and some would "set up" with the grieving family members throughout the night. Although the doctor had no family close by, he was known throughout the region, so there would be an unusually large crowd. Some wanted to pay their respects to the friends and family of Charlie, even though they did not know him. Still others were just curious and wanted to be there for the big event, visit with neighbors, and hear the gossip.

There were certainly stories to tell and to hear. One of the dead men was a kidnapper who had attempted murder—but wasn't the boy his son, after all? The other was apparently a suicide; and on top of all that news, the preacher's wife had just had twins. Many brought food; some brought musical instruments; some brought gifts for the preacher's new babies. Several brought jugs of whiskey, but they left them out of sight, in their wagons. They knew that the preacher and the deacon would not approve. Still, late at night, out in the shadows, some drinking would go on, because this was a wake.

The summer day was long and mild. As time passed, people made their way through the house, viewing the bodies and talking to the mourners before moving back outside. Musicians gathered on the front porch and started playing and singing softly. Small clusters of people stood around the yard, eating and talking quietly among themselves. Harry had met many of them in the past year, and he did his best to learn the names of the new people he met as he walked from group to group. In addition to his own church members, there were people from the other churches in the county.

Harry greeted Collinses, Dyers, Duckworths, Hunters, Englands, Browns, Southers, Millers, and many others, and he tried to remember all their names. He felt they were all his people. As he walked among them, shaking hands, asking about sick relatives and answering questions about the events of the week, he tried not to say anything about the doctor's mysterious death. He did well until he reached one group of men who were arguing about where to bury the two bodies. "If the doc committed suicide, he doesn't belong in the church graveyard," declared one man with a long white beard. His name was Moses, but people called him Mose.

Another added, "And neither does a murderer who's not even from around here."

Harry did his best to reason with them. "Charlie didn't actually commit murder, although he did try to. And I know that he asked forgiveness before he died." That silenced them for a moment.

"But what about the doc?" Mose demanded.

"Well, as far as I know, our church doesn't have any rule about barring people from the cemetery. And think about it. The doc served the people of this community to the best of his ability for his entire career. There's no telling how many lives he saved or how many times he sat with a family while someone was dying. No telling how many babies he delivered. And the truth is, nobody saw him die. We don't really know the circumstances of his death. I believe we should let him be buried next to his wife in the cemetery."

Just then, Eldridge Payne walked over to join the group. He was listening to the discussion.

"But we do know he killed himself, don't we?" demanded Mose.

"No, we don't," answered Harry, meeting Eldridge's gaze before turning back to Mose. "I don't know about you, but I just can't believe the doctor would do that, and until someone proves he took his own life, I think we should give him the benefit of the doubt." Then the Captain spoke firmly, his mind made up: "His body will be buried in the cemetery."

Harry had brooked no argument, and although some people looked at each other with raised eyebrows, there was no more discussion right then. They had all liked the doctor. Most of them were happy that Harry had made the decision, and they were willing to go along with it. Just then, Walt came over, offering Harry his fiddle.

"How about some music?" he said. "The people on the porch want you to play."

"Well, I can't turn that down," he said, smiling. Then he nodded to the group and headed back toward the porch. "Just in time," he said softly to Walt.

"I thought so."

"Who's looking after Carlotta?" Harry asked.

"A whole room full of women. She's told the story about finding the body half a dozen times. I decided I wasn't needed."

"Well, that's good, I guess. What about Molly?" asked Harry.

"Michael is still there. You can't pry him away from her. He's standing right beside her, wearing his badge, looking like a bodyguard. Everybody knows him and likes him, so they're all talking to him. There's a crowd of women there, too. Not sure if they're more interested in Molly or Michael, but they all seem sympathetic."

Harry nodded. "The people are good-hearted, but they want to know the truth, and you can't blame them. I do, too. I may have told more truth than I should have back there. I told them I didn't believe the doctor killed himself. That will get around. Now they'll start wondering, if the doctor didn't do it, who did? I'm not sure how Eldridge will react to that."

They stopped to greet more people, then finally made it to the front porch, where they joined in singing a hymn that was already in progress. The singers were friends and neighbors—country people of all ages—wearing their Sunday best or their farm clothes, sitting on the porch or standing out in the yard. In the glow of the late summer afternoon and in the presence of that amazing view, they might have been a great choir singing on a stage. Their voices rang out to the mountains and the heavens beyond as they sang four stanzas of "Amazing Grace." Harry held the silent fiddle on his lap and joined in the singing.

> Amazing Grace! How sweet the sound
> That saved a wretch like me!
> I once was lost, but now am found;
> Was blind, but now I see![2]

The song leader from the Choestoe church had a hymnbook, but the rest sang from memory. As soon as they finished one hymn, someone would call out the name of another. They sang all the verses that they knew of "Be Still My Soul," "Abide With Me," "Rock of Ages," "What a Friend We Have in Jesus," and "Nearer My God to Thee." The adults knew the words because these were songs they had sung all their lives, and the children knew them well enough to sing along. In time, they, too, would pass the old hymns and the message they conveyed along to their children and grandchildren. They continued singing until the sun settled behind the house, and the sky and the hills before them blended into pale shades of blue, pink, lavender and gold.

As sunset approached, many families took their leave, especially the ones with small children, elderly parents, or a long way to travel. They visited Carlotta and Molly again, said their goodbyes to Eldridge Payne and the preacher, and walked or rode away. Lanterns marked their progress down the hill, and some groups of people kept on singing or talking as they walked, greeting others who were still making their way up the hill. There were distant calls of "Good-bye!" and "See you tomorrow!" as people parted ways when they reached the road. As the sky darkened, fireflies sparkled in the dusk, mirroring distant lanterns, and more lanterns were lit and hung in trees around the house.

Of the ones who stayed, some would remain until sunrise, while others would leave by the light of the moon. The crowd would grow smaller throughout the night. Right now, most went back to the tables for food. Someone on the porch tuned a dulcimer, another a banjo. After some conversation about keys and tunes, the musicians were ready. Harry and Walt lifted their violins and played with them, and the music wrapped itself around the house, bringing ease to the hearts of the listeners.

All except Eldridge Payne, who hated the sound, hated the preacher, and wished he had never invited all these people to his house. But he smiled, shook hands with the nearest person, and went on being the deacon for one more never-ending night. If the preacher had accepted his offer of the house and the raise in pay, he would have known he was on safe ground. He'd have had the man where he wanted him, like a dog on a leash. But as long as the preacher kept his distance and said he needed time to pray, Eldridge had to worry that he had plans of his own. He was beginning to feel like a fish that was being played, being drawn closer and closer to a net. Maybe it was time for him to put his own plans into play. He walked into the house through the back door and began greeting people who were helping themselves to food in the hallway.

When Harry saw Ned and Rafe approaching the front porch he put down his violin and went to meet them. They had a brief conversation. They told him Liam's mother, Ivalee, was staying with Winifred and Sarah. Rafe didn't feel right hiding out when he could be here looking after Carlotta. He felt that she was in more danger than he was. Right now they were planning to check on Molly and Carlotta and let them take a break to eat and stretch their legs. They had also brought Liam with them, but he was avoiding the crowd. And they had seen Jimmy standing with a group of men beside the house. He wanted to talk to Harry. Harry made his way around the house to meet him.

CHAPTER 20

The Deacon's Undoing

Eldridge stuck his head into the parlor, where Carlotta was holding forth to a rapt group of women about finding the doctor's body in the smokehouse.

"Where's Rafe?" he asked her.

"I don't know. I haven't seen him all evening."

"That's odd. It's not like him to run off without saying anything," he said, frowning. He looked around at the convenient audience he had and thought how best to plant the rumor that the boy had fought with the doctor the night before and now had run away. If the doctor hadn't killed himself there had to be a killer. Rafe would do just fine.

Just then, Rafe walked up behind him. "I'm right here, Mr. Payne. What do you need?" he asked.

Eldridge looked startled. "Where've you been, boy?" he asked. "You had me worried."

"He's been helping me with some things," answered Ned, who came up behind Rafe. "We've been sifting through the ashes at Harry's house, trying to find some shirts so Harry will leave mine alone," he said.

"Ah, yes. The shirts. Did you find some?"

"As a matter of fact, we did. That end of the house didn't burn. The clothes were still safe."

"That's a good thing," said Eldridge. So, there was Rafe, then behind him Ned, and behind him, Michael Gibson had stepped out into the hall and come to join them. Eldridge was beginning to feel trapped, and the

The Captain Seeks the Lost

rumor he had hoped to spread died in his throat. "Well, you fellows go on down the hall and help yourself to some food. I'm sure you've worked up an appetite," he said, then he turned and began greeting the people who were in the parlor. He made his way through the room to the far doorway that entered the dining room and walked quickly through there with just a wave to the people who were sitting at the table and eating. He moved steadily out onto the back porch into the yard. He felt like a fugitive inside his own home, and he didn't like it.

* * *

Back in the parlor, Carlotta was tired of the strain of talking to everyone and curious to see what was going on elsewhere in the house. She asked Florence Ward, who was standing nearest, if she would mind taking her place for a little while so that she could have a break.

"Sure I will," said Flo. "You shouldn't have to stay here all night. The doctor was our friend, too. We can take turns," and she immediately got some other ladies to help.

Carlotta felt a little shaky when she stood. It had been such a long and tiring day. She gave herself a moment to get her balance, and then walked out of the room, across the hall to the living room. There, Ned, Rafe, and Michael were talking with Molly in a tight group over by the casket, and, for the moment, no one else was in the room. Carlotta walked past them practically unnoticed as she headed for her room. She pushed the door almost closed behind her. She had intended to lie down, but she found that there were two sleeping children on her bed, along with an assortment of baby gifts, purses, jackets and hats.

She sighed and sat down on an upholstered chair beside the bed, but even that had a bag she had to move. As she pulled it out from behind her, she realized it was Molly's medicine bag, and her curiosity got the better of her. She settled back in the chair with the bag on her lap and pulled a lamp closer so that she could see. She looked toward the door to make sure she was alone. Then she opened the bag. It was an interesting carpetbag with lots of sections, and inside it were smaller cloth bags and several deep pockets full of assorted things.

At first glance Carlotta saw cloth bandages, scissors, bags of dried herbs, a pocket watch, a small notebook and a pencil. Something heavy was at the very bottom, so she reached down to see what it was and was mildly shocked when she pulled out a derringer. She dropped it immediately, back among the bandages. Imagine! Molly carried a gun. But maybe that wasn't too surprising, since she went alone to deliver babies at all times of the night. What an interesting person Molly was! She heard someone approaching the door, leaned back in the chair and closed her eyes, pretending sleep. That had worked earlier in the day when she had gotten nervous about all of Molly's questions. Someone opened the door slightly and watched her for a moment, then left, pulling the door almost closed again.

Carlotta put the bag back down and walked over to the door. She found that even though their voices were low she could hear the conversation quite plainly. She stood still to listen.

"So he'd killed other people before he killed Fred Banks and the doctor," Molly was explaining to Rafe.

Ned added more information. "The reporter thinks he killed four people on the boat. One was his father-in-law."

"But why would he do that?" Rafe asked.

"It was all about the money," answered Ned. "Carlotta and her sister got paid by the insurance company for the loss of the boat and for her father's life insurance. Not only that, but they were hauling gold from the New Orleans mint to Memphis, and that supposedly went down with the ship. When the drought caused the water level to go down this summer, they finally recovered the wreck, and the gold was gone. Not only that, but there were skeletons in the hold, and their skulls were fractured. It looked like someone had hit them in the back of the head. That's when a U.S. Marshal re-opened the investigation."

"But how did he get away with it?" Molly asked.

"Jimmy said they'd had trouble with a boiler and had gotten it worked on when they were in New Orleans, so it was reasonable to assume the explosion was an accident. Jimmy thinks Eldridge rigged the boiler to explode and then took the gold off in a smaller boat and hid it on the shore. Then for some reason he went back to the paddleboat. The explosion must have happened before Eldridge expected it, because he got blown off the ship into the water and nearly drowned. It's one of the reasons he got away with it. He seemed innocent."

"Do you think Carlotta knows any of this?" asked Molly.

"No," said Rafe. "She's told me about the explosion before, and how she lost her father and how she almost lost her husband. It broke her heart when her father died. I'm sure she had no idea Eldridge was involved."

"And this explains the knots that hanged the doctor and Mr. Banks," said Molly.

"Yes," said Ned. "It's called a bowline knot. It's for tying up boats."

It was the detail about the knots that settled it for Carlotta. She felt a dark certainty descend over her. It all made sense. Eldridge had done all of it. It explained so much that she had wondered about all these years. It explained Eldridge's distant attitude toward her and the business trips he would never explain and his silence about his early years. He had a secret life. It explained everything. He had killed her father and all the men on the ship, and Fred Banks, and the doctor.

She turned woodenly and walked back to Molly's medicine bag to get the gun.

Outside the door, voices were raised back to normal again as someone else came into the room.

"We're going to leave. I just need to get my things," someone was saying.

"But Carlotta's resting," said Rafe protectively.

Carlotta put the gun in her dress pocket—a derringer was such a handy size—and walked to the door.

She smiled brightly as she opened the door and walked into the living room. "It's all right. You can come in. I just needed a little rest, but I'm fine now. I'm just fine."

Molly watched her as she left the room. "She's not fine," she said. "Do you think she heard what we said?" Ned and Rafe hurried out into the hall to try to catch up with her, but she was already out of sight.

"Let's go this way," said Ned, and they went out the front door and around the house to where Harry was standing among a group of men, talking seriously. Jimmy was there, and he pulled Harry to one side just as Ned and Rafe reached them.

"The sheriff is here somewhere. He was asking questions. I think he and Eldridge are getting nervous."

* * *

Eldridge had made a trip to the outhouse and used that as an excuse to linger in the shadows of the outbuildings for a few minutes, watching people from a distance. He was glad that the crowd had thinned out. It was all such a charade, and he was sick of playing the part of someone who cared. The sheriff had come, and they had stood in the shadow of the barn making a getaway plan to be used if things went wrong. He had finally started walking toward the house and had just passed the smokehouse when Mose intercepted him, smelling like whiskey.

"I still say the doctor should not be buried in the churchyard if he committed suicide. And if he didn't, who killed him? I don't understand the preacher saying he doesn't believe it if he doesn't have anything to back it up. It's all well and good to say, *but the doc was such a nice man*, but nice doesn't matter if he killed himself. And if he didn't, well, who did? That's what we have to ask."

At that moment, Eldridge would have gladly added another murder to his list of crimes if there hadn't been so many witnesses around.

"I don't have any answers, Mose. Maybe Rafe? Maybe Liam? Do you have any ideas about who could have done it?" He looked beyond Mose's head to see a group of very serious men in conversation under the lantern that hung from an oak limb beside the house. The stranger named Jimmy was there along with Elder Dyer. They were talking to the preacher. Now Ned and Rafe were joining them, all looking somehow like a posse. And there came Michael Gibson with his ridiculous badge and that woman who was never out of his sight. What was going on?

Mose suddenly got his attention by stomping on the ground. "You aren't even listening to me!"

"I'll look into it, all right?" Eldridge said angrily. "Look, Mose, this has been a terrible day. I don't have all the answers. Can we just leave it there for now?"

"All right, all right," said Mose, stepping back. "Sorry I bothered you."

And then there was Carlotta, of all people, holding out what looked like a toy gun. "You did it, didn't you?" she said. "You killed my father."

"Your *father*?" he asked stupidly. "What in the world are you talking about?" He looked over at Mose. "There's a young doctor here. He may be playing music on the porch. Why don't you go get him? She's out of her mind." Mose turned and hurried off in the direction of the front porch.

"Now it's just us, Carlotta. Give me the gun." He held his hand out, expecting her to do what he said, just as she had always done. She fired the gun at his feet. At the sound of the gunshot, all eyes turned toward them, and the preacher came quickly.

"Don't do it, Carlotta. Don't shoot him," he called.

"I will, you know. I'll shoot you," she said to Eldridge. "I would have done it years ago if I'd known. Did you have to kill my father? What about Fred Banks? He was my friend!"

"Carlotta!" Eldridge reached out to her, as if to beg her forgiveness, then he snatched the gun from her hands and grabbed her, dragging her close, pointing the gun at her side.

"You'd better stop there, Captain, or I'll kill her," he said, just loud enough for Harry to hear.

Harry stopped, holding his hands up in submission. "Stop and think about this," he said. "Look how many people are here. A lot of them are armed. If you shoot her, you'll never leave this place alive."

"But I'd have the pleasure of shooting her before I die. That's worth something," he said. "Besides, I don't think that will happen. I think you'll let me leave."

"But I won't," said a voice from above, and there was the unmistakable click of a rifle hammer being pulled back. Eldridge looked up to see the silhouette of Liam, the sniper, who was just above his head on the roof of the smokehouse. Liam was holding Harry's Winchester. "I won't miss from here," he said.

Eldridge looked at the tiny derringer in his hand and knew he was beaten. He dropped his arm and let Carlotta go. It was Rafe who grabbed her and hurried her out of harm's way. Out of nowhere, the thought came to Eldridge that he hadn't been paying enough attention to Rafe. The boy had grown up. And then Harry was disarming him, backed up by Ned and Michael, and they were all holding guns.

"I didn't do anything," Eldridge said, raising his hands.

"I'll get a rope," said Michael. "To tie him with," he added, because it sounded like he meant to hang him.

Just then, Sheriff Oaks rode over from the barn, leading Eldridge's horse.

"I'll take him in for questioning," he said.

"Where did you come from?" asked Ned.

The sheriff didn't answer.

Michael didn't trust him. "You just happened to have two horses saddled and ready to go. Were you already planning to arrest him before Carlotta came out with her gun?" asked Michael, frowning.

"Yeah, Michael. I'm not as stupid as you thought," said the sheriff, dismounting.

"I never thought your were stupid," said Michael, "Just corrupt."

"Well, you were wrong about that, too." The sheriff led Eldridge's horse toward him.

"So, you've been working on this for awhile?" asked Ned. "You could have told us, and we would have helped."

"I didn't think I needed help from a revenuer and a bootlegger, thank you very much," said the sheriff. "Not even a bootlegger with a badge," he scoffed. "I heard what the writer's been saying. Now that someone's presented me with evidence, I agree that we need to question Mr. Payne. I'm just doing my job, like I've always done it."

There was a crowd growing around them.

"Well, are you just going to stand around and talk about it or take me to jail?" asked Eldridge petulantly, holding his arms out for the handcuffs.

"Whatever you say, *boss*," said the sheriff sarcastically. He locked the handcuffs on Eldridge's wrists, letting the deacon keep his hands in front so he could hold the pommel of his saddle, and helped him to mount. Then, without another word, the sheriff remounted his own horse and rode off, leading the deacon behind him.

"Follow them," said Harry, and both Ned and Michael ran to the barn to get horses.

The boss. As he rode away, Eldridge looked back at Harry and smiled smugly, and for Harry, the pieces of the puzzle fell abruptly into place. Eldridge was *the boss*—the boss who had tried to kill Sarah and almost killed Harry on their journey to the mountains. He was the head of the gang of counterfeiters that had included Sarah's guardian. The man had killed a musician *with a blow to the back of the head.* No wonder they had tried so hard to keep Harry and Sarah from reaching Choestoe. That's where the boss had lived all along.

There wasn't time to saddle a horse. Harry ran down the hill in the silvery light of a full moon that hung like a giant lantern over the lane. From a distance he saw the sheriff stop to unlock Eldridge's handcuffs and give him his gun as well as his freedom. He saw Eldridge shoot the sheriff and ride off, leaving him for dead.

When Harry reached the sheriff, he found him slumped in his saddle, bleeding badly from a wound to the neck. He stuffed his handkerchief into the wound and applied pressure to stop the bleeding, but it didn't stop. When Ned and Michael reached him, he said, "Take him up the hill to Walt. See if he can save him. You'll both need to go. Keep pressure on the wound or he'll bleed to death."

Harry ran on, trying to catch up with Eldridge, who must not escape. He saw him meet a wagon as it turned up the hill to come to the wake. Saw that it was *his* wagon, and Winifred was driving, and Ivalee and Sarah were seated on each side of her, each one holding a baby. Harrison must be riding in the back because his dog was trotting alongside. Harry saw the deacon stopping to talk to them. Saw him ride close to admire a baby, then take it from Ivalee. The baby's blanket was made of granny squares. It was Annie.

"No!" he cried out and ran toward the baby.

Harry was panting when he stopped running, his breath tearing at his throat. The deacon was still on his horse, holding Annie, waiting for Harry.

"Hello, Harry. What a pretty family you have," said the deacon in a voice that was as cold and deadly as an icicle dripping poison.

Harry fought to gain control of himself as he walked the remaining steps. He stopped before he reached the wagon. He must not let this man know that he held Harry's heart in his hands. "What do you want?" he managed to ask.

"I want you to throw your gun over into the bushes. Right now."

Harry did it without hesitation. Then he said calmly, "Now give me the baby."

"What if I don't?" asked Eldridge.

Harry hesitated, as if thinking it over, then he shrugged and made a weak joke. "I have another one. That one's the girl," he said, offhand, as if he didn't care about girls.

All the women in the wagon gasped and Sarah moaned, "Oh, Harry!"

Eldridge laughed out loud and looked at him with glee. "*Oh, Harry!*" he repeated. "You are in so much trouble with your wife! I almost wish I could hang around and see what happens to you when you get home tonight!"

"Will I get home tonight?" Harry asked.

"That's a good question. That's the *real* question, isn't it? Never mind the baby. What happens to *you*?" Eldridge made a face and abruptly thrust the baby back into Ivalee's arms. "It's wet!" he said, disgusted. "Take it." Then he waved his arm at Winifred. "You women get on your way. You're more trouble than you're worth." He was wiping off his hands as he spoke.

"*Do it,*" Harry commanded Winifred. She smacked the horses with the reins, and they went rapidly up the hill, but the dog remained, snuffling at something in the bushes beside the road. Harry knew that Harrison had climbed out the back of the wagon and stayed behind. He talked quickly so Eldridge wouldn't notice the boy. "You're the boss, aren't you? The one everyone was so scared of—the big man behind the scenes. You were behind the whole counterfeiting plot. You gave the orders to kill Sarah."

"Not just Sarah. You assumed we were after Sarah, but from Atlanta onward, it was *you* we were after." Eldridge looked around carefully to be sure they were alone. "I told you I'm not a marksman. I was the one who missed you at the buggy shop. And in Gainesville, the man who broke into your room at the hotel was after *you*, not Sarah. Without you, she would never have been a threat. All we needed from her was a suitcase. But you! You had to come here. After all the time I'd spent building the perfect hiding place, you had to come to *Choestoe*. I couldn't believe it. Then my men failed me."

"And they all died, didn't they?" said Harry.

"Not quite all." Was he talking about Dawson, who was in jail, or were there others? No time to ask.

"So, how many people have you knocked in the head and killed?"

"In Georgia?" asked Eldridge, grinning.

"Georgia will do for a start," answered Harry.

The Captain Seeks the Lost

"Well, not counting Fred Banks, it started with Robert."

"*Robert?*"

"You know, Harry! The man Sarah was supposed to marry, back in Macon. The man you stole her from."

"Oh, *that* Robert. You *have* been a busy man. I'd put that one down to Jake. Did you kill Leonard, too?" Harry asked.

"Of course. You didn't think Jake would do it, did you?"

"Actually, I did."

"You're quite good at this, Harry," said Eldridge.

"At what?"

"Keeping people talking until it's too late. I've gotta go now. Just one more thing I need to do."

"What's that?" asked Harry.

"I have to kill you, Harry. You know too much."

At that, Harrison cried out from the side of the lane, "No you don't!" Harrison was sitting cross-legged on the ground to keep the weight off his ankle, holding Liam's Sharps rifle to his shoulder, and he was invisible in the shadow of trees and brush. "Get on your way," he said angrily.

"Harry!" said Eldridge. "You're letting your boy do the dirty work! I'm proud of you!" Then he swung his gun toward Harrison, and Harry made a leap for it. From the roadside, Harrison fired, and the recoil knocked him backward just as Eldridge's gun went off. Eldridge's shot went over the boy's head, and the horse reared, knocking Harry to the ground. Then Eldridge whirled the horse around and rode hard, up the road toward Blairsville.

It was difficult to see what had happened in the shadows.

"Harrison! Are you all right?" Harry cried, fearful that the boy had been shot.

"Dad! Are you okay?" the boy asked at the same time.

Neither of them had been hit. Harry faced toward the hill.

"Liam!" he bellowed. "The rider on the road!"

Then they heard two quick shots from the side of the hill. Liam had fired Harry's Winchester, but the hoof beats didn't stop. Apparently, in the darkness, even Liam had missed.

"Sorry, Cap'n," came a distant cry from Liam. "He got away."

Harry helped the boy stand up. Suddenly, horsemen surrounded Harry and his son. They were led by Michael Gibson, who seemed relieved to find Harry and his son still standing.

"We're fine!" Harry assured him. "See if you can catch him. Let people know there's a murderer on the loose." At Michael's signal, they rode off into the darkness. As Harry watched them go, he felt certain that Eldridge would not be caught. He had been practicing invisibility for years. He was a master at it. He had already vanished into the darkness.

Only Ned remained behind, and Harry looked gratefully at him as he dismounted, took the Sharps from Harrison, and helped him up into the saddle. The boy rubbed his shoulder as the two men started trudging up the hill, leading the horse.

"That Sharps has a kick," Harrison said ruefully.

"That kick probably saved you," said Harry.

"Yeah?"

"And you saved me again," Harry said.

"Yes sir. You know something? I'm gettin' pretty tired of doing that. You need to start looking after yourself better, Dad."

Ned laughed. "You tell him, Harrison," he said. "Maybe he'll listen to you. I've been saying the same thing for years, and he never listened to me."

"What does a man have to do to earn a little respect around here?" Harry asked solemnly.

Then he noticed a large rock beside the path. "Hey, hold up a minute here. I think this is where I left my Colt." Harry went past the rock and felt around in the darkness until he found his gun. He dusted it off and put it back into his holster. Then he rejoined them and carried on the conversation. "Since you don't appreciate me, next time you get yourself stuck on a ledge I'll just leave you there," he told the boy.

"No, you won't," said Harrison. "You had too much fun rescuing me."

"That's what you call fun?" Harry shook his head. "That was not fun."

"I'd love to have seen that rescue," said Ned. "Did you know that your dad is scared of heights?" he asked Harrison.

"Really? I didn't think he was scared of anything."

"Of heights—yes," said Harry. "But there are other things that scare me even worse than heights."

"Like what?" asked Harrison.

"Like the thought of losing you or Sarah or the babies or Ned or Winifred—"

Harrison continued the list. "—or Molly or Michael or Walt?"

"Or Molly or Michael or Walt. Or Liam," Harry added. He turned to Ned. "How's the sheriff?"

"He was still alive when I left, but it didn't look good. Molly and Walt were working over him. He was bleeding bad."

"Heaven help them."

They were nearing the top of the hill, and the lanterns made a cheerful glow of welcome. Harry stopped, suddenly overcome by exhaustion. He looked down and sighed loudly.

"What?" asked Ned.

"I've got to figure out how to ask for Sarah's forgiveness."

"For what?"

"For pretending I didn't care about our baby girl."

"She knows you love her, Harry. She knows you did what you had to do."

"But what if Eldridge had killed her? Dashed her little body to the ground? How would I have gone on? And how could Sarah ever have forgiven me?"

"There's no point in worrying about what might have been, is there? We have to go on with what *is*," said Ned. "And be grateful, Harry! You've survived again! We've all survived."

"Thank God," Harry said fervently. "Thank God!"

Just then there were hurried footsteps in the dark, and Sarah ran down the driveway and threw herself into Harry's arms.

"Harry!" Sarah cried. "And Harrison! You're both alive! When we heard the shots, we didn't know."

Apparently no apology was necessary. Harry held her close, then frowned and pulled away from her.

"Are the babies okay?"

"They're fine," she answered.

"What are you doing out here in the middle of the night? You should be resting!"

"I'm all right, Harry. We were all awake anyway, and I wanted to be with you," she said.

"Oh," said Harry, holding her close again. He couldn't think of an answer to that, except that he was glad. "All right, then." And they walked arm in arm up to the house, following Ned, the boy, and the horse. Ned stopped beside Harry's wagon to tie up the horse and get Harrison's crutches. Then they all went inside.

They found Molly and Walt sitting at the kitchen table, looking grim. There was blood on their clothes. Molly gave a sigh of relief when she saw her son.

"The sheriff?" asked Harry.

Walt shook his head. "There was nothing we could do."

"Where's the body?"

"Some of the people from Blairsville are going to take him home. His family is there," said Molly.

"They've carried him out to a wagon," said Walt.

"I'll go see," said Harry. As he walked out, he was still quietly giving orders. "Sarah, you sit down, now, and rest, and Harrison, you need to prop up that foot." As he walked past Ned, with a nod toward the weary group, he suggested, "Maybe you could make some coffee?"

"Sure thing."

"I'll be back." Harry walked quickly out, letting the screen door slam gently behind him.

Ned was the only one who actually paid attention to Harry. He started filling an enamel pot with water.

"I want to see who else is here," said Harrison, looking at his mother for permission.

"Go ahead," she said, and the boy hobbled off.

"Lindy Jones," explained Sarah, after he left.

"Ahh," said Molly. "I'm glad he has a friend." She indicated the chair beside her. "Have a seat, Sarah."

"In just a minute." She walked out the door into the hallway and came back carrying a plate that held about three-fourths of a three-layered cake. "If I'm not mistaken, this is Mrs. Puett's black walnut cake.[3] This is just what we need."

Sarah set the cake on the table, then went to find some small plates and a knife. There was a stack of clean dishes on the counter. Some of the church ladies had washed and dried them not long ago.

The Captain Seeks the Lost

When Harry came back in just a few minutes, they were all drinking coffee and eating cake, and they waved him toward an empty chair. But before he would join them, he wanted to check on the babies and see what else was going on in the house.

There was a small group of ladies sitting with Carlotta in the parlor, consoling her and asking for details of her life in Memphis, and how she had met her husband, and what the real story was. Jimmy, the writer, was sitting among the women, taking notes in his notebook. He and Elder Dyer were the only gentlemen present, the rest having gone home or joined the men on horseback who were searching for Eldridge. Harry didn't interrupt the conversation, only nodded approvingly to Jimmy, and walked on.

In the living room, Winifred and Ivalee were talking quietly, minding the twins, who were swaddled in their blankets in an oval laundry basket, sound asleep.

Harry knelt in front of the babies, but did not wake them. He watched to see that they were breathing peacefully, then he quietly thanked Ivalee and Winifred, and left.

On the porch, Liam was still on guard, seated on the steps beside Harrison and Lindy Jones. Harry was gratified to see that Harrison's foot was propped up. Liam was telling Harrison the proper way to hold the Sharps rifle in order to control the recoil. He was not stuttering much at all. When Harry invited him to come to the kitchen and have some cake, he turned him down. He was keeping watch, and he took his duty seriously.

"He might still be out there, Cap'n," Liam reminded him.

"You're right. Thank you for keeping watch. If you need a break, tell me, and I'll take a turn."

"I can sit here. You rest while you can."

Harry nodded. "Can we talk just a minute?"

Liam looked surprised, but he got up and walked away from the children so they could talk privately.

"You never told me. What exactly happened at the foot of the falls? What did Charlie say to you?"

Liam told him how he had helped Charlie, and what Charlie had said, and Harry only nodded, holding back tears. "Thanks, Liam. Thanks."

Then he returned to the kitchen to eat cake, drink coffee, and enjoy the quiet company of his wife and his friends.

Before long, the horsemen returned, and most of them said their goodbyes and took their wives home. There was nothing else to be done tonight, and they wanted to travel while the moon was still bright. Tomorrow would be another busy day, and some of the men would dig the graves early in the morning.

Michael Gibson joined Harry and friends in the kitchen. He reported that there had been no point in continuing the search. Even in the moonlight it was too dark to see anything, and they could have ridden right past Eldridge hiding in the shadows and wouldn't have known it. Instead, by riding down the road they were destroying whatever tracks they might have been able to see by day.

Harry agreed with his decision to call off the search. "I don't think you'll be able to track him, even in daylight," he said. "The road has been so heavily traveled all day, there would not be much chance of following him, anyway."

Michael also explained that Rafe had decided to head on up to North Carolina to find Abigail and look after her. "He wants to tell her about her father and talk to her about marriage," said Michael.

* * *

Outside the kitchen window, on the ground beyond the side edge of the porch, Eldridge Payne sat in the darkness, listening. So Rafe wouldn't be home tonight. That was convenient, since Eldridge's horse was still tied up in the woods behind Rafe's house, and he had to go back there. Eldridge had gone to Rafe's cabin after escaping the preacher and his son. That had been a close one, there. The boy had almost blown his head off with that Sharps—had knocked his good hat off, and there had been no time to recover it. And then Liam had sent bullets whizzing by when Eldridge had thought he was well out of range, galloping down the road.

Once out of sight of the house, he had stopped at Rafe's cabin, and had still been there in the darkness when the horsemen went galloping by a few minutes later, but none of them had stopped. It was a good thing. He would have had to kill anyone who had stopped. After they had passed, he had lit one small lamp and taken time to change clothes. Rafe's clothes

The Captain Seeks the Lost

would blend in better than his. They were worn and patched—the clothes of a laborer, not those of a gentleman farmer.

And then he'd climbed the hill and approached the house through woods and fields, avoiding the front entrance. He had dug up a small box of gold coins from its hiding place behind the barn and retrieved his saddlebags from the tack room. This wasn't his main stash of gold. That was safely locked away in a bank vault. This was his emergency money.

Eldridge had been hiding in the shadows beside the porch when the horsemen came home, and he had heard Michael's voice clearly through the window. Knowing Rafe was gone gave him some time. All he had to do now was walk back to Rafe's cabin carrying the gold, load that and some other things into his saddlebags, travel north through the quiet countryside to the nearest railroad, and he'd be gone. Eldridge looked carefully around and saw no one. He got up quietly, walked back to the barn, and then, unnoticed, went back the way he had come.

When he was a safe distance away, he looked back at the farmhouse on the top of the hill and realized he would miss the place. He thought he might even miss Carlotta. He shouldn't have let himself get attached to her, but thirty-five years was a long time, and they had been through a lot together. That had been his undoing. If he hadn't been jealous and lost his head and killed Fred Banks all those years ago, none of this would have happened, and he could have gone on living here indefinitely, in spite of that annoying preacher. No one would have known—but then there was that writer, Jimmy. If the writer had actually figured it all out, it would have been time to go, anyway.

When he got back to Rafe's cabin, Eldridge shaved off his mustache. He had always taken pride in that tidy mustache, but people would be looking for a gentleman with a mustache. That would never do. He washed the hair oil out of his hair, dried it with a towel, and mussed it, so that it hung loose around his face, then he put on Rafe's corduroy cap. If he rubbed a little dirt on his face, no one would recognize him. He had gotten some dirt under his fingernails when he dug up the gold. That would help the disguise, too.

He kept his own clothes and packed them into the saddlebags, then added some more things he found that might come in handy—some changes of underwear and worn out socks and the shaving gear. It was too bad that when he was at home he couldn't have sneaked upstairs to pack, but the place was still full of people, and it would be foolhardy to waste any time getting away. He had plenty of money to start over somewhere else. Might as well make the change of identity complete by leaving his clothes at home.

Eldridge cleaned up the mess he had made in the cabin. He was a tidy man. Maybe Rafe wouldn't notice right away that his things had been disturbed. By the time he did, Eldridge should be long gone.

Finally, Eldridge found paper and a pen, and he sat down to write a note, which he tucked out of sight in a place where it would be found, but not immediately. When he had finished, Eldridge blew out the lamp and went out the back door, got on his horse, and vanished into the darkness.

Day Five: Friday

CHAPTER 21

Two Funerals and a Reunion

On Friday morning, Harry conducted the funeral service for Dr. Carter at the church, followed by a brief graveside ceremony at the cemetery. A Methodist minister assisted him, because the doctor had attended church with the Methodists as well as the Baptists, and there were people from all the local churches in attendance. The crowd overflowed the church, so people stood at the back and outside the open windows to hear. The congregation participated in the singing of hymns and recitations of scripture, including the Twenty-third Psalm.[4]

Both pastors read scripture passages and spoke kindly of the doctor, whose life had ended so cruelly. They also expressed their outrage at the actions of the murderer who had pretended to be a good man. People were stunned by the deacon's treachery.

Carlotta was there, dressed in a plain, black dress, with many friends close by to comfort her. Her grief was profound; this might as well have been her own husband's funeral. She sat silently with head bowed and tears streaming down her face throughout the service. Her husband had brought this tragedy upon them all, and now that he had left her, she was truly alone. But now that the truth was revealed, she realized she had been alone for a long time. She wondered if she had ever really known her husband, or if he had ever really cared about her. She wished she had shot him when she had the chance, but she also wondered what she would do without him.

After the church service, pallbearers carried the coffin to the cemetery as mourners walked behind. As was traditional in the southern Appalachians, the cemetery had been located on the side of a hill with the graves facing east so that at the Second Coming resurrected souls would see Christ in the eastern sky. After people had walked respectfully by the open casket one last time, men nailed the lid onto it and lowered it into the grave. Many people wept openly. The doctor had been a part of their lives for many years, and he would be missed. The shock of his murder intensified their grief.

Harry ended the service with these words:

"As you all know, our community has been shaken by three deaths this week: that of our doctor, the sheriff, and a man named Charlie Baldwin. There will be a private graveside service for the friends and family of Mr. Baldwin this afternoon. The wake for Warren Oakes will be held at his family home in Blairsville tonight, and the funeral will be at the Blairsville Baptist Church tomorrow. Also, please remember that since this will be a fifth Sunday, there will be no service this Saturday, but on Sunday we will celebrate Communion at the eleven o'clock service at the Choestoe Church, and that service will be followed by singing and dinner on the grounds. And at three o'clock on Sunday afternoon we will celebrate the Ordinance of Baptism down at the river.

"Now, to close the funeral service for Dr. Carter, I'd like to read several scriptures which remind us that we should not despair. At times of great tribulation, God still loves us and brings comfort and peace to our hearts.

> "Romans 8:35, 37-39
> 35 Who shall separate us from the love of Christ? shall tribulation, or distress, or persecution, or famine, or nakedness, or peril, or sword?
> 37 Nay, in all these things we are more than conquerors through him that loved us.
> 38 For I am persuaded, that neither death, nor life, nor angels, nor principalities, nor powers, nor things present, nor things to come,
> 39 Nor height, nor depth, nor any other creature, shall be able to separate us from the love of God, which is in Christ Jesus our Lord.
>
> "John 14:27

27 Peace I leave with you, my peace I give unto you: not as the world giveth, give I unto you. Let not your heart be troubled, neither let it be afraid."

Harry looked out over the people who were crowded around the casket and asked them to bow for prayer before reading the benediction.

"The grace of the Lord Jesus Christ, and the love of God, and the communion of the Holy Ghost, be with you all. Amen."

* * *

That afternoon there was a much smaller group in attendance for Charlie's funeral. Pete and Alice Nix were there, along with several other members of the church who served as pallbearers and gravediggers. Pete was still suffering from the broken ribs that Charlie had given him, and there were bruises on his head, but he was on his way to recovery. He was happy to have outlived his attacker and not sorry to see him gone.

Carlotta was back. Sarah, Ned, Winifred, Ivalee, and the babies were there. Ivalee, who would have preferred not to get out among people, had offered to stay home with the babies, but Harry had insisted that she and Liam come. The two of them stood together beside his family. They had brought a chair for Sarah so that she could rest, and the babies were there in their basket.

Michael was present, of course, still staying within reach of Molly, but he seemed quiet and he was careful to keep a respectful distance from her.

Michael was uncertain about how Molly felt, and he found Walt intimidating. Walt was well dressed, apparently wealthy, and educated. It was obvious to Michael that Molly had more in common with Walt than she did with him. With their medical backgrounds, they had so much to talk about. What had he ever talked with her about? Fairies! How silly he must seem to her. And Michael had decided he had made a mistake when he had kissed Molly in the buggy. He had rushed her, and he shouldn't have done that. It was obviously too soon. Then, yesterday afternoon before the wake, when he and Molly were finally alone together on Ned's porch, sitting in the wicker loveseat again, they hadn't talked at all. The one time they could have talked, they had sat quietly together and fallen asleep again, just as they had the night before. So today he was quiet. He was there for her if she needed him, and he had promised not to leave her alone, yet he wanted to give her space. He stood on one side of her at the gravesite, and Walt stood on the other. Harrison was at Michael's other side, leaning on his crutches.

Harry addressed this small group differently than he had the people at the doctor's funeral. His words were more personal. This was his family. These were his closest friends. He talked briefly about the importance of finding what was lost, and he read the parables of the lost sheep and the lost coin.

> "Luke 15
> 3 And he spake this parable unto them, saying,
> 4 What man of you, having an hundred sheep, if he lose one of them, doth not leave the ninety and nine in the wilderness, and go after that which is lost, until he find it?
> 5 And when he hath found it, he layeth it on his shoulders, rejoicing.
> 6 And when he cometh home, he calleth together his friends and neighbours, saying unto them, Rejoice with me; for I have found my sheep which was lost.
> 7 I say unto you, that likewise joy shall be in heaven over one sinner that repenteth, more than over ninety and nine just persons, which need no repentance.
> 8 Either what woman having ten pieces of silver, if she lose one piece, doth not light a candle, and sweep the house, and seek diligently till she find it?
> 9 And when she hath found it, she calleth her friends and her neighbours together, saying, Rejoice with me; for I have found the piece which I had lost."

After Harry read the scripture, he paused before beginning his remarks. Finally, he took a deep breath and began.

"I've always loved these parables, but I don't think I've ever fully appreciated their meaning until this week. When Harrison was lost, I feared for his life, and I searched and searched until, by God's grace, I found him. I was standing on a muddy little path beside a cliff in the rain, and I looked up, and I could see his foot moving back and forth on a ledge. And when I called out to him, he answered me. I can't describe the joy that I felt!" Harry looked at Harrison. "I'm thankful for you, son. You are the son that I've lost twice, and I rejoice that I've found you again!

"Later that day, I came home to find that his mother, Molly, whom I had not seen for Harrison's lifetime, was still alive. This woman had been my friend, and more than my friend, and had been lost to me for all those years, and yet here she was alive, and—amazingly—still my friend." He looked at Molly. "I'm thankful that I've found you again, Molly. I'm so glad you've survived all these difficult years and that we can still be friends." Molly's eyes filled with tears, and she took a step closer to Michael for his support. He took her arm to steady her when she swayed slightly on the uneven ground, and when she moved closer to him, he put his arm around her and gripped her shoulder. At the same time, Harrison moved close to him, so Michael put an arm around Harrison, too. And suddenly he felt that he had a family.

Then Harry looked at Sarah, who was wearing her striped shawl over a black dress. The amazingly efficient Winifred had found time to wash the shawl and let it dry, and Sarah had worn it for modesty's sake with a wooden pin to keep it together in the front. She couldn't button the dress at the waist, and there were milk stains on the bodice, but it was the most appropriate dress she had for a funeral. The shawl covered the imperfections. Harry looked at her with love.

"My biggest fear this week was that I had lost Sarah. Charlie led me to believe she had died in the burning house, and he carried her shawl for proof, and it was bloody and smelled like smoke. But when I got back home, not only was she alive and well, but she had given birth to twins! I thought I had lost her, but not only did I find her, I found I had gained a family with her, as well." He spoke directly to Sarah. "Sarah, you are my heart and my home, and you bring me joy every day that I'm with you. I thank God for you. Without you, I would be lost."

Harry stopped and wiped his eyes with a handkerchief. "In each of these cases, I thought I had lost someone that was precious to me, but I found every one of them, and each time, I was overjoyed. The Bible teaches us that just as we are overjoyed when we find the things—or people—we had lost, so there is joy in heaven when a sinner repents. We should never underestimate how important it is to God when a sinner comes back to him. Behold, how much he loves us! How he longs for us to be reconciled with him! We can even come to him like a little child." Then he read another scripture passage.

> "Matthew 18:2-6
> **2** And Jesus called a little child unto him, and set him in the midst of them,
> **3** And said, Verily I say unto you, Except ye be converted, and become as little children, ye shall not enter into the kingdom of heaven.
> **4** Whosoever therefore shall humble himself as this little child, the same is greatest in the kingdom of heaven."

"You may be wondering how all of this relates to the funeral of Charlie Baldwin, so I'll tell you. Charlie has been lost for his whole life. He searched for the wrong things and usually found them. He didn't appreciate the good things he had, and he lost them. He had opportunities to be successful in relationships and in life, and he threw all of those away. We could have been friends; instead, we learned to hate each other. I'm sorry about that. His friendship is something that I lost and never recovered. I feel very strongly that where Charlie is concerned I was a failure.

"But I've found solace in something that Liam told me yesterday. I was never able to help Charlie, but Liam did. It was Liam who found Charlie's body after he fell from the waterfall. Liam picked him up while he was still alive and carried him to the side of the creek. It was Liam who told Charlie he should make his peace with God and helped him to pray. This is the prayer that Charlie prayed while he lay dying. I'm sure he learned it when he was a child, and maybe it was the only prayer he knew."

> "Now I lay me down to sleep
> I pray the Lord my soul to keep.
> If I should die before I wake,
> I pray the Lord my soul to take.
> God bless Molly and Harry and Harrison and me.
> Amen.

"Then Charlie told Liam he was sorry for the things he had done.

"I don't know for sure what was in Charlie's heart. But I choose to believe that in those final moments of his life, like a little child, Charlie made his peace with God, and I pray that God has had mercy on his soul. I believe that in Christ he is a new creature, and that one day we will see him in heaven."

Several people around the coffin cried quietly. Pete Nix was respectful, but dry-eyed. Harry asked them to bow.

"Dear Lord, we pray that you have welcomed Charlie home to be with you, and that there is rejoicing in heaven, for this one that was lost has been found. And we pray that you will make us ever grateful for your goodness and mercy, which will follow us all the days of our lives, and we thank you for your assurance that we will dwell in the house of the Lord forever."

And then he led them in repeating The Lord's Prayer.[5]

After they finished the prayer, as people greeted Molly, offering their condolences, there was the sound of a carriage coming down the narrow road that ran alongside the cemetery. The carriage turned in through the trees that surrounded the cemetery and pulled to a stop. Liam, with his sharp eyes, recognized them first.

"That's Rafe," he said.

With Rafe was a young, red-haired girl.

"And Abigail," said Carlotta. "And who is that with them?"

Another tall young man walked beside Abigail, and an older couple followed them. As the group approached, walking carefully around gravestones, Carlotta suddenly cried out, "That's my son! That's my son!" and she ran across the cemetery to greet him. The young man swept her into his arms and swung her around. When he finally put her down she looked up at him in disbelief.

"Theo?" she asked.

"Yes, Mama. I've come home." She hugged him again, now crying tears of joy that this oldest son who had fought for the North had returned. Next she greeted her sister and her brother-in-law, and then she hugged her daughter, Abigail. "I'm so glad you've come home. We shouldn't have sent you away."

As they watched the family reunion in the distance, Ned slapped Harry on the back. "You messed up, Preacher," he said.

"How?" He waved his hand at the scene. "I'd say I got it right. Another lost person has been found."

"You should've read the story of the prodigal son."

"Well, there's still time. You want me to make the sermon longer?" Harry asked.

"No, no. That won't be necessary!" said Ned, backing quickly away.

"I thought not." Harry smiled and went to speak to Molly. After that he went to greet Carlotta's children, who had come home.

Day Six: Saturday

CHAPTER 22

A Conference on the Porch

On Saturday they rested, and Rafe came around in the morning to invite everyone to come back to the Payne house that night for a celebration. The prodigal son was doing the barbecuing himself, and inviting all the neighbors to come. More covered dishes were needed! Rafe also let them know that he thought Eldridge Payne had been in his house the evening before and that some of his things were missing.

That afternoon, Marshal Joel Underwood and Agent Raymond Whittaker arrived together, and while the women were inside cooking and tending to babies, the men congregated on Ned's porch to talk out the events of the week. After they had filled the newcomers in on all the details and Jimmy had given them his report, they fell into easy conversation.

Harry was upset about losing Eldridge Payne. "We had him, Joel, but none of us had the authority to arrest him. It was frustrating."

Ned agreed. "I deal with that all the time! I manage to catch people, then have to wait on the sheriff to make the arrests."

"It would be different if you had a reliable sheriff to work with," said the Marshal. He and Raymond Whittaker looked questioningly at Michael.

"What?" said Michael, as all eyes focused on him.

"Well, you looked pretty comfortable in that badge," said Ned. Michael had handed the badge back to Agent Whittaker when he arrived.

"You think I should run for sheriff?" asked Michael, surprised.

"Why not?" asked Harry.

"Well, for one thing, it would seem a little strange to start chasing down people who've trusted me all these years. It sounds unfair. It'd be like baiting a field and making pets of the deer and then shooting them."

"You could give them fair warning," suggested Harry. "Let them know you're running for sheriff. If they were worried about it, they could move their stills—or rush to turn themselves in," he said with a grin, "—or move to Towns County."

"Don't suggest that," said Ned. "I'd have to chase them down there, too."

"Chasing down moonshiners isn't the only job of the sheriff," said Harry. "He has a lot of other law enforcement issues to deal with. I think you'd be good at it. I think you should consider it."

"Well, thanks," said Michael, at a loss for words. "I'd love to have the pleasure of throwing people like Eldridge Payne into jail." He looked around, still uncomfortable with all the attention. "I'll think about it," he said. "But I might want to see what's available down in Dahlonega. You mentioned that, Mr. Whittaker." Everyone knew that he was wondering about how things would work out with Molly.

Walt spoke up then. "I've made a proposal to Molly." Michael looked at him, startled, but didn't speak.

"What? You asked her to marry you?" asked Ned.

"No, of course not. I'm still engaged to Elise," said Walt, blushing. "At least I think I am. It's hard to keep in touch, with her living in Macon and me in Atlanta. But that's beside the point. If all goes well I'll have my degree soon, and I'd like to come up here to start my practice. I wondered if Molly would like to come and work with me as a nurse. She's a good nurse, and I think she's interested. She and Harry could both be close to Harrison that way."

"Assuming I still have my job!" said Harry. "The church elects the pastor every year."

"And you've lost the chairman of the deacons," said Ned. "I'm sure he would have supported you."

"You say that in jest, but he actually offered me a house and a raise and said I'd be elected for sure," said Harry.

"When was that?" asked Ned.

"Just before the wake Thursday afternoon. I think if I'd said yes, he would have considered me bought and paid for. He might not have decided to leave town."

"Except Jimmy came forward," said Walt.

"And Carlotta took a stand," said Michael.

"Wasn't that something?" said Harry. Then he sighed. "The sad truth is Eldridge Payne was a good financial supporter of the church. I'll probably have to get another job to support us now that he'll be gone. Maybe they can use me at the sawmill and pay me in lumber."

"You'll need a house, for sure," said Ned.

"Pete says we can use his house as soon as they leave, at least until we get something else figured out. They'll rent it to us."

"When's he leaving?" asked Ned.

"Why? Are you in a hurry?"

Ned grinned. "You can stay as long as you need to. Although sleep used to be good, as I recall."

They were still talking when Rafe came by again. He walked up onto the porch to deliver a note he had found that was addressed to Harry. It was from Eldridge Payne.

Harry took it with some apprehension, opened it, and read the message aloud.

> Dear Harry,
> Just so you know, I wouldn't have hurt your baby girl for the world, and I know perfectly well how much she means to you."

Harry looked up, disgusted. "The man will say whatever he has to to get what he wants. What's he playing at?" Then he continued reading.

> "I intentionally missed when I shot at your boy, too. I've almost grown into the good deacon I pretended to be, but not quite, obviously. I want you to know that you're the best preacher I've ever been forced to listen to. 'Almost thou persuadest me to be a Christian.' But being good is just so boring!

"To prove that there is still some kindness in me (and to thank Harrison for not blowing my head off), I'm giving your boy that gray horse he's so proud of. I'm the one who bought it and hired your good friend Charlie to deliver it. I had hoped he would stir up trouble for you, and that went pretty well, but Charlie got so sidetracked he never managed to deliver the horse. And he missed the whole point: He didn't kill you! The best laid plans…

"Anyway, you'll find the bill of sale among my papers. The horse is your son's, and the saddle, too. He can have my hat too, if he can find it, although I'm pretty sure it has a bullet hole in it.

"One word of advice, Harry. Don't cross paths with me again. The next time I might not be so merciful.

"Sincerely,
"Eldridge Payne"

"He's threatening my family," Harry said grimly. "He's saying, 'I spared them once out of the kindness of my heart, but next time I won't show mercy.'"

"That arrogant, no-good—" sputtered Ned.

"Exactly," said Michael. "All that good will makes you wonder what he's up to. He must think we're complete idiots. Makes me want to join the Marshals Service and chase him down."

"Well, that might be a possibility," said Joel Underwood. "Maybe that job would be better for you than sheriff. We'll have to look into it."

Michael nodded at him, looking very serious.

Harry wondered if there was any truth in the letter—if it was possible that he had actually given Eldridge Payne second thoughts, and if it was true that Eldridge had intentionally spared the lives of his children. Or was he just "playing nice" because he was afraid that Harry was mad enough to come after him? Did he think he could use flattery to control Harry's behavior? Did he think he knew Harry's weaknesses better than Harry did, himself, and that he could take advantage of them? His attempted manipulation made Harry angry, but the implied threat to his family made him furious.

The Captain Seeks the Lost

He spoke directly to Marshal Underwood. "We have to stop this man, Joel. Eldridge Payne will kill again. He doesn't seem to have a conscience or any attachment to anyone—not his children or even his wife. He has to be stopped, and I have a mind to go after him myself."

The others frowned at him, shaking their heads.

"You need to leave that to the lawmen, Harry," said Ned. "You have a family to think of."

"I'm thinking of my family. My family won't be safe until he's locked up."

"We'll get him, Harry," said Marshal Underwood. "We'll get wanted posters out all over the country. Raymond and I are going to spend the next several days with the Payne family, looking through all of Eldridge's papers and talking with them. We'll find something to help us track him down."

"I want to be there with you when you ask your questions."

"We'll be happy to have the help, but I want you to know we're taking this seriously, Harry. And it's not just the Marshals Service that's after him," said Agent Whittaker. "The Secret Service is interested in what happened to the gold that was on the riverboat. And now that we know he was the boss of the counterfeiting ring year, that's another reason for the Secret Service to go after him. The insurance company will be after him for fraud. And all the families of the people he's killed will demand justice. We'll get this man."

"I'm going to try to find out about his early life," said the writer, Jimmy McClanahan, who had been listening quietly. "No one knows who he was before he went to work on the riverboat and met Carlotta. He was young, but he may have committed crimes under another name, in another place. Carlotta says he would never talk to her about his past. He said his life began when he met her, and she believed him, bless her heart."

"Maybe we can offer a reward," suggested Walt. "I'd be willing to help with that."

"Good idea," said Ned.

"Still, I'd like to go after him." Harry said grimly, remembering the terror he had felt when Eldridge held little Annie in his hands. "I want to see him hang."

* * *

207

That evening, the lanterns were all lit again at the Payne house, this time for celebration. There was food and fellowship, fiddle music, and dancing on the well-swept yard. It was a smaller crowd than the night before, but many of the neighbors were there. There was no more talk of Sarah "lying in." She sat beside Harry on the porch while he played his fiddle, and when he took a break from playing, they watched contentedly while others danced. When Molly asked if he wanted one last dance for old time's sake, Harry squeezed Sarah's hand and replied, "No, Ma'am! My dance card is full!" and Sarah smiled at him. Then Michael, looking stormy, whirled Molly away.

"What do you think?" Sarah asked Harry. "Will they get together?"

"I wouldn't be surprised. He's thunder and she's lightning. They're suited to each other."

"A perfect match?" she asked.

"Or a perfect storm," said Harry. "I just hope he'll find a way to make an honest living, so he won't end up in jail. She deserves better than that."

"I think he'll settle down and make her happy," Sarah predicted.

Both Harry and Sarah were glad that Carlotta was not alone after all. She seemed strong and happy, and had told them all the news. Now that Eldridge was gone, Rafe and Abigail were free to marry, and Theo, who had left fifteen years earlier to fight for the Union army, had finally come home to stay. He had been living near Carlotta's sister but had made her promise not to tell where he was. When Theo had left home, Eldridge had told him he could never come home again, that he was no longer his son, and that if he came back on the property Eldridge would shoot him on sight. Carlotta was overjoyed to have her son and daughter back home again and a wedding (even a grandchild!) to prepare for. No one knew what had happened to the younger son, but now Carlotta hoped that he would be found, as well.

Harry and Sarah left early, along with Ned, Winifred, and the children, so that they could all get some rest and be ready for Sunday.

Day Seven: Sunday

CHAPTER 23

New Beginnings

On Sunday the morning service was very emotional, with many people rededicating their lives and giving testimony of the "moving of the Spirit" during all the troubling events of the week. Later, old-timers would say that a revival broke out that Sunday morning. The preacher spoke with absolute conviction, and there seemed to be a new light in his eyes, as if he had gone to the mountaintop and come back with stone tablets in his hands.

Harry exhorted the people to beware of falling prey to the evil that had walked among them and to give themselves fully to the service of God. He warned that they should not come to the Lord's Supper unworthily, and before the communion service some people who had held grudges for a long time finally made their peace with each other. It helped that Theo Payne was back and that he wanted to be part of the fellowship again. When the altar call was given, Harrison made his profession of faith, and Harry announced that he would baptize him that afternoon. Others came forward asking if they could be baptized, as well.

After the regular service, there was singing, dinner on the grounds, and then the baptism, down at the river.

Harry had talked with Harrison about this decision before the service, and even though his ankle was still very sore, he wanted to be baptized while his mother was there, before they returned to Dahlonega.

Harrison had decided to go back home with his mother for the time being because he thought it would be wrong to leave her alone right now. Harry had to agree that it was the right thing to do, even though he hated to see the boy go, even temporarily. Michael would escort them on the trip and see them safely home. They would leave on Monday, accompanying Walt for part of the way. Harrison would ride in the buggy with Walt while he could, to spare his ankle, but after they parted ways, he'd ride Moonshine. Sparky was coming too.

In a couple of weeks, if Pete's ribs were better, he and Alice would be moving out of their house, starting their journey to Colorado. Harry, Sarah, and the twins would move into their house for the time being. Their next steps were still uncertain, but they thought they'd like to tear the old cabin down completely and rebuild on the same spot. The family home place was part of his heritage, and that meant something to Harry. He also liked the view and the water supply, and he liked being close to Ned and Winifred. They could help Sarah when he was away.

Harry planned to build a study for himself and a room in the house where a person could actually take a bath, and he looked forward to having some space where he and Sarah could make a home together and adjust to their new life with twins.

* * *

Late that day, as the sun went down, Harry sat alone in one of the rocking chairs in front of the ruins of his cabin, looking at the view, writing in his journal, and thinking about the highly emotional events of the day. Baptizing Harrison had been the crowning moment for Harry. Old Preacher Brown had baptized Harry in that same spot many years ago.

Today Harrison had been the last person to be baptized. Harry had stood in the river in water to his waist and watched as Michael and Ned helped Harrison walk out into the cold water. They had worried that he would hurt his ankle again. The two men stood to one side as Harry placed his right hand on his son's back and stood beside him with Harrison facing to his left. As he had been instructed, Harrison grasped Harry's left wrist with both hands. Then Harry had addressed the crowd of people who watched from the bank of the river.

"When Jesus was baptized by John the Baptist, a voice came from heaven saying, 'This is my beloved Son, in whom I am well pleased.'" Harry stopped, finding it difficult to speak. "I mean no irreverence when

I say that I think I know how God felt." He turned to Harrison and asked, "Harry Richardson Baldwin, have you accepted Christ as your Savior?"

The boy answered, "Yes, sir."

Then Harry held up his right hand and spoke so that the crowd could hear. "In obedience to the command of our Lord and Savior Jesus Christ, and upon your public profession of faith in Him, I baptize you, my Brother, in the name of the Father, the Son, and the Holy Ghost." Harrison held tight to Harry's wrist as Harry covered his son's nose and mouth with his hand. Then Harrison bent his knees as Harry lowered him backward into the water, then raised him back up. Water streamed off the boy, and he stood up, wiping water out of his eyes.

"Are you okay?" Harry asked softly, holding him steady.

"I'm fine," said Harrison, smiling broadly.

"I'm proud of you, son," Harry said as he hugged him.

Then Ned and Michael helped him back to the riverbank, and people surrounded them, expressing their happiness in Harrison's decision.

Now tired, but satisfied, Harry sat in the stillness of a beautiful sunset treasuring the memory of that experience, hiding it in his heart so that no matter what happened, he would never forget. Ignoring everything that had come before in his life, and with no thought about what would come after, in that perfect moment, he had known joy—and the peace that passes understanding.

Harry stood and walked down the hill toward Ned and Winifred's house, where his family waited for him. Tomorrow would be another busy day. He would have to say goodbye to Harrison, Molly, Michael, and Walt, and begin to figure out how he would bring an evil man to justice. He had promised himself that, with God's help, he would do it. But for now, he would enjoy the company of his family and his friends and be thankful that they were all safe.

When he was about halfway down the hill, Sarah met him, and they walked the rest of the way together.

END NOTES

1 **Choestoe** (pronounced Cho-ee-sto-ee) is a community located east of the Nottely River in the southern part of Union County, Georgia, in the valley between Brasstown Bald Mountain and Blood Mountain. Its name came from the Cherokee "*Tsi-stu-yi*" which means "Rabbit Place" or "Rabbit Town." Local tradition says that the name means "The Place of the Dancing Rabbit," or "The Land Where Rabbits Dance."

2 **These are the four verses of Amazing Grace that they sang:**

Amazing Grace, how sweet the sound,
That saved a wretch like me.
I once was lost but now am found,
Was blind, but now I see.

T'was Grace that taught my heart to fear.
And Grace, my fears relieved.
How precious did that Grace appear
The hour I first believed.

Through many dangers, toils and snares
I have already come;
'Tis Grace that brought me safe thus far
and Grace will lead me home.

When we've been there ten thousand years
Bright shining as the sun.
We've no less days to sing God's praise
Than when we've first begun.

3 Recipe for Black Walnut Cake

1 stick butter or margarine
½ c. shortening
2 c. sugar
5 egg yolks
2 c. self-rising flour
1 tsp. soda
1 c. buttermilk
1 tsp. vanilla
1 c. coconut
1 c. chopped black walnuts
5 egg whites, stiffly beaten

Cream butter and shortening. Add sugar and beat until smooth; add egg yolks and beat again; combine flour and soda and add to mixture with buttermilk; add vanilla, coconut and nuts. Fold in egg whites. Bake at 350 for 25 min. Bake in 3 layers.

Frosting
1 ½ (8-oz) packages of cream cheese
¾ stick butter or margarine
1 ½ boxes confectioners sugar
1 ½ tsp. vanilla
1 c. chopped black walnuts

Mix above ingredients and spread between layers of cake and then on top and sides.

Patsy Efird

4 Psalm 23

1 The Lord is my shepherd; I shall not want.
2 He maketh me to lie down in green pastures: he leadeth me beside the still waters.
3 He restoreth my soul: he leadeth me in the paths of righteousness for his name's sake.
4 Yea, though I walk through the valley of the shadow of death, I will fear no evil: for thou art with me; thy rod and thy staff they comfort me.
5 Thou preparest a table before me in the presence of mine enemies: thou anointest my head with oil; my cup runneth over.
6 Surely goodness and mercy shall follow me all the days of my life: and I will dwell in the house of the Lord forever.

5   The Lord's Prayer

Matthew 6:9-13

9 After this manner therefore pray ye: Our Father which art in heaven, Hallowed be thy name.
10 Thy kingdom come, Thy will be done in earth, as it is in heaven.
11 Give us this day our daily bread.
12 And forgive us our debts, as we forgive our debtors.
13 And lead us not into temptation, but deliver us from evil: For thine is the kingdom, and the power, and the glory, for ever. Amen.

READER'S GUIDE

Discussion Questions for Reading Groups

1. As the book's title suggests, the story is about finding what was lost. Cite examples throughout the book, using characters, Harry's message at the funeral, and specific scenes. What people/things have been lost? What people/things have been found?
2. What issues do the characters face in 1876 that are similar to struggles we face today as married couples, parents, adolescents, families, or community members? What issues do they face that are completely different?
3. Discuss the ways that some characters grow and change throughout the story. Consider Carlotta Payne and Michael Gibson, among others. Does Harry change?
4. Discuss the way that some characters' perceptions of other characters change during the course of the story.
5. How are Charlie Baldwin's dying moments significant to the theme of "Finding What Was Lost" and to Harry's message of salvation?
6. In the years following the Civil War, the concept of Post-Traumatic Stress Disorder was unknown. From today's perspective, do Harry or Liam exhibit signs of PTSD? Explain.
7. What about Ivalee Banks? Why do you think that Ivalee and Liam have become hermits? Will their lives change because of the revelations in the story?

8. Discuss the personality of Eldridge Payne. How was he able to hide his true nature for so long? In hindsight, what clues may have indicated that things were not normal?
9. Could Charlie have changed his life and avoided the tragedy that resulted, or was everything beyond his control? What could he have done differently?
10. How are Charlie and Eldridge alike, and how are they different? Why do you think Harry and Harrison both feel sorry for Charlie? Does Harry feel sorry for Eldridge?
11. Would the story have changed significantly if Molly had not lied and had let Harry know her situation when she sent Harrison to him? What might have happened if Charlie had known from the beginning that Harrison had gone to be with Harry? Would Harry's relationship with Sarah have been harmed? Could the kidnapping have been avoided?
12. Carlotta was known as a gossip. How is gossip harmful? Is there anything good about gossip? How did Eldridge make use of Carlotta's tendency to gossip?
13. What changes do you predict Michael will make, if any?
14. Was the deacon being truthful when he wrote the letter to Harry? What was his purpose? Why did he make a point of giving the horse to the boy?
15. Should Harry go after Eldridge Payne, or should he leave that to the lawmen?

Praise for Doris Durbin's
The Captain Takes a Wife

"An ex–Civil War soldier–turned-preacher aids a young woman in danger by marrying her, but their troubles aren't over.

Waiting for the train that will take him to his new job as preacher, Capt. Harry Richardson encounters a young woman in danger. Sarah Franklin, a teacher, begs for his help in escaping her pursuers, who want to force her into a marriage arranged by her scheming guardian. Snowballing circumstances—the innocent girl's plight, Harry's sense of responsibility, the villains' relentlessness, suggestions of darker crimes afoot—make an impromptu wedding seem the best solution to protect Sarah. It helps that Harry and Sarah share an instant attraction, and after a few probing questions for one another, Harry asks, "Will you marry me today on this train?" Harry's friends, who had accompanied him to the station, get in on the act, and together, they organize an onboard wedding while dodging gunmen from town to town until they can see Harry and his new bride safely home. Using many elements from Victorian melodrama, Durbin's debut novel handles characterizations well, with both heroes and villains being more than just cardboard cutouts. The camaraderie between Harry and his friends is believable and helps define his character while making Sarah's trust more understandable; he's the kind of man friends would do anything for. Durbin also complicates the plot in interesting ways beyond the forced marriage…."

—*Kirkus Reviews*

Printed in the United States
By Bookmasters